In Search of the Hidden Moon

Praise for
In Search of the Hidden Moon

With a combination of faith, humor, romance, drama, and suspense, *In Search of the Hidden Moon* keeps you turning the pages, while also reminding you that a Biblical parable's lesson still applies to today's real-world problems.

—Dr. Leighton Ford, founder of Leighton Ford Ministries

In
Search
of the
Hidden
Moon

Tim Eichenbrenner

NEW YORK

LONDON • NASHVILLE • MELBOURNE • VANCOUVER

In Search of the Hidden Moon

A Novel

Published in New York, New York, by Morgan James Publishing. Morgan James is a trademark of Morgan James, LLC. www.MorganJamesPublishing.com

Proudly distributed by Publishers Group West®

A **FREE** ebook edition is available for you
or a friend with the purchase of this print book.

CLEARLY SIGN YOUR NAME ABOVE

Instructions to claim your free ebook edition:
1. Visit MorganJamesBOGO.com
2. Sign your name CLEARLY in the space above
3. Complete the form and submit a photo
   of this entire page
4. You or your friend can download the ebook
   to your preferred device

ISBN 9781636984681 paperback
ISBN 9781636984698 ebook
Library of Congress Control Number:
2024934141

Cover Design by:
Rachel Lopez
www.r2cdesign.com

Interior Design by:
Chris Treccani
www.3dogcreative.net

Morgan James is a proud partner of Habitat for Humanity Peninsula
and Greater Williamsburg. Partners in building since 2006.

Get involved today! Visit: www.morgan-james-publishing.com/giving-back

For my good friend, the Rev. Dr. J. Thomas Kort.
Tom, many thanks for the lessons, laughter, and love.

Chapter One

The exam room door suddenly swung wide, the first in a series of events that would change my life's trajectory. A gaunt and elderly man rushed out and down the hall, his thin strands of gray hair swirling in disarray. I turned and joined the chase, with my nurse Sarah ahead of me calling out, "Mr. Harrelson, please . . . stop!" The man ducked and weaved like Tom Brady avoiding a pass rusher, his gown flapping open behind him and revealing way too much backside for the little ladies in the waiting room witnessing the race. We caught him at the front door. I grabbed the door handle and Sarah gently secured his forearm. She looked at me, nodded once, and said, "We make a pretty good team, Dr. Gil."

Yes, we were a good team. I had first met Sarah Taylor two years earlier, during the interview process for a position I was after at Hillsborough Family Care. She'd been with the practice for twenty years. Lucky for me, she drew the short straw and was assigned to be the newbie's nurse. I'd heard in my residency training that nurses not only kept doctors straight, but also kept them out of malpractice court. As a rookie physician, I'd scoffed at the notion, but since discovered it to be true. If I could count on my fingers, I could always count on Sarah to save my bacon. But chasing down a half-naked patient before he escaped from the office—that took our work relationship to a whole new level.

We finished the first half of our day's schedule and sat in the lunchroom, rehashing some of that morning's encounters.

"Did you see the look on Mrs. McIntyre's face when Mr. Harrelson streaked across the waiting room? I thought we were going to have to do CPR," Sarah said. "What was that all about, Dr. Gil?"

"When we returned to the exam room, Mr. Harrelson told me he saw something out the window that spooked him, so he ran."

She arched her eyebrows. "What in the world was it?"

I chuckled, shook my head, and then looked back at Sarah. "Mr. Harrelson said he got bored waiting for me and started looking for things to keep him busy. He snuck a peek through the window blinds and saw a guy in a hoodie and sunglasses walking down the street, carrying a large backpack. Thought it was unusual to be dressed that way on a late summer day, and that he looked like one of those suicide bombers he's seen on television."

"Seriously?" Sarah said. "A suicide bomber in our little town? How funny is that? It'd be like spotting Jeff Bezos in a soup kitchen. I think Mr. Harrelson's been watching too much cable news."

I nodded and started to speak when the loudest sound I'd ever heard rattled the office windows and interrupted our lunch. I grabbed Sarah and threw us both to the floor.

I'd moved to Hillsborough from Chapel Hill the previous year. It was north of the university town, not far off Interstate 85. I commuted my first year of work, waiting to commit to a move until I knew the practice and I were compatible. The charm of a town morphing into a small city, with restaurants, breweries, and specialty shops popping up like mushrooms after a wet spell, drew me in. My medical office was near the end of Main Street, surrounded by the few surviving trade and manufacturing businesses that employed many people in our community. They were good people. Ordinary Americans. People who went to work every day to provide for their families. A furniture plant sat back from the road a short distance from my office. Scattered buildings thinned and gave way to the Piedmont's flatlands, with fields of soybeans, cotton, and tobacco dotting the landscape. It was a town where neighbors knew one another, watched out for each other, shared meals, and worshiped together. Doors weren't locked at night—it wasn't considered the neighborly thing to do. So a bomb exploding didn't even make the top ten of things I thought could've caused the noise.

I rushed outside with my co-workers. The furniture plant was in flames, with cotton balls of smoke billowing from holes in the roof into the Carolina-blue sky. My senior partner, Dr. Arnie Schmidt, yelled at us to get to the scene, adding that he'd handle the patients still at the clinic. Wood and wires crackled and sparked, people yelled, and victims screamed. Instinctively, we all ran toward the danger. I stopped and fumbled for my phone, dialed 911, and resumed running, knowing whatever we'd find wouldn't be pleasant.

People staggered from the building, some bleeding. Clothing smoldered. Burning and partially shattered wooden beams lay strewn on the ground like pickup sticks dumped on a dusty carpet. The smoke and the smell of burned flesh brought tears to my eyes and seared my nostrils. I grabbed my handkerchief from my pocket and covered my nose and mouth. Victims lay on the ground, some clearly beyond triage and others moaning in agony. The scene was chaotic and unorganized.

Focus and stay calm. This is what I was trained to do. "Do your best to find survivors and triage them so the medics will know who to prioritize for routing them to Chapel Hill . . . but please be careful," I yelled.

I found one man crumpled on the ground, lying on two charred wooden beams, one crossed over the other. I quickly assessed his injuries, their enormity almost overwhelming. His face's olive complexion was streaked red from a gaping head laceration, and blood from a side wound ran like red paint through what remained of his shirt. I left him against his wooden cross, fearful of injuring him further were he to be moved. Beneath singed eyebrows, his pitch-black eyes stared back and pleaded with me before he even spoke. In a whisper, he said, "They . . . after me . . . the girls, Peru . . . please, find . . ." I asked him his name, but before he could answer, he assumed a fixed stare—those black eyes now open windows to an empty room.

I lost him. He was in my hands, and I lost him.

Other victims' screams snapped me back into focus. It was then I noticed something in the man's shirt pocket. Instinctively, I grabbed a tattered photo of two girls and the victim, stuck it in my lab jacket pocket, bowed my head, and said a brief prayer. More accurately, I registered a complaint: *I realize death is a natural part of life. I've faced it professionally and, even more pro-*

foundly, personally. But this, God? Why do You let such awful things happen in this world?

A ray of sunshine reflected off a small, silver cross necklace dangling to the side of the victim's neck. I removed it and stuck it in my pocket too.

He was gone, but the other victims needed my attention. I had to stay on task, but this sense of sudden loss was stirring emotions I'd done my best to suppress. With work still to be done, I'd have to subjugate those feelings once again.

Chapter Two

Somewhere near Moyobamba, Peru
Two weeks earlier

Luna

T he truck bounced and swerved. I'd walked pot-filled roads like this many times, going to the outdoor market for my mum or to school in the village when there was no field work for us children. Sometimes we picked cotton or cut sugar cane. I thought school was my only escape from my village people's way of life. Until now.

The men came as unwelcome guests to Campoflores during the night, when the village men were off at remote agriculture sites, roaming and looking for work to feed our families. There were many of these intruders, and they overwhelmed the women and children, threatening to kill anyone who resisted. They rounded up the girls who were of working age and younger and herded us like sheep onto the bed of a truck. An overhanging green tarp gently undulated in the breeze as they drove us away. A Jeep full of kidnappers followed. Our mothers' screams gradually faded, yielding to those of howler monkeys and night frogs, cicadas and crickets—the chorus of the jungle.

Crowded together with the other girls in this envelope of black, I felt disoriented. Occasionally, a beam of moonlight snuck through the spaces between the side slats of the truck, briefly illuminating the shroud of darkness to reveal sad, crying faces. Much later, as the sun rose, shards of rays shone through, orienting me to the east. That meant we were headed south. Several of the girls still cried, their sobs punctuating the warm, stagnant air hovering over us the way a dense fog sits on the mountains. As one of the older girls, I tried to remain calm and reassure the others. I dared not cry. Ava, a neighbor and close friend, sat next to me with her arms wrapped around her knees pulled to her chest, rhythmically rocking.

The jarring and bumping improved as I heard the sounds of a town: a few vehicles, street vendors, and other voices. As little as we'd traveled, we must have been in Moyobamba, due south of Campoflores. The truck skidded to a sudden stop. A man jumped into the truck's bed, carrying a rifle and warning us to keep quiet. He was missing several teeth. The smell of gasoline permeated the air. They were refueling.

Another man climbed in with a large jug of water. He looked around until his eyes fixed on me. He handed me the jug and told me to pass it around. After every girl had taken a few sips, I took mine. The cool water pried the dust from my mouth and tingled my dry throat when I swallowed. He offered no food.

We began moving again soon afterward, the town's sounds gradually growing more distant until extinguished. Morning light flickered through the lush jungle overgrowth, finding its way into our prison. I had questions: Why were we taken? Where were they taking us? Why us?

Once my mum and I had moved from England to the village, I'd never ventured far from home. Rarely, we went on a church trip to Tarapoto, in a bus driven by a man named Johnny, and I traveled several times to nearby Moyobamba to purchase provisions, but that was it. Simply by age and my mum's education, I'd had more schooling than most of my younger friends. My Spanish was adequate, and I could communicate well in both languages. Maybe I could use that to our advantage at some point, even though I'd heard nothing but crude Spanish from our captors.

The truck stopped again. Men threw the back of the tarp over the top portion and ordered us out. The truck's driver, a large man with a hideous scar snaking across one cheek, climbed down from the cab. A man stepped from the passenger side and walked toward the edge of the road, not making eye contact with my friends and me.

We were allowed to relieve ourselves, three at a time, with one man standing close enough to keep us from running. I counted fifteen girls, including me. They told us to sit in the grass by the road. It was good to be in fresh air with blue skies overhead, even with rifle-toting men standing around us. They gave us banana leaves stuffed with rice and small pieces of fish. We ate eagerly, grateful for any nourishment. Once again, they ordered me to pass the water jug around. The girls whispered and whimpered among themselves. The men used their weapons to poke those who cried out for their mamas and papas, a veiled warning to keep quiet. As we climbed back into the truck, I glanced at the impressions our bodies had made in the tall grass, now just vacuous images, as though we were never there. Was that a foreboding of our fate?

The tarp was pulled down, and our journey to an unknown destination resumed.

Chapter Three

Hillsborough

To say it was a taxing day would be a gross understatement. Once medic arrived and our work was finished, we all returned to the clinic. Regular appointments were canceled so we could tend to the workers who were fortunate enough to escape with injuries not requiring hospital evaluation. When I finally got home that night, my modest ranch and Dutch, my black lab mix, were a sight for sore and tired eyes. When I walked in, he jumped up excitedly, his front legs landing at my waistline. Just my opinion, but when God was drafting His image of love, He gave it four giant paws, floppy ears, and a tail that incessantly wags. Dutch was a rescue, pedestrian in appearance, with a long snout, ears too big for his head, and sad, brown eyes. His posture, demeanor, and loyalty, however, were as regal as any AKC champion. I scratched his ears and then collapsed on the sofa.

Too busy earlier to worry about my phone, I checked for messages. One, from "Dunk" McElroy. No surprise.

> Brother, you alright? Heard about the explosion and know your practice is nearby

Duncan McElroy was the popular minister of my church, Second Presbyterian. The stout redhead's Scottish brogue incongruously resonated with his small Carolina congregation. More importantly, he was a great friend. He was there for me whenever I needed him and, to borrow from *The Godfather*, I knew he'd go to the mattresses for me.

8

I clicked Dunk's name in my Favorites, and he answered immediately. "Hey, Dunk. Thanks for checking. I'm fine but exhausted from a very long and tragic day. Sorry, but there was no time to stop and call from the office."

"Don't worry about that, Gil. I'm relieved you're okay. I want to hear all about it next time we're together. We need to meet soon at the Caffeine Scene. We're overdue for some coffee and Christianity, you know."

"I'd love that. To be honest, I'm angry about what I saw this morning, so I could use some religious wisdom to help me with it. Of course, you're my source for all things spiritual."

———————

For a town Hillsborough's size, the bombing was major news that spread faster than spilled milk on a kitchen table. Dozens of our citizens were injured or killed in the explosion and fire. Our community was hurting. Soon, there'd be the added grief of daily funeral services—salt poured repeatedly into the town's wounds. In the ensuing days, our office was open only for emergencies because so many of our staff were out for funerals or tending to family members affected by the disaster. Notwithstanding the personal loss so many were feeling, the plant was also a major source of employment, and now people were without jobs.

News teams were in town from CNN and Fox News affiliates, as well as local stations' teams from Wilmington, Asheville, Charlotte, and Raleigh. We received daily updates on the explosion, providing details as they were verified. None of the locals could remember so much buzz and attention in our little town, all for the wrong reason.

The North Carolina State Bureau of Investigation bomb squad was on the scene the same day as the explosion, doing its best to reconstruct what happened. Fortunately, the plant's office was in a separate building that sustained no damage. Things became clearer once the plant's owner, Hank Martin, turned over the security tapes to the authorities. They were taken to Raleigh, where experts could piece together the time-stamped video showing a man in a hoodie approaching the entrance and dropping his backpack to the ground before walking off. His face was concealed, making facial recognition impossible. The only mistake he possibly made was sporting a hoodie with a striking image of a dragon on the back, its mouth spewing flames like those that shot from the furniture plant. Not your typical garb.

Slowly, life returned to normal in Hillsborough. Reporters moved on to the next "breaking news" crisis, people healed from their emotional and physical wounds, and Hank Martin announced plans to begin reconstruction of his plant. The mayor cited our medical clinic for the work we did as first on the scene. The explosion was still a major topic of conversation, especially when people talked in hushed tones as they huddled over coffee and comfort food at Shorty's Diner, the go-to place for morning fellowship. But it remained a mystery why someone would want to destroy a furniture plant, peoples' livelihoods, and, most importantly, so many lives. The intrigue of one victim's life remained with me—haunted me, even—as I struggled to understand my responsibility in honoring the victim's last request.

Find the girls in Peru.

Chapter Four

Alexis "Alex" Morgan was waiting outside her house when I pulled up. Her natural blonde hair in French braids and her hot pink lipstick likely would've caught any guy's eye from two blocks away.

"Hey there, sweet boy," she said as she batted her big blues at me. She climbed into the car before I had a chance to get out and open the door for her. Seated, Alex tugged at the hem of her black shift, a vain attempt to pull it to her knees. She sported a multicolored silk scarf and carried a teal Dooney & Bourke clutch. I couldn't see her shoes, but I complimented them anyway. That's what guys should do, right?

"Hi, Alex. You look stunning. But you do realize this is only dinner with friends, nothing fancy. Right?"

"No reason to own dress-up clothes if you don't wear them once in a while. It's kinda nice to get away from my work and school outfits and wear something nice. Besides, I thought you and Bobby might shock us ladies and take us somewhere classy for a change." She hesitated and then grinned. "I'm messin' with you!"

Alex was the first woman I'd seriously dated since college. Other girls hit "undependable" on my radar, and with my personal history, that plane wouldn't fly. But Alex seemed like the real deal. New to town, I'd met her when I ducked into Stately Raven Bookstore, where she worked part-time. The place smelled of old wood, musty paper, and coffee. I remember the conversation like it was yesterday.

"Help you?" she asked.

"Yeah, but first help me understand the store's name."

"You read poetry?" she'd asked.

"Not unless I have to. Why?"

"The owner, Nancy, is a closet poet. She loves Poe, so Stately Raven was a natural choice. We even have a small corner called 'Nevermore.' It's where the out-of-print books are displayed."

"Clever."

"Yeah, we thought so too." She shrugged.

She then helped me find the latest Baldacci thriller. I loved the guy. Not only a solid writer, but he lived in my home state of Virginia, not far from where I grew up. Alex and I got to talking; one thing led to another, and I asked her to dinner. That was a first for me with someone I'd just met, but something triggered chimes in my head, pealing like the bells of Notre Dame on a Sabbath morning. We'd dated regularly since.

She grabbed my arm. "Sweets, you missed the turn to Pizza Palace."

"Very funny. Actually, we are doing Italian tonight but at Gino's, that nice restaurant close to campus. If that's okay, that is." I loved Alex's sense of humor. It took the edge off my tendency to take everything seriously. We shared a love of dogs, hiking, and Jesus—not necessarily in that order. But a love for dogs was almost sacred to me. We attended church together, and she'd taken to my Dutch like he takes to any water he has a chance to belly flop into.

"You know anything's fine with me. I don't complain 'bout any night out, especially going to the big city of Chapel Hill." She rolled her eyes. "Chrissy's at a friend's house for the weekend, so I don' have to worry about her. And I don't have to fret over how much wine I drink, since you're practically a teetotaler and my designated driver."

"Sounds great. How's Chrissy doing, by the way?" Alex had gone through a bad marriage to an immature and irresponsible young man named Virgil. It ended poorly, but not before something good came out of it: their daughter Chrissy, now fourteen. Her ex still lived in the area and had a decent job driving an eighteen-wheeler west on Interstate 40 to Asheville and into Tennessee, or down I-85 to Charlotte and on through as far as Atlanta. He occasionally resurfaced, like a sub coming up for fresh air, and pretended he was interested in Alex and Chrissy. He'd even mentioned reconciliation, a nonstarter for Alex.

"She's doing okay."

"Any problems with her anxiety since the plant explosion?" I asked.

"Probably no more than anyone else her age. Hard to understand for all of us, actually. Of course, I can call Dr. Greer if I see any signs of trouble—you know, like I've done when she gets angry with her dad."

"You do remember he said you can call him Jim, not Dr. Greer, especially when we're away from the office? Besides, you've known him a lot longer than you've known me."

"True that. Guess you're lucky he's a confirmed bachelor, right?" She winked. "Listen, he's Dr. Greer, not Jim, at least for as long as he's taking care of my little girl."

I nodded. It was nice to hear a mom praise her child's doctor, as it reminded me that my patients, or at least most of them, appreciated me too. Don't get me wrong. I'm blessed to do what I do and wouldn't trade it for any other job. There was a time when I was laser-focused on becoming a physician and didn't bother trying to make long-term friends, much less consider a girlfriend. But I'd since learned the science of medicine and interpersonal relationships overlap one another—a Venn diagram sharing common ground. Sometimes a doctor has to go beyond the problem with the skin, heart, or other organs and get to a person's soul to heal them. That requires the art of medicine, and it's a lifelong learning curve. I guess that's why it's called the practice of medicine. Always practicing but never perfecting. Even my seasoned senior partner, Arnie Schmidt, admitted that . . . and constantly reminded the rest of us.

"Gil, are you with me? You just drove past the restaurant, and this time, I'm not kidding."

"Sorry, babe. You caught me daydreaming again. I guess I've driven this route so many times, I went on autopilot."

"Sometimes I worry about you, sweet boy." Alex shook her head.

Bobby and his wife, Jill, sat on an ornate metal bench outside Gino's, huddled face to face in what appeared to be deep conversation.

"Well, you never know who you might run into around here," I said.

Bobby turned to me and jumped up. "Gil! Great to see you, my man! It's been way too long. Sorry we didn't see you two. We were talking about my possible campaign for mayor."

Truthfully, we'd had coffee the week before, but Bobby was given to cliches and other insincere overstatements. Robert Archibald Culpeper IV was the latest iteration in generations of Orange County attorneys who bore his surname. He'd worked on patents for many companies in the state's Research Triangle Park, developed a solid reputation, and now had all the work he could handle. Of course, it didn't hurt that his dad was the US congressman for our district. I guess Bobby's aspirations of being Chapel Hill's mayor came honestly. His square face, topped with close-cropped blond hair, was set off by tortoise-shell glasses. He was dressed in jeans and a polo shirt tonight, but his work outfit this time of year typically consisted of a white shirt, bowtie, and seersucker suit, tailor-made by Brooks Brothers yet still appearing to cling to his thin body for fear of falling off.

Bobby had been one of my best friends since college. I guess we had similar career goals—both of us driven to succeed in our respective professions. Beyond that, we really didn't have much in common. He'd had a silver-spoon childhood, but mine had been, well, anything but. He married young—said a marriage helped his image—but got lucky when he chose Jill. The only god he seemed to worship was the almighty dollar. Often, he talked first and thought later, whereas I kept things to myself. In fact, Alex had asked me several times why we were such good friends. I wasn't really sure. He could be so superficial, but he had a knack for understanding how my heart and mind worked, and he'd helped me through some tough times.

Entering Gino's, the scented waves of cheese, garlic, and freshly baked bread washed over us. Guided by the hostess, we made our way through the subdued lighting, maneuvering around seated guests until we reached our table. Once we took our seats, Bobby started in on me as though it were a billable hour.

"Well, Gil?"

"Well, what?"

"Tell us all about the explosion and the clinic team's heroic rescue efforts."

The depravity of that act wasn't a topic I wanted to discuss. But I knew Bobby, and like he always did, he was asking for all the details. I'd have to give him something, or he'd never relent.

"Utter carnage is the best way to put it. Listen, there was nothing heroic about what we did. We responded the way any medical personnel would and did the best we could for those who were injured." I massaged my temple muscles and looked down at the menu, hoping to end the conversation.

"It must have been awful," Jill said. "I'm so glad your clinic was close by, but I'm sorry you had to witness that . . . and Bobby, why don't we talk about something else? Maybe it'd be better to give Gil some time to get past all this."

Thank goodness he had Jill to reign him in.

Mercifully, the conversation shifted to more mundane topics. Jill, a Georgia transplant who taught history in the local high school, was enjoying her time off and had just returned from a visit with her parents in Athens. For me, the only difference summer made in family practice was more sports physicals and school checkups, more injuries, and fewer infectious disease visits.

"Well, Jill," I said, "One thing we have in common is we both deal with a lot of teenagers and their surging hormones, right?"

Before she could respond, Bobby said, "That's what I love about patent law, ladies and gentleman of the jury. Steady work year-round, dealing with facts, not emotion. No hormone-laden teenagers who'd rather be anywhere than in a classroom, or handling the emotional toll of seeing sick or dying people all day. I've got the best job in the world." He slammed the table. "I rest my case." When Bobby looked at Alex, she closed her eyes and shook her head.

Emotional toll. I had to give Bobby credit for that insight. Medicine was taxing, especially when sharing the final, intimate moments of someone's life.

"Hey, my man, just some playful pontification. You lost in thought?"

"Yeah, he does that a lot," Alex said.

"Guilty." I shrugged. "Guess I was thinking that, even with everything you think is wonderful about patent law, I'd rather face reading Leviticus or Numbers every day than deal with that stuff."

Our orders were taken. And soon, I was staring at a huge pile of spaghetti, with bread and a salad drowned in Italian dressing. Bobby ordered beef lasagna and a double serving of bread. The girls, both so thin they probably had to run around in the shower to get wet, predictably split an order of veggie lasagna. The three of them shared a bottle of Moscato.

"Veggie lasagna?" Bobby said, looking at Jill.

"Well, I can't speak for Alex, but I need to keep myself slim and fit for when you run off with your mistress, Patent Law." Everyone laughed, and, for once, Bobby had no retort.

"Hey, no one's asked about my work," Alex said, faking a pout.

"Alex, how's work?" we said in unison.

"Peachy. Actually, pretty slow now, as everyone's already bought their summer beach reads. We're taking inventory, restocking, and moving some genres around to create a new look for fall. You know what? I don't make a lot of money, but I love working there, and it's the perfect job for me while I finish my social work degree at Carolina."

Our conversation dwindled as we turned our attention to polishing off our entrees.

Before we knew it, dinner was over and it was time to go. We declined Jill's invitation to go by their place for coffee and dessert, as Alex had an early day at the store the next morning.

On the way home, I thought about how nice it was to get away and have a night out with friends. Like all of us, Bobby had his shortcomings, but he was a true friend, and Alex and Jill treated each other like sisters. But even with the distraction of a night out, I couldn't get that victim's last words, or the photograph I took from his shirt pocket, off my mind. *What did he mean?*

"Gil, you're doing it again. What on earth are you thinkin' about? Is somethin' wrong?"

I shook my head and glanced at her. "Nope, everything's perfect, babe."

Yeah, I know. I lied.

Chapter Five

Our town had a decent-sized population of Latinos, and we were the better for it. They were ordinary folks who valued family, work ethic, and religion. Most were devout Catholics who'd purchased and restored an old warehouse as their place of worship. The local priest was Father Jose, a patient in my practice. The families also bought or rented houses throughout Hillsborough, choosing to blend rather than become insular. My next-door neighbor, Xavier, an Argentine, was bilingual. He was a great guy who sacrificed his sanity by attempting to teach me conversational Spanish. But, hey, give me credit. I was trying, and I practiced it on my Latino patients, who shook their heads and humored this gringo. Xavier worked at the furniture plant and was mercifully spared from serious injury in the bombing. As he had excellent carpentry skills, he'd gotten a job with the contractor rebuilding the plant.

I'd not shared the photograph with anyone but decided I needed to find out what I could about its owner. On a free Saturday morning, I had Xavier over for coffee . . . and a little prying.

Xavier stared at the photograph, looked up, and said, "Dr. Gil, that Carlos. He work at plant, but start not many days ago. His life . . . gone. *Bueno hombre*. Very sad." He looked down and reached for his coffee cup.

I explained how I got the photo. "Tell me more about him, Xavier."

"He not say much. On break and at lunch, he read from very small book that fit in palm of hand. Don't know his last name or the *ninas* in photo."

"Did he have friends at work?"

"No *amigos*. He keep to himself. Very serious."

He went on to say he rarely heard him speak, but on one occasion, they were both in the plant office and Carlos was talking with the secretary. She was checking his files—probably looking at his work visa information. Apparently, Hank Martin was very careful not to violate any federal laws or regulations related to temporary-status employees.

That might be my answer. "Xavier, do all of you have a work file, even those of you who've become naturalized?"

"Oh, yes, Dr. Gil. I fill out name, address, family information, and address back home when I start there. Same for all workers."

"This has been helpful, Xavier. Thank you so much."

"You very welcome." He hesitated. "A question, *por favor*. I know you are man of God. You maybe visit our *iglesia* . . . uh, church? We love to have you."

I thanked him for the gracious invitation.

"I must go, Dr. Gil. You keep practice Spanish, and I keep practice English. Yes?"

"Absolutely, and thanks again for your help."

After Xavier left, I pulled up our office's electronic medical record and found the number for Hank Martin, who saw one of my partners. I knew it was a HIPAA violation, but I justified it as me trying to do the right thing. I grabbed my cell.

> Dr gil sullivan here. May I come by your office monday at lunch? It's very important

The reply came right away.

> Sure doc. 12:30?

> I'll be there. thx

On Monday morning, I asked Sarah to have the front desk staff clear an extra thirty minutes for my lunch. That would allow for plenty of time to get the information Martin was hopefully willing to share with me.

I found him alone in the office, up to his elbows in blueprints, work orders, and sticky notes with scribbled messages on them. Construction noise and the odor of freshly cut wood blew through an open side window, its panes shadowed by sawdust like a three-day-old beard.

"The secretary's at lunch. That lunch train has left the station without me, though, as busy as I am right now. I'll eat when I get home. Anyway, what can I do for you, Doc?"

I told Martin about my encounter with Carlos and what he said to me right before he died. Then I pulled out the photo and showed it to him.

"Yep. That's Carlos all right. Never seen the two kids. If he had children, I didn't know it."

"I've spoken to a friend who works here. He identified Carlos, too, but said he didn't know much about him."

"Well, he hadn't been here long before the day of the explosion. He was definitely a loner. Kept to himself. Hard worker and never caused trouble. Heck of a woodworker too. But he's gone now, Doc, so what can I do for you?"

"I need to find out more. I need to find these children who might be his kids. I couldn't help him, but at least I can try to honor his last request. Can I look at his files? This is important to me."

This was important. I'd experienced something like this once before, when I stopped at an accident and tried to help a woman who died at the scene. I'd failed, but at least I followed through on her last request to contact her family with a message. I'd struggled with her death until I finally realized that sometimes I can't heal or fix a physical problem, but I can help with what's broken in that person's life—to honor a last wish, powerful enough to escape through their dying lips, but also to help those left behind. To put some of the pieces back together and make a family whole again. *I wished someone had done that for me when I lost my mom.*

"Doc, you with me? Seemed lost in thought there."

I looked up at him. "Sorry."

"As I was saying, I don't know. Employee files are privileged information. We aren't supposed to share them with anyone. I'm sure you know that, being in the medical business." He hesitated and nervously shuffled some papers on his desk. "Of course, Carlos is gone, and far as I know, no one has stepped up as family, so it might be okay. But you can't leave with it. You gotta look at it here."

He stood and turned to a green metal filing cabinet that looked older than the dirt scattered on the floor beneath it. He gave the drawer a hard tug, sorted through a mass of papers, and grabbed a file. "Here you are, Doc. You're welcome to use my assistant's desk."

The information on Carlos was sparse but useful: Carlos Aguilar. Year of birth, 1988. He listed Campoflores, Peru as his place of residence but gave no contact information or any family members' names in Peru. He also listed his address in Hillsborough. I knew the street—within walking distance to where the plant once stood. I made notes and returned the file to Martin and thanked him.

"You know, he was thirty-three when he died. He appeared much older at the scene, but a hard life, not to mention an explosion, could probably account for that."

"Reckon so, but you're the doctor," Martin said.

As I headed back to the office, I thought about something that caught my attention: his date of employment. He'd hardly settled into our town before we lost him forever.

Chapter Six

Chapel Hill, North Carolina

Alex

The high sun beat down on me when I stepped outside, my pale, freckled arms faring no better than the quad's grass wilting under the dry summer heat. I tucked a rogue strand of hair behind my ear and donned my Ray Bans. After three hours in an advanced social work class, I was ready for some downtime. Summer sessions were brutal, but they were an easy way to meet the requirements for my social work degree while still working at the bookstore. Suzie and I agreed to meet at the student union and grab a quick bite before I headed to my externship in family court. I loved court because it felt close to what I would do once I put my degree to work full-time. I dreamed of the fulfillment it would provide, not to mention the extra income Chrissy and I could seriously use. There was Gil, and that relationship was firing on all cylinders, but who knew if it would last? I'd been burned before, but he seemed different. My heart was happier and my step lighter when we were together. Romantic, right?

I hadn't seen Susannah Rose Dutton in over three weeks. She was an Air Force brat—an only child whose family left Charleston, South Carolina, and lived all over the country, even as far south and west as Texas and California. Once her dad opted for early retirement, they returned like homing pigeons and settled in Mt. Pleasant, South Carolina. Suzie's goal was to get her undergrad degree in journalism within three years, so she was in town year-round. She'd explained there was no reason to be back home when it was hot, humid, and full of tourists spilling over from Charleston. Chapel

Hill wasn't much cooler, but at least one could walk to the car without immediately dripping in sweat.

The union was busy. Chairs scraped the floor, trays rattled, and utensils clinked as students ate, checked their phones, and chatted. The odor of grease hung in the air, rivaling that of Shorty's Diner.

I went through the line and grabbed my usual Caesar salad and can of Cheerwine. From a table against the far wall, Suzie waved her arms at me. As I walked up, she withdrew her long, slender legs from under the table, stood, and greeted me with a quick hug.

"Girlfriend, it's wonderful to see you," I said. "How's your off-site going?"

"And I'm glad to see your sweet face, Alex . . . I'm really loving my externship. You know, seeing how the real world works. But the course work? Not so much, 'cause it's rigorous. Thank heaven I only have one class this semester." She brushed from her face wayward curls of black hair that would've made *Seinfeld's* Elaine jealous. "How you doing, girl?"

"Peachy. Hectic, of course, between Chrissy, school, and work. But loving it and grateful to almost be finished with my degree."

"And Gil? How's that tall hunk?"

Suzie was my best friend, my confidant. Somehow, we'd both been assigned to the courthouse for our off-sites, where she was shadowing a court reporter and I was observing one of the county's social workers. She was one of the few people with whom I'd shared my background regarding Chrissy's dad and our sorry marriage. Still, I was reluctant to be too optimistic about romance, even with her. I scooted croutons around with my fork like pawns on a chessboard and took a sip of soda.

"Gil's great. We're good. You know, he's busy too, but we make time for each other when we can."

Suzie's eyes lasered in on mine. "Well, don't let yourself get too busy. Busyness—"

"I know . . . busyness is the work of the devil or a sin we create for ourselves. I've heard you say it a thousand times, like you're quoting out of Proverbs or something. Have to admit, though, it's good advice."

"What can I say, girl? I'm biblical." She laughed and then took a bite of her tuna wrap.

Spending any time with Suzie always elevated my mood. She was the most positive person I knew, and sometimes a dose of her was exactly what I needed. We finished lunch as we girl-talked.

"Well, I've got to get to court, girlfriend."

"I know, Alex. You're always going somewhere. I'm gonna sit here a spell and finish my tea. Now remember, busyness—"

"Yeah, I got it." I gave her a peck on the cheek and walked outside to my car.

The Orange County Courthouse was a flurry of noisy activity, all of which came to a screeching halt with a single bang of the judge's gavel. The musty smell of worn, cloth-covered seat pads wafted through the room filled with heavy yet ornate oak furnishings. Folks from throughout our county congregated here to handle everything from minor traffic violations to domestic violence, or worse. My objective was to observe how the court system worked, how the various participants in the process—including advocates for the disadvantaged—managed their roles, and gain some real-world insight into the pitiable plight of people's lives.

My assignment was family court, where custody claims and foster home placements were negotiated. I sat inconspicuously in the front row. An oak railing, its top surface no doubt worn from decades of distracted hands nervously traipsing its surface, separated me from the table where the clients and their lawyers sat.

That day, my case study was a mother trying to get full custody of her young child. Claiming the woman's ex-husband drank too much and worked too little, her attorney made a strong case for the father's unsuitability for even a grant of partial custody. After hearing the case for both her and her ex, including the testimony of a county social worker, the judge took a thirty-minute recess and returned with her judgment: full custody for the mother, with an allotment of supervised time for the father and child, as long as a court-approved third party was present. This was a win for the parents and the child. He would live with his mom, a worthy provider despite her blue-collar job, but still get to see his dad in a safe environment. I left the court feeling good about my future work. That wasn't always the case.

Before walking out, I checked my messages. One from Suzie, telling me how awesome it was to spend a little time together, and one from Gil:

> Maybe dinner tomorrow night?
> Think on it. Will call this evening

Hmmm. That sounded good, as long as it was okay for Chrissy to tag along. She adored Gil, and the two of them always had fun together. Another dinner to look forward to, almost like a family night out. *Hopeless romantic strikes again.*

Chapter Seven

Hillsborough

I owed Bobby a call. We hadn't talked since dinner at Gino's. I'd been busy at work and preoccupied with Carlos's last words. After Dunk, Bobby was my go-to person when I needed to talk through something. He could be loquacious and self-serving, but when he focused, he could laser beam his attention on me. He couldn't help me fulfill Carlos's request, but he might provide some clarity for me, and maybe some legal insight.

"Gil! What's up, my man?"

"Just touching base to make sure you're behaving yourself, buddy."

"Dude, when's the last time you heard of a patent attorney getting into trouble?"

"Fair point," I said. "But I've accepted looking after you as my assignment in life."

"Oh, so you're working for Jill now, huh?" We laughed.

I took a deep breath. "Actually, there is something I want to discuss."

I told him about finding Carlos in the rubble and what I'd learned since. Keeping it vague, I told Bobby I'd gotten information on Carlos's personal life through some acquaintances. The lack of interruptions on Bobby's part meant he was fascinated by the story—or bored, thinking it wouldn't lead anywhere. Turns out, it was the latter.

"Gil, you're a doctor, not a minister, detective, or social worker. It's not your job to track down those kids, if that's even what the guy meant. This whole thing reminds me of the times you've gotten over your skis with patients' problems. We both know you tend to drift from your lane."

"Don't even go there, Bobby. You know I feel obliged to honor what my patients share with me."

"Yeah, I know. Didn't mean any offense. Hey, why don't you talk to Alex about it? It's more her area of expertise than mine, right?"

"I plan to but wanted to run it by you first. Figured if it sounded outlandish, I'd have to re-think it. You've always helped me with things when I'm confused, so I called you first. I appreciate your insight, buddy."

"That's what brilliant minds are for. And, if you want to talk about patents and violations."

"I'll take a hard pass, but thanks." Classic Bobby. We disconnected the call.

I needed to go for a run. I put the lead on Dutch, and we took off down the street. It was lined with live oaks that offered partial shade from the evening sun. Beams of light flickered through gaps in the leafy canopy like a strobe light, and the scent of summer flowers from neatly manicured front yards filled the air. An occasional car passed us, moving over to give us safe passage. Jogging was about the only exercise I had time for, and even in the summer heat and humidity, it was a welcome respite from work. Running helped me think. Perhaps it was the endorphin release, or maybe it was simply jogging along as I watched Dutch's eyes widen as he set our pace. If only humans enjoyed running as much as dogs did, and could do it as effortlessly.

Bobby was right. I had a practice full of patients to care for and no experience or qualifications in tracking missing persons. Maybe the best course would be to stay in that lane Bobby referenced and pass the info along to someone more qualified. Alex would probably know somebody in the legal or social work world who could help. I'd approach her about it from that angle. With a good thing going, I didn't want her to suddenly think I lacked sound judgment.

We completed the loop and walked to the front door, with me dripping sweat and Dutch's tongue hanging sideways from his mouth. I grabbed my phone from the table in the foyer as Dutch went for his water bowl.

> Change of plans if okay with you. Eat at my place tomorrow night. need to talk. 6?

Alex was never without her phone, especially when Chrissy was away from the house. She answered immediately.

> Of course, sweets. See you at 6

This needed to be a private conversation, at home and not in a restaurant with Chrissy sitting there. She'd suffered enough desertion in her life without hearing about the possibility of missing children. Regardless, I kept hoping Carlos was delirious from his injuries and was talking nonsense.

As a bachelor, I'd settled for microwaved food, ramen noodles, or anything else not requiring even the most basic culinary skills. Back then, there were parts of my kitchen and things in the drawers I wasn't even familiar with. But I'd picked up some tips from Alex, and I knew she would appreciate my effort to prepare a meal rather than ordering something from Eats To You. A chicken and rice casserole was fresh out of the oven when she and Chrissy arrived. I'd also tossed a spinach salad and warmed some whole wheat rolls. Green beans were available as a side because I knew Chrissy wouldn't eat the salad—she said she didn't put in her mouth anything that looked like tree leaves. Teenagers. You gotta love them . . . I guess.

"Oh my, something in here smells yummy," Alex said as she dropped her purse in a chair. She gave me a hug and a kiss on the cheek. Chrissy gave me a single chin-nod "hello" and then glanced at her mom and rolled her eyes.

"How'd you have time to cook all this after working today, sweets?"

"Actually, I prepared the casserole and partially cooked it this morning, so all I had to do was stick it in the oven while I got everything else ready."

"Well, Dr. Sullivan, I do say, I'm impressed." She winked.

As Chrissy reached for a roll, her mom's arm shot out and grabbed hers. "Remember, Chrissy, we say grace first."

Over dinner, I asked Chrissy about her upcoming final year of middle school. Her answer showed she hadn't given school much thought and was really more focused on soccer. As she picked at her food, she mentioned she was also working out with weights and running under the soccer coach's supervision. I was happy for her. I'd never gotten into sports, having decided my future was in academics and not on a field or court, especially since muscle strength, coordination, and agility weren't exactly my fortes. Probably explained why I wasn't good at much more than pounding the pavement at a reasonable pace.

I still wasn't over my childhood. There was the loneliness of a fatherless home and living with a mom who tried—but who often seemed more focused on her next drink, male conquest, or both. I was pretty much a loner, strangely comforted by my school books, and that never changed. In fact, I had only one friend who still lived back home in Christiansburg, Virginia.

"Sounds great, Chrissy," I said. "Sports are fun. Also, they may not admit it, but boys dig athletic girls."

"Whatever, Dr. Gil." She rolled her eyes again and shook her head.

After dinner, I suggested Chrissy take Dutch out for some backyard play time and then a walk. Once she left, I turned to Alex, who'd already started clearing the table.

"Don't have to twist Chrissy's arm to get her to play with Dutch."

"You kiddin'? Think about it: a fourteen-year-old with two adults—one being her mother—versus a dog? Not a hard choice."

"True. Hey, I'll clean up after you leave. Let's sit down. I have something I want to discuss."

Alex arched her brows. "You're making me nervous."

"No, it's not that, babe . . . another time and place." She sighed then stared at me, locked in, waiting for me to continue. "I've told you about our clinic's response to the explosion, but there's more."

I went through the entire series of events, like I had with Bobby. Reliving that moment etched it deeper into my brain, like an image carved into granite. Someone had died, practically in my arms, and I knew I'd never forget it. Confronting death wasn't unusual for a doctor, but this one had occurred emergently and felt different—thrust upon me with emotional impact.

Alex's eyes never left mine. Other than an occasional raised eyebrow or slight shake of her head, she was expressionless.

"So, what do you think? Anyone you know at the courthouse who could help?"

"Yeah, actually, there is an international office, if you want to call it that. It's one person at a desk in a room with a landline. He has the number to call in Raleigh when we have a case involving something with overseas implications. I'm happy to run it by him."

Chrissy and Dutch came in, both of them panting and apparently thirsty. Dutch went to his bowl, Chrissy to the fridge's water dispenser. As she filled her glass, Alex told her they needed to go soon.

Turning to leave, Alex stopped and looked back at me. "I'll get back to you soon, Gil, but please put it on hold 'til I do, okay?"

"Sure."

I cleaned up our dinner mess, took Dutch out for one last "business" walk, and got ready for bed. I was glad I'd shared everything with Bobby and Alex, and I'd finally decided Bobby was right—better to leave this to the people who do it for a living. I climbed into bed and put my cell on the nightstand. A chirp sounded, then the screen came to life with a text. I read it and dropped the phone to the floor, the illuminated screen still silently screaming the message.

> You better stop now or there will be more tragedy

Chapter Eight

Sundays in Hillsborough were as sacred as college basketball in nearby Chapel Hill, where the name Dean Smith ran a close second to the Holy Trinity. Seriously. Most businesses closed on the Sabbath. My office had one doctor available for emergencies. People in small towns tended to be a close-knit group, and never were they closer than when they gathered with the church flock on Sunday mornings.

Folks would enter their respective churches, drawn like moths to the bright light of the Holy Spirit. They'd take their seats—almost always in the same spot on the same pew—Sunday after Sunday. That fascinated me, and I loved to watch the choreographed seating from my favorite perch toward the back of Second Presbyterian. I know what you're thinking: Why not First Presbyterian? Local historians said First Pres was burned to the ground by the Union in the Civil War, and when it was rebuilt, the brethren didn't have the heart to put an old name on a new church. Something having to do with Jesus saying we don't put new wine in old wineskins—one of those confusing parables. Anyway, down here, it was never a bad option to blame something on Grant's boys in blue.

Little old ladies wore flowery or polka-dotted dresses and colorful hats resembling plumes on a bird's head. Not to be outdone, the menfolk generally wore their Sunday finest as well. This was the South, after all. Only the millennials dared to come casual, and some even ventured to enter God's house carrying a Yeti filled with their favorite coffee—no doubt thought to be an unpardonable sin and a ticket to purgatory by the older members. Truth be told, I had tried, but Alex had nixed that idea.

Second Pres was all brick and mortar, now painted off-white. I suspect the sanctuary would hold about three hundred people, not counting the seats in the balcony. Those were typically occupied by the teens and tweens, and that was usually where Chrissy landed. Alex sat with me, one ear listening to the preacher and the other aimed toward the balcony, making sure she didn't hear Chrissy cutting up—either moved by the Holy Spirit or, more likely, tempted by Satan himself.

There were rarely empty seats, in part because the members took their religion seriously, but also because of Reverend Duncan McElroy. He still sported the slight brogue he inherited from his parents, who'd moved from Scotland to Washington, DC when Rev. McElroy was a child. After seminary, Rev. McElroy accepted his first pulpit call to our church, finding his way to Hillsborough because Second Pres was a perfect starter church and the town was close to Chapel Hill and Durham. He had a love for basketball and wanted to be close to his adopted school, Carolina. Of course, he had the wisdom not to disparage Duke—at least publicly. He frequently said traveling down Tobacco Road was akin to a pilgrimage for him. I guess it was more than fitting that I and others affectionately called him "Dunk."

On that morning, as the sermon began, I looked around and saw many people I knew from the neighborhood or clinic. Alex elbowed me. "Gil," she said quietly, "You're not even paying attention."

"Yes, I am," I said, through clenched teeth.

As Dunk droned on, I thought about how I'd ended up here. When the mistrust and loss that characterized my youth led me to prioritize my studies, I missed out on so much. But, by God's grace, I got a mulligan and realized before it was too late that I needed people in my life—not only co-workers and neighbors, but real friends. And now here was Alex. What to do about Alex?

After the service and on the way out, I had three informal consults with patients of mine—one of the hazards, or joys, of being a doc in a small town. When we got to the minister, I shook his hand. "Nice sermon, Dunk. Your message hit nothing but net." He laughed at the metaphor.

Walking to the car, Alex grabbed my arm and stopped me. "'Nice sermon, Dunk?' Seriously, Gil? Lyin' to a preacher? You weren't even listening."

"Busted . . . well, kinda listening, but I did have my mind on something else."

"What was it?"

"Nothing."

"Well, you said it was something else."

"Busted again." I forced a smile. She looked away and shook her head.

———————

We were downtown at one of our favorite cafés for Sunday lunch. Chrissy had gone home with a friend. The place was bustling, the waitstaff hopping. We'd been here so often, we didn't even need a menu. I took a deep breath and a sip of my Coke Zero.

"Actually, Alex, I couldn't tell you a thing Dunk said this morning."

She tapped her knuckles on the table. "I knew it," she said, nodding slowly. "What's got your mind goin' like ninety, headed south?"

"The other night, right after you and Chrissy left, I got a weird text."

"Weird how?"

I pulled out my cell to show her the message. "Look at—"

"Doc? That you?"

The measured footsteps and the clicking of paws on linoleum had to mean Tom. I knew it before I even looked up.

"Hey, Tom. Yep, it's me. I'm here with a friend. Meet Alex. Alex, Tom Waters. Tom and I go way back to my residency days."

Tom Waters was one of the most respected men in Hillsborough. He'd founded Waters Pharmacy and ran it himself for years. During my residency, whenever I phoned the drugstore with a prescription for my patients who lived in that area, Tom always answered. Once his son, Rich, finished pharmacy school at Carolina, he joined the business. Tom said things were getting too busy for one pharmacist, but later, we learned he was developing macular degeneration. Gradually, he couldn't type the bottle labels. Claimed he could tell a pill and its medicinal merit by simply rolling it in his fingers but couldn't make out the keys on a typewriter. Tom still went in to work, but mostly to hold court and hobnob with his many loyal customers. Now he needed his trusty guide dog Scout to help him navigate a town he'd lived in most of his life.

"Oh, Miss Alexis and I go way back. You got you a good one, Gil." He turned to Alex. "And Gil's a smart doctor and a fine man."

"So I've heard, Tom. Jury's still out, though." She laughed. "Now, if we could just keep him awake and paying attention in church."

"One nice thing about being legally blind—I can wear my sunglasses in church and no one can tell if I'm awake or asleep." He cackled and then turned his head toward me. "On a serious note, Gil, how's work? Rich says he's sure filling a lot of prescriptions for anti-anxiety drugs. Guess the explosion is still rocking the town. What an awful shame."

"No surprise, based on patients I've seen who either were in the plant or had family members there at the time. Gotta say, I've also sent Rich more prescriptions lately."

"You reckon they'll ever catch the devil who did it, Gil?"

"Who knows? I imagine the person's long gone."

"Well, I'll let you two get back to your lunch. Miss Alexis, so good to see you again. Come by the store sometime and bring this fella. That old soda fountain's still in operation, and we whip up some pretty mean shakes."

"Sounds yummy. We might do that, Tom. Thanks."

Alex looked wistfully at Tom as he walked away. I wanted to ask her how she knew Tom, but as soon as he was gone, she pivoted back to the text.

"Gil, let me see that again."

I pulled up the text. As she read it, her eyes widened. "This is a threat. You've got to go to the police. That creep might still be here."

I explained I was considering going to the authorities, but I wanted to give it a little more thought. Maybe it was a prank. I didn't want to be an alarmist and make a fool of myself.

"If that's what you think, you're not as bright as everyone believes you are. Why on Earth would it be a prank? And even if it is, so be it. But if it isn't . . . well, I don't even want to think about that."

So much for a nice, quiet Sunday lunch.

Chapter Nine

Arnie Schmidt and I had a rough beginning, mostly because I didn't understand what motivated the man. As the senior partner and founder, he saw the practice as his baby, and everything he did was in the best interests of his patients, the staff, and his partners. Sometimes, he simply had a hard time showing it. Arnie was a short and bookish man, his readers usually perched precariously on his nose. You'd take him for an accountant were it not for a shirt pocket full of tongue depressors and the stethoscope hanging from his neck like a prized necklace. His size was a mismatch with the large shadow of influence he cast. I'd learned a lot from him, and one thing he did that I emulated was to keep the last two hours of Friday afternoon schedules open for emergencies. Seemed a lot of folks didn't think about their medical problems or prescription refills until they realized they were facing the weekend, and then everything became a crisis.

On this Friday, my last hour was taken by George Owens, a middle-aged, gentle giant of a man who typically sported a big smile and an even bigger laugh. Both were missing today. When I shook his hand, a workingman's calluses pressed into my palm. As I closed the door to my personal office, he took a seat and hung his head, slowly shaking it like a pendulum.

"George, what's going on?"

"It's our young'un Tyler, Doc. We lost him in the explosion, you know." His eyes moistened.

Actually, I didn't know. The final list of the victims hadn't been made public because the medical examiner was still identifying remains. And I didn't know Tyler—he wasn't a patient of mine and, as George explained, he lived outside of town.

"I'm so sorry for your loss, George. I don't have children, so I can't imagine how you must feel. I'm so sorry." I repeated myself because sometimes "I'm sorry" is the simplest and best thing to say to someone who's grieving.

"I don't get it, Doc. He was a good boy. He loved carpentry and thought he'd found his life's work at the furniture plant. Then this. How could anyone . . ." His words halted as his tears began to flow.

The silence was uncomfortable but necessary. I got up from my desk and took a seat beside George, placing my hand on his shoulder.

"Things happen we don't understand, George. Life doesn't always make sense. Sometimes the natural order of things goes off the track, at least as far as we can discern as humans."

He pulled out a handkerchief and wiped his eyes. "I go from being sad and crying to being angry . . . even mad at God. That don't feel right, either. Leastways, that's not how I was raised."

"Don't worry about God, George. He can take it. And He expects us to have questions and doubts. We all do, especially when something like this happens."

"What do I do, Doc? I'd like to crawl into a deep hole and let the darkness just cover me up."

"Let yourself mourn and keep talking about it. I'm going to refer you to a grief counselor—someone you can talk to who's an expert in what you're going through—and I'm sending a prescription to the drugstore for a mild anti-anxiety medication, just to take the edge off your pain. Now, why don't you and I meet again next Friday afternoon?"

George nodded, and we both sat there silently for a few minutes. Finally, he looked up at me, said thanks, stood, and shuffled out of the office, his head hung low again. I'd done the best I could with him. He didn't know my full back story, and he didn't need to, at least not right now. The questions he'd posed and doubts he'd expressed were eerily similar to those I'd had after I experienced my deep and personal loss. It's hard to understand, but as Rev. Dunk often quoted from the Bible, "The sun rises on the evil and the good, and the rain falls on the righteous and the unrighteous." I'd experienced that, and now it was my turn to help someone else with something I'd been through myself.

First Carlos, and now George's son, Tyler. It seemed more personal now. I was angry—angry at this person who willingly destroyed innocent lives.

I could no longer ignore the text message and the possibility it could help identify this monster. I had to act.

———

The Hillsborough Police Department was small but the perfect size for a city with little or no major crime. The explosion was the biggest event to hit the town in anyone's memory. Chief of Police Jasper Riddick had made it known that anyone with information regarding the plant explosion could come directly to him—any time, any day. I scheduled an appointment for the next morning.

As I walked in, Chief Riddick came out of his office to greet me, carrying an issue of *Firearms News* in one hand and a cup of coffee in the other. Middle-aged girth spilled over his belt buckle, and wisps of graying hair strayed to all points on the compass, as though they hadn't seen a comb in years. Riddick and I knew each other from serving on a community forum about crime prevention and personal safety the previous year.

"Gil, good to see you. Coffee?"

"Morning, Chief. Don't mind if I do. You minding the store by yourself?"

"Got one officer out on patrol. Otherwise, I'm solo. What can I do for you?" He filled a mug and handed it to me, his yellow-stained fingers gripping the handle. "Take a seat, please. Mind if I smoke?"

I shook my head. *Of course, I mind, but it's your office.* I reviewed the role I'd played at the scene, my discussions with the plant owner and my neighbor Xavier, and the threatening text I'd received. I explained my reluctance to come forward sooner, thinking the text might have been nothing, and then my change of heart when a patient came to me about losing his son in the tragedy.

"How could the perpetrator have gotten your number, Gil?"

"Probably foolish, but I make it available to all my patients so they can contact me if they really need something. Most people never call, but those who do really appreciate my accessibility. Guess the number's gotten around."

"Well, any possible lead is just that, Gil—a possibility. Did you save the text?" he asked through a smoke ring. I nodded. "Great. Hey, look at that. You know, it took me a lot of years to learn to blow a perfect ring—"

"Chief, you were saying?"

"Right. Sorry. If you'll let me borrow your phone, I'll send it to Raleigh. The state crime lab has sophisticated electronic forensic capabilities they can use to track that message. Unreal equipment. 'Course, I could never learn how to do all that stuff. I remember when I was in metal shop in junior high, trying to build a simple—"

Focus wasn't the chief's strong suit. I didn't want to give up my cell, but I also didn't want to get in the way of anything that might help catch the bomber. "Sure, Chief, but first let me call a couple of friends and record a message letting my patients know I'm temporarily without my phone."

I left voicemails for Alex and Bobby, recorded my message, and handed the phone to Riddick.

"Shouldn't take but a few days, Gil. Appreciate you coming forward. I'll be back in touch."

———

On the short drive to Chapel Hill, I mulled over what I'd done. I was encouraged. Maybe the mistake of boldly texting a message would lead to this creep's undoing.

The Walmart Superstore in Chapel Hill was a beehive of activity, typical for a Saturday morning. I made my way to the electronics section, told the clerk what I wanted, and bought a pre-paid phone with enough minutes to get me through the next few days. I called Bobby on the way out of the store.

"Hey, buddy. I know it's last minute, but I'm in Chapel Hill and wondered if you could meet me at the Grind."

"Sure, Gil. Jill's at some kind of event at her school, so I'm all alone. Perfect timing."

The Coffee Grind was an institution in Chapel Hill. During my training, when Bobby and I were both living in the town, we'd spent untold hours there enjoying coffee and discussing life's issues, large and small. Walking into that shop was like coming home, greeted by the rich aromas of coffee beans and short orders simmering in the kitchen. Bobby strolled in, his phone trapped between his ear and his shoulder. He took a seat across from me but kept talking for another few minutes before he clicked off.

"Sorry, Gil. Really important call. Patent law never takes a holiday, you know. Whatcha doing in Chapel Hill?"

I explained the last two days and my need for a temporary phone.

"My man, I'm so glad—"

The waitress brought us our coffees and pimento cheese sandwiches, with chips, of course.

"This looks good, Gil. Beats the old days of ramen noodles, right? Anyway, I'm so glad you did that. That's gotta take a load off of you, and it's better to let the experts figure it all out than for you to sit on it. And who knows? Maybe they'll catch the idiot. Assuming you discussed this with Alex, how's she taking it?"

"She was all for me taking the phone to the police. She'll be glad it's out of my hands too."

"Never a bad idea to follow a woman's intuition. I've learned that in the two years I've been married to Jill." He held out his hands, palms up, and shrugged.

We enjoyed small talk while we ate lunch. As we got up to leave, Bobby gently grabbed my forearm.

"Hope it all works out. Keep me posted, Gil."

We shook hands before walking out. Driving back to Hillsborough, I thought about what had transpired that morning. Very productive half day, capped off by a visit with a good friend.

Chapter Ten

Despite my amateurish attempt at criminal investigation, I still had my day job. Something I worked at and enjoyed tremendously. Life's road is good, but it has speed bumps we don't always see coming. George Owens was going through that now—through the valley of the shadow of death—and I prayed he'd come out on the other side as healed and whole as anyone can after a tragedy. Maybe some people are blessed to never have to descend into that valley and fight to rise back to the mountaintop. Sadly, some who descend never make it back, with no opportunity for a do-over.

That Monday morning, I walked into the clinic, greeted by the usual sights and sounds: the mindless banter at the front desk that would cease once the first patients arrived; triage nurses on phones, already putting out "fires" and scheduling visits; and partners grabbing coffee from the break room. The post-explosion, somber mood had slowly lifted, and things seemed back to normal. Even with its antiseptic smell and unique hubbub, the office was my comfort zone. I could manage most of my patients' problems and, at the end of the day, I knew I'd done some good. Not every job came with that reward. I felt blessed.

After an uneventful morning schedule, I sat in my private office charting and answering messages. My temporary cell chirped. Alex, with a reminder.

> Tonight at 7. Meet at my favorite place.
> Will be fun. Got it. C u there

A relaxing evening with Alex. Something to look forward to after what had been a stressful few days. Often, with plans to do something after work, I'd have a few work-ins or a patient would take more time than expected, and I'd go well beyond the usual quitting time. Murphy's Law, but not today if I could help it, even with Miss Wainwright on the schedule.

Eleanor Wainwright was an elderly and dignified spinster who insisted on being called "Miss," not "Ms." She was single and wanted would-be suitors to know it. Said she had no intentions of "saddling up with some cowboy," as she put it.

I walked into her exam room where she sat gowned and upright, one varicosed leg crossed over the other. Her silver hair was pulled into a bun—permanently, I think. I suspect a bird could have nested in it and she wouldn't know until the babies hatched. Before I could speak, she started with her standard moniker for me.

"Young man, I'm here simply to be seen by you."

"For?"

"A look-over, please. Just to be sure all my parts are still where they need to be and working properly."

"You mean a 'physical exam,' right?"

"Oh, that sounds so . . . *ordinary*. But call it what you must."

"Are you experiencing any problems or having any symptoms?" I asked.

"My only problem is the people, men especially, who are after me. They want to be friends, but I know they're only interested in Wainwright money." She looked away and shook her head. "It'll be a cold day in . . . I won't say it and sully your young ears. Let's just say they will never touch my assets, physical or otherwise. My family earned our wealth, and I plan to keep all of it, thank you very much."

It was well known that Miss Wainwright was loaded. Her grandfather had founded Wainwright Mills, and in its day, it produced an untold amount of spun cotton goods. As that business shipped overseas, the mill died a slow death, especially when Eleanor's father inherited the company but not his father's business savvy. The Wainwright family's saving grace was the mill's location on prime real estate, strategically situated between Hillsborough and the Research Park. He sold it for millions to a developer who built a mixed-use commercial complex that was now thriving and contributing to the success of our town. Kind of a win-win.

Today, I found Eleanor to be in perfect health, with no issues that would require any follow-up. She seemed satisfied, and I was happy her visit didn't delay my schedule.

After finishing on time, I went home and took Dutch out to do his business, fed him, and changed into something more appropriate for tonight's destination: El Capitan Loco. The Crazy Captain, as Xavier had taught me. Alex and I'd been there a few times, but the idea of a Mexican honky tonk in downtown Hillsborough still seemed weird. It symbolized the artsy, hip vibe the town was developing as more professionals and young college grads moved into the area. Bars, breweries, and boutiques abounded, and I loved it.

I walked into a noisy, dimly lit bar with a raised wooden dance floor covered with years of scrapes and scratches, no doubt from taps and heels. It was the only bright spot in the building. The smell of spilled beer filled my nostrils. People were line dancing to the Maca-something. I looked around and found Alex, already seated and rhythmically pumping both arms. Honestly, I wasn't sure if she was signaling to me, jiving to the music, or communicating with the Trinity.

"Hey, sweets. Glad you made it—and on time to boot."

I gave her a peck on the cheek, sat down, and shouted, "What's that music?"

"It's the Macarena, silly. Wanna dance?"

"That's a no, but thanks. I still can't believe you like this place."

"It's fun, and you know what they say: blondes have more fun! Anyway, I ordered some tortilla chips and salsa and asked for a Coke Zero for you and a Fat Tire for yours truly. Hope that's okay."

I arched my eyebrows. "What's a Flat Tire?" I said over the din from the band. The song ended and the band went on break. Patrons returned to their seats and our conversation returned to a normal decibel.

Alex laughed. "No, Gil, *Fat* Tire. It's a beer."

"Oh. Sorry. I don't know much about—"

"I know, you're practically a teetotaler, and I admire you for it. By the way, I also admire you for going to the police and letting them handle this whole text message thing."

"Gotta admit, it is a load off my mind. The chief said we should hear something from Raleigh today or tomorrow."

Our food and drinks arrived. As Alex grabbed a handful of chips, I looked over her shoulder at a table in the corner. Some guy seemed to be staring at me, or maybe Alex. With his sitting in the shadows and wearing a ball cap, I couldn't make out his features. I didn't mention it for fear of upsetting her. Maybe I was imagining something.

People got up from their tables and migrated to the dance floor. The band was back. The music started.

"And this is—"

"'Boot Scootin' Boogie.'" She laughed.

I shook my head. "Can we go? This noise is giving me a headache."

"Well, if a girl's not even gonna get one dance, we might as well." She shrugged and stood up to go. "Such a party pooper."

As we walked out, I glanced toward the corner. The guy was gone. My eyes bounced around the room until I spotted him at the bar, looking over his shoulder in our direction. He really did seem to be watching us.

Chapter Eleven

Tuesday afternoon, Chief Riddick left a message at the front desk that my phone was back from Raleigh. As the office manager handed me the message, Bonnie, my scheduler, wrinkled her forehead and tilted her head.

"Trust me, Bonnie, it's a long story."

"But everything's okay. Right?"

"Of course. Everything's fine." She didn't need to know the details.

When I called the chief, he told me he planned to go by Carlos Aguilar's apartment to look around, but he'd wait until after I stopped by to pick up the phone.

"Doc, Raleigh got nowhere. Traced the phone back to an electronics store in Charlotte—a burner bought as a cash purchase. They contacted the store manager. No video surveillance."

"Well, that's a bummer. Hey, Chief, any chance I could go with you to Carlos's? I'm very curious about what you might find."

"Well, it's not regulation for a civilian to go on an official visit, but don't reckon it would hurt nothing. In fact, I saw this gangster movie where the police chief allowed—"

"I'll be there as soon as I finish seeing patients, Chief Riddick."

He was waiting on me outside the police department. As we walked to his squad car, I couldn't hide my disappointment that the phone had been a dead end.

"Everything okay, Doc?"

"Yeah. Guess I'm just frustrated the phone was a dead end."

As we neared Carlos's street, we passed by the furniture plant site. Most of the debris was gone, but the death and destruction would linger for a long time. Large earth movers, used to scrape and level the lot to ready it for re-building, sat quietly like steel dinosaur fossils, their work for the day now over.

Carlos's rental was one of several in a row of so-called mill houses, all identical and once used as residences for factory workers, allowing the people quick commutes to work. His was a simple, concrete block house. Bicycles lay on the ground out front, abandoned in favor of a baseball game in the street, its participants begrudgingly stopping play and moving to the side of the road to allow us to pass. We pulled into a gravel driveway. The front door was slightly open. Riddick motioned for me to stay back as he gently pushed the door wider, his firearm in hand. After a quick walk-around, he came out and told me it was safe to come inside. Furniture was turned over and drawer contents were scattered on the floor. Pictures hung crookedly on the walls. In the small bedroom, a print of the Mother Mary and baby Jesus hung perfectly level over the head of the bed. A wooden cross and a Spanish Bible lay on the nightstand.

"Looks like Carlos was a religious man," the chief said.

I thought about the cross necklace I'd removed at the scene. "Well, Chief, the place has obviously been tossed."

"Agreed. I'll ask the boys in Raleigh to take a look, but I'll bet ya they'll be hard pressed to find any clues here. Reminds me of one of those old Hardy Boy books, when Frank and Joe—"

"Chief, I think we're done here. Let's go." We left frustrated, with no new clues about Carlos's backstory.

As I climbed into the chief's car, my phone chirped. "Well, at least I know it's working . . . oh my gosh!"

"What is it?" he asked.

"A new text. Look at this."

No more warning. Stop now

"That's two warnings, Doc. All due respect—maybe you ought to stick to doctoring and leave the detective work to me."

No way could I stop now. Carlos and his family deserved more.

———

As usual, Dutch greeted me at the door, his tail wagging rhythmically to the beat of canine happiness and his beefy, wet tongue hanging out and poised to lick. I needed to think, and jogging with my faithful companion was the best way to accomplish that. "Come on boy, let's get you some supper, and then we'll go for a run." He must have understood; he scampered away to the pantry, his nose stuck against the space between the floor and the door. "Yeah, you know where I keep your food, don't you?"

I loved late summer runs. The air was no longer as heavy and sticky, but grass, trees, and flowers still held the promise of life, not yet moving into their cool-weather dormancy. A few miles in, with Dutch loping along, my strides grew shorter and more labored, but I could still think without interruption and ask myself questions. What was Carlos's story? Who were these children—his children or someone else's? How could I ignore a man's final request? Was it the hand of God that put me there in the last moments of his life? Was God speaking through one of His own to tell me something? Being a believer was a privilege but also a heavy responsibility. Jesus called on us to help others, especially the "least of these." Is that what this was all about? Scripture came to mind. "To whom much is given, much is demanded." I'd been given a lot. *Maybe that verse is meant for me right now.*

"Great run, boy." I rubbed his ear, and he preened in response. Dogs don't ask for much, but they sure give us a lot. Once I rescued Dutch, I couldn't imagine life without him.

We were back home, and I'd made my decision. I would not abandon Carlos's request. While I might not solve it, I'd see that it wasn't forgotten by those who could investigate further. That was enough, I told myself. After all, I couldn't ignore my medical practice.

Dutch lapped up his water while I chugged Gatorade. My phone rang. Alex.

"Hey, babe. What's up? Everything okay?"

"Yep. Had coffee with Suzie today. That girl hasn't moved on since the whole 'Todd thing.' Hardly dates, which is weird for a beauty like her in a college town. But she had some good advice for me." I'd heard about Suzie's breakup with her latest guy, Todd.

"How so?"

"Said I should tell Virgil there's no chance for any relationship between us other than getting Chrissy to him for his court-appointed time with her. 'Course, that's how I feel, but it's complicated with Chrissy caught in the middle. Anyway, I was callin' to see if you got your phone back and, if so, what Raleigh found out."

"Good news and bad news. Obviously, I got my phone back, but they couldn't trace the text message. One of those phones people get when they don't want to be found."

"Oh, a burner."

"Okay, I'm impressed."

"Well, I do watch those *NCIS* shows on television. Love that delicious Leroy Gibbs." She sighed, and then we both laughed.

"Hey, how 'bout dinner and a movie Thursday night?" I asked.

"6:30?"

"Perfect." I'd bounce my decision off Alex and hope for affirmation. I needed to get it off my chest and, hopefully, out of my head. An evening with Alex was always something to look forward to.

Chapter Twelve

Somewhere north of Tarapoto, Peru

Luna

Wherever we were headed, our progress was slow, and our captors didn't seem to be in any hurry. Heavy rains had washed out parts of the earthen road, causing mudholes and ruts as the truck strained to pass through. The bigger girls and I were enlisted to help push the truck to get it moving again when it became stuck, the mud splatter adding to our filth and misery.

Our water was now a large lidded barrel, and we each took a turn, one scoop per girl. Food consisted of two meals a day—plain rice now, wrapped in a large leaf and eaten with our dirty hands. We were allowed to go into the woods to use the bathroom, still three at a time, tied together, with a guard nearby.

Two of the guards took one girl, Andrea, the one next in age to me, into the woods. A flock of Black-collared hawks flew out of the trees, apparently disturbed by the human intrusion. Papi taught me they love water, even the marshlands. The Ucayali, which flows down the Andes from what my people call the Great River, had to be nearby. The birds' flight to freedom reminded me of what we'd lost—and had never appreciated before it was taken from us. We were captives, with no chance of flying away to safer perches.

Muffled screams pierced the jungle's natural noises, an unwelcome reminder of our captors' cruelty. When they returned, the men tugged at their pants, and my friend had tears rolling down her dirty cheeks, leaving tiny trails on her face like the rows men plowed in the fields back home. Her torn dress betrayed what had taken place. As the oldest, I wondered why my fate was not similar. My mum always said I looked younger than my age. Perhaps that was it, or maybe it was because I spoke English and they needed me to cooperate. If we encountered an English-speaking authority, maybe they needed me to lie for them and say we were traveling by choice. But only one who couldn't plainly see would believe such a tale.

The younger girls looked on in horror, the anguish of their squeals interrupting the calm of the deep woods. I tried to reassure them and comfort Andrea. Even at age sixteen, I had trouble keeping a brave face. I wasn't sure how much longer the youngest could go on—or the rest of us, for that matter.

In our Sunday classes at our makeshift church, Papi had taught us to trust God in all circumstances. That seemed so easy when "all" didn't include captivity and abuse. What we were experiencing now tested my faith. I prayed I could endure.

An engine's noise interrupted my thoughts. A van broke through the brush, with a young man driving and an older man next to him. Our captors ordered us to line up side by side. The older man walked up and down the line, his driver armed and at his side. The one with authority leered at each of us, like a lion stalking its prey, and then stopped and glared at the youngest girl among us, Ava.

"Ah, *chica joven*." Young girl.

Please. Not Ava.

He walked over to our driver, Scarface, and the guard who rode as his passenger. Whenever we stopped, Scarface always kept a close eye on us while he smoked a cigar, but the passenger seemed disinterested in what went on and occasionally pulled a notepad from his pocket and jotted down something. The old man and Scarface talked and laughed, and then the visitor handed him some cash.

The man's driver tied Ava's wrists together, grabbed her by the arm, and led her away from the group. When I tried to run after Ava, one of our captors knocked me to the ground. The two men threw her into the back of the van, climbed in, and drove away.

Amid a chorus of cries and screams, we were rounded up by one of the men I'd named Toothless and taken back to the truck bed. The engine sputtered to life, causing more birds to soar from the trees. We moved again, leaving behind one little girl and a piece of our collective heart, both possibly lost forever.

Chapter Thirteen

Hillsborough

Thursday evening. Date night. Alex had her heart set on Monterey's, a gastropub located in town and within walking distance of the movie theater.

"A gastropub? Seriously, Alex? Sounds too much like some kind of lower intestinal thing to me."

"Appetizing thought, Gil. Thanks for that. It's actually the latest and best, with some of the yummiest food in town. Here I am, a little ole country girl showing my doctor boyfriend the finer things in life!" She winked.

The place was loaded with chrome and wood . . . and people filling the tables and crowding together at a noisy bar. Until now, I'd missed out on this craze. Alex ordered for both of us. The waiter soon returned with a pinot for her, coffee for me—a combination that made for a weird toast. We discussed my decision regarding the investigation. How I wanted to stay in the loop and ensure Carlos's concern for those girls wasn't lost.

"Makes perfect sense, Gil. Let Chief Riddick handle it. I don't think he'll drop the ball, but you'll be here so he can keep you updated. I know how much it means to you to honor Carlos's last wish, but that'd be like somebody coming into the bookstore and asking me to perform surgery. We all have our talents, and the chief's no exception. Lucky to have him in our little town. Yeah, he loses focus sometimes, bless his heart, but he's as solid as a fence post."

The food came. I guess I eyed it suspiciously because Alex looked at me and laughed.

"What's wrong, sweetie?"

"What is this?"

"Well, that's bean sprouts right there, with butternut squash—"

"Alex, I know that. I'm asking about the entrée."

"Foie gras."

"Which is?"

"Tell you later." She hiked her eyebrows and giggled again.

A guy shooting glances our way from the far end of the bar caught my eye. His cap and posture sent me back to the night at El Capitan Loco when I thought someone was eyeing Alex and me. I looked over intermittently until he stood and left the restaurant.

"How's your food, sweets?"

"Food was good. I'm getting seconds on coffee. Want some?"

"Think I'll go with hot tea."

I didn't want to admit it, but dinner was great. Of course, being with Alex would have made a peanut butter and jelly sandwich seem regal. She had a way of grounding me. I was glad she agreed with my plan to turn over this sordid mess to Riddick, especially since I was seeing the bomber everywhere, or so I imagined.

"Gil, you seem lost in thought again. Everything all right?"

I jerked my head toward her. "Yes. I'm fine. Hey, this coffee is good, but I've had enough. Let's go."

Alex knitted her eyebrows and said, "Well, okay. If that's what you want." She took one more swig of her tea and stood to leave.

When we walked out of the restaurant, Alex asked me again if everything was okay. I promised her it was. *I need to forget this dude who probably isn't even watching us and focus on Alex instead.*

We were met by music flowing out of the nearby bars, pedestrians thick on the sidewalks, and patrons eating outdoors at the small cafes. Our little town was abuzz once again, and I loved it. Seemed we'd put a lot of distance between the bombing and where we were now.

"Hey, babe, we could go for a stroll to, you know, walk off our dinner."

"No way, Sullivan. You promised me a movie, and I've already made my choice."

"And the winner is?"

"Spider-Man: No Way Home."

"Seriously?"

"Oh yeah. Spidey's cool. And I love action flicks. Even guns, killing, blood and guts—all that gory stuff, you know?"

"I would have never pegged you—"

"Ha. Wait until you see me on the shooting range, sweets. A girl's got to be able to defend herself, right?"

"You never cease to amaze me, Alex."

I bought our tickets, and we went in and found our seats. Right before the movie started, I asked, "By the way, what was that grass stuff we had tonight?"

"Duck liver." She held out her hands, palms up, and shrugged.

I nodded and tried to look cool.

Full disclosure, the film was pretty entertaining. Once it ended, I took Alex home. We pulled up to a dark house, except for the front porch light. "Chrissy already in bed?"

"No, she's at a friend's house. Come on in." She took me by the hand as we walked up the front sidewalk.

"Coffee?"

"Sure, I'd love some."

We took a seat on the couch, with Alex scooching up to me. Nervously, I placed my arm over her shoulders, and she leaned over to kiss me. It was awkward. Not her fault, but mine. I worried that any act of even the slightest intimacy might lead to something more. Alex must have read my mind.

"You've got to move on, Gil. I respect that you're not ready to completely do that, but it sure puts a monkey wrench in our sweetest moments."

"I know, Alex. I'm working on it. Give me time."

After small talk and two more cups of coffee, decaf this time, I was ready to go. "Alex, I'm beat. It's been a week, and I think I need some sleep. I really enjoyed our evening—even the duck liver grass." She shook her head and then kissed me.

As I reached the door, Alex grabbed my arm and turned me. She got within a few inches of my face, and her eyes zoned in on mine like lasers. "I can wait, Gil. Not forever, but for now, I can wait." We shared one more kiss.

As I pulled into my driveway, my phone chirped, illuminating the car's interior. The text sent chills down my spine.

> I warned you to stop

I'd gotten home much later than I'd planned. I knew Dutch would have to go out, and he'd likely be at the door. As I entered the house, he wasn't there to greet me. That was unusual. I turned on the den lamp. Still no sign of Dutch. *Must really be sound asleep.* As I walked into the kitchen, my feet, heart, and breathing all stopped in unison. Dutch was lying on the floor near the back door, a puddle of blood under him and broken glass scattered close by. A glass pane on the door was shattered, its jagged edges crimson colored. I knelt to Dutch's side. A large clot of semi-solid blood was matted in the fur of his neck. His big, brown eyes were staring and distant, his breathing rapid, and his body quivering. Shock.

"Dutch!" I cried out. No response. What to do? *Think, Sullivan.* I needed help. I grabbed my phone. "Xavier, Dutch is hurt . . . badly! Get over here right now! Please hurry." He was in my kitchen in a flash. "Here, take my keys and drive us to the emergency vet office. Here's my phone but call on the way. We gotta go."

I lay Dutch in the back seat and got in beside him, constantly keeping pressure on his neck wound. There was no change in his appearance, but he was alive—that was something. My tears fell onto his snout as I leaned close to reassure him.

We were met at the office door by the veterinarian and the nurse on duty, a gurney at their side. We gently moved Dutch to the stretcher. Dr. Griff Benton and I were casual acquaintances, having both been featured recently in the local paper's story on young professionals. "Gil, we'll take it from here. Let me do a quick assessment, and I'll come back out to update you. My partner's on the way in, just in case surgery's necessary and we get into something complicated."

Xavier and I took a seat in the waiting room, furnished with hard plastic chairs and an artificial Ficus plant sitting in the corner. "Dr. Gil, I so sorry for Dutch. I love that dog, you know."

"I know you do, Xavier, and thanks so much for your help. Without you to drive me here, I don't know what I would have done."

"Dutch be okay?"

"I don't know, *mi amigo*. I honestly don't know." I kneaded my temples.

"Dr. Benton—he good doctor. Saved life of friend's *gato* . . . uh, how you say . . . cat?"

Griff walked out, a concerned look on his face. "He's lost a lot of blood, Gil. His mucous membranes are pale. If his thick coat hadn't helped the blood to clot, I don't think he'd still be with us. We're getting him prepped for surgery, and we'll get started as soon as my partner is here. Don't know how long it will take. Gotta get in there and assess the damage first. Why don't you go home and try to get some rest? I'll text you when I know more."

"Please, call me, Griff. No matter the time, call me. And thanks."

Chapter Fourteen

I'd called the police station while we were sitting at the vet's office. Chief Riddick had answered. No surprise. When Xavier and I returned home and turned into the driveway, he was parked in the street. From our phone conversation, I knew he was anxious to hear what I had to say and to see the crime scene.

"Did you touch anything, Doc?"

"Only Dutch."

"Good. Let's take a look." He entered the kitchen and stopped, looking at the scene intensely. "Pretty obvious this was a break-in. Must've broken a pane and reached in to unlock the door. From the looks of what's left, the idiot probably cut himself as he stuck his arm through the opening." He looked down at the broken glass near the pool of blood, now purplish-black and gelatinous. "See that large shard with blood on it? My guess is Dutch surprised him, the person picked up that piece and used it as a knife to stab him. I'll gather glass from the door and the floor and send blood samples from both to Raleigh. While I dust the glass for prints, why don't you take a look around and see what's missing?"

I was impressed with the chief's attention to detail, as I'd never seen this side of him. While he delicately picked up glass fragments and put them in evidence bags, I walked around the house, looking for anything damaged or missing. Nothing.

"Everything's in order, Chief."

"Good. Hopefully, that means the perpetrator might have been hurt bad enough that he had to get out of here pronto. Maybe even seek medical help, especially if he's as stupid as he seems to be. You know, I read this book on true stories of dumb crook—"

"Chief, please."

"Right. I'll alert the hospitals in Chapel Hill and the surrounding areas to be on the lookout for someone with the injuries we're suspecting. You need to get some rest, Doc."

"Yes, sir. I'll do that." But I lied. I still had to clean the floor and somehow patch the damaged door pane. Besides, I was running on adrenaline and worried about Dutch. No way I'd fall asleep right now.

Once Xavier and the chief left, I was alone with my thoughts. I couldn't lose my dog. He was family, and I'd lost enough family already. As I swept the glass and wiped the floor with moist cloths, I cried like I hadn't cried since my mom died.

I wanted to call Alex, but it was late. She was opening the store in the morning and then would be in Chapel Hill at the courthouse for the rest of the day. I'd call her tomorrow after work. If Dutch survived, I would spare her the worry. If he died, there would be no good time to tell her—or Chrissy. If he survived or died? Could he really die? What would I do if I lost my Dutchie? Who would do such a thing? Why wasn't bombing the plant enough? Who, or what, was he after? Was all this related to my searching for the truth about Carlos? If so, he could come at me with guns blazing, but don't hurt my dog. This is our pets' world, and we're lucky to live in it. There'd be a special place in Hell for people who hurt animals. I know, not very Christian, but who could blame me? Even Rev. Dunk would understand my feelings . . . maybe. If God was testing me, I was failing badly. I needed to forgive, but I'd never forget. But how could I forgive a killer? I did the only thing I knew to do as a believer. I prayed.

Prayer always calmed me, even when I didn't hear an answer right away. I fell asleep for a few hours, waking frequently. Dr. Benton's call came before dawn, but I was already up and drinking coffee.

"Gil, it's Griff. Dutch is out of surgery. The wound extended to his jugular vein, nicking it. I don't need to tell you how close that is to his carotid. Hit that, and he doesn't survive."

"How is he, Griff?"

"He lost a lot of blood. We've replaced some of it, but his blood pressure's still low, and he's tachycardic. Too soon to say how he'll do. He's still coming out of the anesthesia, and his pain meds are keeping him asleep. But I'll keep you posted. You'll be at your office later today, right?"

"Right." I knew I had a full Friday schedule, and I needed to be there, even though I'd rather be at Dutch's side. "But call me anytime."

———

My plan was to not burden anyone at the office with my news. That lasted about five minutes. Sarah, my nurse, knew me better than anyone but Alex, and it must have been obvious to her something was wrong.

"Dr. Gil, you okay?"

"Yes, Sarah . . . actually, no, I'm not. Can you step into my office, please?" I closed the door behind her and motioned to a chair by my desk.

"What's wrong?"

"It's Dutch." As I explained what happened, Sarah's eyes moistened, and then the dam broke. She loved Dutch, having kept him for me on those rare times when Alex and I could get away for the weekend.

"I am so sorry." Her voice caught. "I'll pray for Dutch, and I hope they catch the son of—"

"You don't have to say it, Sarah. I know what you mean, and trust me, I feel the same way. Dutch is recovering from emergency surgery. Dr. Benton promised me updates, but I don't know if he'll call or text. Please let the front desk know to pull me out of a room if he calls."

"Dr. Benton's great. I know Dutch is going to be fine, Dr. Gil." She bit her lower lip. "At least, that's my prayer."

"That's all we can do right now. Really appreciate your concern. Now, we need to get to work, try to focus, and make it through the day."

Miss Wainwright was on my schedule again. Maybe that was good. She always distracted me; maybe I'd actually stop thinking about Dutch temporarily.

"Hello, young man," she said as I opened the exam room door. "Didn't expect to be back so soon. After all, I recently saw you, and you told me I was perfectly fine." Sarah followed me in. "Oh, hello, Sarah. Guess I don't get this young man all to myself."

"No, ma'am. I'm here for the exam and to help Dr. Sullivan if he needs anything." She cleared her throat and glanced at me.

"What brings you in today?" I asked.

"This dreaded cough. Started a few days ago. No big deal until I brought up some blood yesterday. Feel a little winded too."

"Uh-huh . . . hemoptysis."

"Hem what, young man?"

"Bloody cough."

"Well, why didn't you say that in the first place? Listen, I know you're smart—that's why I come to you. So you don't have to use big words to impress me. Regular Queen's English will do perfectly fine, thank you very much."

"Yes, ma'am." I stepped behind her, shot a glance at Sarah, and rolled my eyes. She smothered a chuckle. I slipped my stethoscope under Miss Wainwright's half-gown and listened to deep breaths over her back and chest. Her breath sounds seemed a little diminished in the right upper chest. "You've probably got viral bronchitis, but let's get an X-ray to be sure. Sarah, can you put the order in, please? Miss Wainwright, I'll step out while you slip your blouse back on."

She grabbed my arm as I turned to go. "Question, young man. What's that large jar half-full of coins and bills doing on the counter by the check-in?"

I explained how the clinic supported a local homeless shelter for women and children, and we not only collected money, but almost every doctor in our practice took a turn working there once a month.

"Well, I suppose what you do with your free time is your business, but I don't understand why you'd expect patients to donate their hard-earned or inherited money to some cause."

"Completely up to you. Now, let me step out so you can get ready to go to X-ray." I slowly shook my head as I walked back to my office.

Between each patient, I checked my phone. Finally, I saw a text.

> No change. Condition stable but guarded.
> I'll keep you posted

Not the news I wanted from Griff, but it could have been worse. Dutch was hanging in there. I said a quick prayer and moved on with my patients.

Finally, the end of the day arrived. Sarah met me in the hall. "Dr. Benton just called. I tried to get him to hold, but he refused. Said it would be best for you to come to his office as soon as possible." She wiped away tears and added, "He sounded serious. I'm scared, Dr. Gil."

Chapter Fifteen

The short drive to the vet's office seemed like the last slow mile of a marathon race. Even though I couldn't wait to get there, I dreaded what I would find, or be told. I rushed into the waiting room, still occupied by owners and their pets. Mostly dogs.

One of Griff's assistants came out and asked me to follow her. "Dr. Benton thought you'd be more comfortable sitting in one of our rooms."

She ushered me into a nicely furnished room that I assumed Griff used for conferences and consolation. "Dr. Benton said he needs extra time with you, but it'll be a bit. He's pretty busy." A framed copy of The Rainbow Bridge hung on the wall. My heart sank as low as the depths of the ocean. With each passing minute, I grew more anxious. When Griff finally opened the door, his solemn look sent my heart even deeper.

"Busy day, but glad you're here, Gil. Sorry you had to wait in this room." Then he smiled. "There's someone who wants to see you. Follow me."

We entered a room designed for dogs recuperating from surgery. A vet tech sat in attendance. Dutch lifted his head and made eye contact with me. His tail wagged and, I swear, I think that dog smiled.

"He made it, Gil. We finally caught up with his blood loss, and he came around. That's a strong dog right there, especially his heart."

I rushed to his side and gave him a hug around his bandaged neck. My tears melted into his coat and moistened his surgical dressing.

"Careful, Gil. I suspect he's pretty sore."

I released Dutch and turned to Griff. "Oh my gosh, I can't thank—"

"You don't have to thank me, my friend. This is what makes my job worthwhile. Now, we'll need to keep him at least another night, but we'll take good care of him." With a smile, he added, "And if you ever decide you don't want this sweet boy, I've got about five employees who'd be happy to take him off your hands."

"Not a chance, Griff. Can I sit here with him for a little while before I go?"

"Sure. Take your time. We'll be here a while longer—still got patients to see."

I sat there with Dutch, who'd put his head back down and closed his eyes. He nuzzled against my hand as I gently scratched his ear. He was weak and needed rest, but he was alive and was going to make it. It was a sweet moment . . . until thoughts of the monster who did this and bombed the furniture plant entered my mind. Why was he after me? The only connection I could figure was my being there with Carlos. He must have stuck around to enjoy the carnage and then seen Carlos talking to me.

When Dutch drifted off to sleep, I slipped out of his room, thanked the staff again, and left the clinic. I had people to call with this good news, with Alex jumping out first in my mind.

I called her from my car and gave her the short version of what Dutch and I had been through since I'd left her the night before. What came next shocked me.

"Dutch's life was at stake, and you didn't see fit to call me, Sullivan? How dare you? And don't give me some line of bunk about how late it was. Listen, I woke up every two hours to breastfeed Chrissy when she was a baby. It's what you do when you love someone. Yeah, I was fourteen years younger, but I can still handle a late-night phone call. And don't you think I'd have wanted to be there?"

"But Alex, I—"

"Don't 'but' me, 'cause I don't want to hear it. If we're going to be a thing—you know, a couple—we need to support each other. That means sharing the good times and the bad. Happiness, yes, but sadness or even grief too. It's what couples do."

I reached for my temple as muscles tightened. I thought I'd done the right thing by not calling her sooner. "I'm really sorry, Alex. I've never been in a relationship where I could share . . . well, you know what I mean. Anyway, lesson learned. I just wanted you to know he's going to be okay."

"And I do thank the good Lord for that, Gil. I can forgive you for this, but I'll never forgive the evil person who hurt Dutch."

A quick mental calculation told me this wasn't the time to say something about the difference between "forgive" and "forget."

"And Gil, long as we're on unpleasant topics, I ran into Virgil the other day or, better said, he ran into me. Came into the bookstore."

"What?"

"Yeah, and it wasn't to buy a book. Said he wanted another chance for us to be a family. He seemed kinda desperate."

"What'd you tell him?"

"Told him there was no *us*, not as a family, in his future; then I asked him to leave. To his credit, he just walked back out the door."

"I thought he was working—you know, on the road most days."

"He had some kind of work injury. Said he hurt his hand and was out for a few days. He even tried using his injury to make me feel sorry for him."

I wasn't happy Virgil had confronted Alex, but she'd handled it well. Her telling me about it also got us off the mess I'd made by not calling her when Dutch was injured. By the time we hung up, I think I was out of the doghouse—no pun intended. I called Sarah and put her mind at ease, and then phoned Bobby, hoping to get a little better response from him than I did from Alex.

"I wish you'd called me earlier, Gil. I couldn't have gotten there quickly enough to help get Dutch to the vet, but I would've appreciated being in the loop."

"Yeah. Alex feels the same way, only she wasn't as nice about it."

"Gil, you've got a lot to learn about women." He laughed. "I can teach you how to read 'em, pacify 'em, play 'em . . . you name it."

Okay, that sounds weird. "Well, I did come late to the game, Bobby."

I'd avoided any kind of meaningful relationship with girls until Alex came along. Though still bothered by my parents' history, I was slowly moving on, and Alex's remarks made me think she was taking our relationship pretty seriously. I needed to do the same or let her know I felt differently.

"Gil, I know it's getting late, but why don't you meet me somewhere for dinner?

"Appreciate it, buddy, but I'm beat. After the emotional roller coaster of the last twenty-four hours, I need to go home and chill."

"Understand completely. Keep me posted about Dutch."

"Don't worry. I won't make that mistake again."

I'd arrived home while talking to Bobby. It was good to be there, even if I was alone. What a day. I'd been worried sick about Dutch but was relieved to now know he'd be okay.

And what about Miss Wainwright? You see enough patients and listen to enough breath sounds and you get a feeling when something doesn't pass the "sniff" test. A cough producing blood with no accompanying fever wasn't likely due to infection. Tuberculosis wasn't likely either, given Eleanor's tendency to isolate herself. A tumor seemed the most probable diagnosis—lung cancer. She had few friends and had outlived most of her contemporaries. This was a battle she'd have to fight alone, except for help from the medical community. But I was getting way over my skis, as Bobby would say. I'd been wrong before. The chest X-ray should tell me something.

Chapter Sixteen

Alex

It wasn't unusual to run into my friend Tom Waters and his dog Scout on Saturday mornings at Caffeine Scene. I think he loved coffee as much as Gil and I did. We were sitting at one of the tables, prepared to solve the world's problems. First, we needed to catch up on each other's lives.

"Great to see you with Gil at the diner last Sunday. Had no idea the two of you are a thing, as you young people call it."

I reached down to pat Scout's head. "Yeah, we're not advertising . . . at least not yet. After my train wreck marriage to Virgil, we're taking it slowly."

"Virgil," he said, shaking his head as he looked away. "Don't know what happened to that boy. I really thought he'd amount to something when he grew up."

"That's just it, Tom. He never grew up. He's a living, breathing Peter Pan." I tapped a finger on my coffee cup, wondering how deep to go with this conversation, and decided to shift the focus to something more comfortable. "You know, I'm going to take you up on that offer for Gil and me to come in for a shake. I know he'd love it."

As kids, my friends and I would rush to Waters Pharmacy on Saturday afternoons and compete for the best seats at the counter. We'd climb onto the cushioned vinyl stools and reach over the Formica top to grab our favorite shakes. Tom—or Doc Waters as we knew him back then—would take our empty glasses, add another scoop of ice cream, and wink at us as he handed them back. The pharmacy was where we girls gossiped about the other girls and, as we came of age, had our serious boy talks.

"How's Chrissy doing, Alex? And, if I can ask, how's she handling seeing her dad so infrequently?" Tom said, bringing me back to the conversation.

"She hardly sees Virgil 'cause usually, he doesn't even make it for his scheduled visits with her."

"Well, I don't mean to bring up old wounds, but I know you understand how a child feels who doesn't have the full support of both parents."

My words caught in my throat, so I simply nodded. This was Virgil's turn to have Chrissy for the weekend. I wasn't surprised when he didn't show up, given how I'd treated him in the bookstore. Chrissy, who seemed to prefer hanging out with her friends, didn't seem disappointed, but I was concerned. Chrissy didn't have a father who served as a role model—a dad in the house, showing her how a man should act and what a man should be.

"Does Chrissy resent Gil or the time you spend with him? Easy for that to happen to a child when they lose a parent, you know?"

"She loves him, and I think the feeling's mutual. They shoot hoops, go fishing, and take Dutch on walks. He lifts Chrissy's mood, and that makes me happy too."

"Well, like I said at the diner that day, Gil's a fine man. And speaking of Dutch, I ran into Griff Benton the other day. Said Dutch was in his hospital, recuperating from an injury. Wouldn't say anything more about it, though."

"At least Dr. Griffin had the courtesy to mention Dutch to someone who'd want to know." Tom lifted both eyebrows. "Sorry. Long story but, yes, Dutch is on the mend."

I took a big swig from my coffee cup, then slowly rested it on the saucer. Was I was being too hard on Gil? Bless his heart, I know he was doing the best he could, or so he thought. My words might have been too blunt, too harsh—one of my faults, and maybe one of the things Virgil never got used to. Matter of fact, maybe I was too hard on Virgil in that last conversation at the store. That was on me. The Bible tells us to be quick to listen, slow to speak, and slow to anger. I needed to work on that. Be a little less critical with people, especially with Gil, but maybe even with my ex. After all, he'd finally found a decent job. Given enough time, Virgil might come around and at least be there for Chrissy. *That's the best I can hope for.*

"Alex? You seem a little preoccupied today. Something on your mind?"

"Oh, just thinking. So much has gone on lately in our little town, what with the bombing and now with Dutch's injury. It wasn't an accident. Someone broke into Gil's house and cut Dutch with a piece of glass from the door pane. We figure Dutch surprised him."

"Well, young lady, don't worry that pretty head of yours too much. Things will settle down. They always do. Hey, I'm going to need to run soon. Guess we'll have to solve the world's problems next time." He laughed.

"Yep, the world will have to wait until—"

My phone chirped. Gil. His message worried me. "I've gotta go, Tom. Gil needs me." I rushed out, leaving Tom with the bill but no explanation.

Chapter Seventeen

I was encouraged by Dutch's improvement. I had the whole weekend off and was ready to bring him home. When my phone rang, I assumed it would be Dr. Benton. Wrong. It was welcome but unexpected news.

"Gil, this is Jasper Riddick. We got him."

"Excuse me?"

"We got the man who broke into your house."

My heart raced. "Who is it? What's his name?"

"Why don't you come down to the station? I think it'd be better if we discuss this in person."

I couldn't get there fast enough. My left foot rapidly tapped the floorboard, while I rubbed the muscles in my temples. My heart pounded. Could this be the end? The guy who threatened me, hurt my dog, and, most importantly, murdered innocent, hard-working people with a bomb is now in custody? When I pulled into the station's parking lot, I was surprised there were no federal or state trooper cars there. The chief's patrol car sat alone. Maybe they hadn't had time to get there, or they'd already picked this guy up. I rushed into the station only to find the chief calmly sitting at his desk.

"Have the authorities already taken him away?" I asked.

"Nope. He's in my cell, at least for now."

"They're on their way to take him to Raleigh, right?"

"No. He didn't bomb the plant, but he confessed to breaking into your house, hurting your dog, and sending you threatening texts."

"How do you know he's not the bomber? Who is this guy?"

"It's Virgil Morgan. Guess I forgot to tell you that."

I froze, unable to speak, as I tried to process what he said. Finally, "Virgil?"

The chief explained that Virgil went to the emergency room in Chapel Hill to get his hand injury treated. While there, the doctor also noticed bite marks on his arm. Virgil admitted he'd been bitten by a dog.

"I'd alerted area hospitals to look for anyone with those injuries, and someone from the hospital called me after Virgil left the ER. I called his work, spooking him. He was getting ready to make a run, but I got there in time. His supervisor checked the logbook, and Virgil was out of town on a trip to Asheville at the time of the bombing, so it couldn't have been him. When I pressed him on those texts, he admitted to sending them. Probably figured they were harmless, as he never specifically threatened you with physical harm. He's probably right."

I looked down and shook my head. "This is going to kill Alex, Chief. Bad enough he's been a terrible father but now a common criminal? And what do you mean he's locked up 'for now'?"

"He called an attorney who's on his way in to work out Virgil's release on his own recognizance. I'll have to let him go since the charges aren't that serious, and his only other crime is being a deadbeat dad."

"In my opinion, they are serious. He almost killed Dutch! Plus, he did break and enter my house—I can't even think straight, Chief. I'm going to text Alex, if that's okay."

I sent her a quick text, asking her to get over to the station as quickly as possible.

The attorney arrived. When the chief opened the door to go back to the cell, I got a quick glimpse of Virgil. It was him—the guy who was watching Alex and me when we were out. Same posture and brooding look, minus the ball cap. I couldn't swear to it, but I was pretty sure.

Alex rushed in shortly thereafter. "What's going on, Chief? Gil?"

Riddick motioned for her to take a seat and explained everything, reiterating what he'd told me. As he talked, her face got redder and redder, and she gripped the chair's arms so tightly that her fingers blanched.

"Is he here? 'Cause I don't want to be here if he's here, even if he's in a jail cell."

"He's with his attorney, Alex," the chief said as he fumbled for a cigarette. "Mind if I light up? They're discussing bail, so it'll be a while longer. You don't have to see him, but I 'spect he'd like to see you. Shoulda heard what he said—"

"Actually, Chief, I do mind. Smoke makes me cough," Alex said. "And I don't hardly care what he said."

"When you led his attorney to the cell, I got a peek at Virgil, Chief. Pretty sure he's the person who was shadowing Alex and me on our recent nights out."

"What on earth are you talking about, Sullivan?"

Sullivan? Uh oh. I knew Alex was about to throw a penalty flag whenever she used my last name instead of the affectionate ones that usually crossed her lips.

I explained to Alex I thought I was being silly or paranoid, and I didn't want to worry her, so I didn't say anything about the guy I'd noticed. She looked away and shook her head.

"This is awful," she said as her eyes filled with tears. "My ex is a stalker, a creepy texter, a criminal, and hurts dogs. I never want to see him again. I didn't even want a relationship with him after we split, but I had to cooperate for Chrissy's sake. Gil, can we get out of here, please?"

Chief Riddick said he'd keep us posted, and there was no reason for us to stay any longer. Before we left, he leaned toward my ear. "Gil, you do realize this means we still don't have the bomber, right? Probably long gone by now." That thought was as unsettling as the thought that someone would send threatening texts, break into a house, and hurt a dog . . . jealousy and stupidity were a dangerous concoction.

Alex plopped into my car, her head in her hands and shoulders sagging. She was too upset to drive herself home. Her crying pushed all the air out of the car. I stayed quiet, figuring she needed time to compose herself.

"Gil, I'm sorry you got dragged into this mess."

"If you're talking about Virgil's actions, forget it. I didn't get dragged into anything. I knew before we started dating that you had an ex who was a loser. He can't let go of you, Alex. That's actually the only thing about him that makes sense to me."

"Meaning?"

"Meaning you're a special person. He blew it when he lost you, but I hit the jackpot." *Okay, Gil, you said it. Now you have to show her how you feel.*

"But he threatened you, broke into your house, and, worst of all, hurt Dutch. Aren't you way beyond angry with him?"

"Sure, I'm angry. But I'm also relieved we now know who was doing all of this. What frustrates me is the bomber's still on the loose. Riddick doesn't have any leads, but I guess there's no reason to think he's still around. The only good thing is, it's over—it wasn't the bomber stalking us and texting me, and now I can get back to focusing on my work and stop worrying about more threats—a couple of silver linings, if you ask me." She finally smiled.

When we pulled into her driveway, Chrissy was waiting on the front porch. Her eyes were red and puffy. As Alex climbed out of the car, she ran into her arms.

"Chrissy, what's wrong, honey?"

"I heard about Dad. Why's he in jail? What did he do?"

Chrissy knew? I looked at Alex and wrinkled my brow.

"Small town, Gil. News travels fast," she whispered.

We sat on the porch as Alex explained everything to her. She got up and paced as she heard the full story.

"I hate him. He walked out on us, barely pays any attention to me, and now this? He almost killed Dutch? I never want to see him again."

"Chrissy, I hate what your father did, too, but I don't hate him," I said. "If you choose to hate him, it will eat away at you, destroy your peace, and you'll pay a higher price for his actions than he will. Why not give this some time, let his prosecution play out, and then see how we all feel? I doubt your dad will show his face, anyway." My attempt at peacemaker was interrupted by a call. I walked a few steps away to take it.

A minute later, I returned to their conversation. "Girls, that was Dr. Benton's office. Finally, some positive news. Dutch has been cleared for discharge. Why don't the two of you go with me to get him, and then I'll drop you off at the police station for you to get your car?"

When we arrived, we were greeted by Griff's assistant and Dutch, leashed and sitting beside him. As soon as he saw us, Dutch stood and limped his way to me. I knelt and wrapped my arms around him, careful to avoid the oversized bandage on his neck. Alex and Chrissy joined us. The four of us must have been a sight as we loved on Dutch and our tears fell into his coat.

"Can I join the happy reunion?" It was Griff. "Gil, I know you're a doctor, but there are some discharge instructions I need to review with you."

I left Dutch with Alex and Chrissy and walked back to Griff's office. He went over wound care, antibiotics, and when to return to the clinic for a follow-up. I tried to thank him, but the words stuck in my throat, crowded in there with my heart.

"Gil, I get what you're trying to say, and you're welcome. That's one special dog, and I'm sure gonna miss the big fella. Now, get out of here and take Dutch home where he belongs."

On our way to the station, Alex said, "Well, I'm not sure 'all's well that ends well' is quite apropos right now, but this *is* a great way to end a very weird day. So much for easy Saturdays, right?"

"I've got my dog and two of my favorite people, so it's all good, babe. I'll see you at church in the morning. Right now, Dutch and I are going home to catch our breath."

Dutch and I walked into the empty house. I could tell he knew he was home as he slowly limped through the living area. At the doorway to the kitchen, he froze. He looked up at the back door's new windowpane and whimpered. The hair on his back stood up and his ears drew back, as though he still sensed the intruder's presence. His eyes seemed to speak to me.

I knelt and whispered in his ear, "I get it, but it's okay, buddy. You're home and safe."

His eyes didn't change.

"Will food help?"

He strolled to the pantry, twice looking back at the door.

I grabbed his food from the pantry and enticed him to his bowl. After a few bites, he trudged back into the living area, looking back a couple more times. Benton had warned me he wouldn't eat much for a while, and I figured he'd also need some time to know he was safe in our house. They say dogs have short memories and forgive easily, but this was going to take a while to get over—for both of us.

Chapter Eighteen

Luna

As the truck bounced along, a thought bounced around in my head: *What bothers me more: that Ava was taken or the way it happened?* A man with money picked her out of the group of girls and bought her like people pick out the freshest fruit to buy when they traveled from the village to the market in Moyobamba. People shouldn't be treated like that, and I'd been powerless to stop it.

I'd assumed the role of protector, trying to reassure the other girls that, as bleak as it seemed, someone would come for us and take us back to the village. I wasn't sure that would happen, but I had to act as though it would. But this? Ava gone? That hurt. She was like a little sister to me. Neither of us had siblings, and we seemed drawn to each other to fill that void. She'd tagged along when we walked to school and when we played in the fields, always at my side and sometimes clinging to my simple dress so as not to be left behind. The older girls laughed at me and asked why I didn't send her away to play with kids her age. I'd never had the heart or desire to do that. Now, she'd not only been left behind, but she'd been captured by a total stranger and would be subjected to whatever his desires and plans would be.

Between sobs and long periods of silence, the girls asked me questions: Why is this happening? Where are we going? Why are they taking some girls away as we travel? Will we ever see our parents, brothers, and sisters again? The questions pierced the innermost part of my heart, and it was all I could do to try to answer them without visibly joining in their despair. Years earlier, my mum had to have been very brave to move with me to Peru, with no husband to help her. I prayed God would grant me similar courage.

Our captors seemed to grant me special favor—for the most part, they kept their hands off or me and their lurid stares on the others, not on me.

Somehow, I would use that to my advantage. As slowly as we were moving, I had plenty of time to think. Time to figure out how we could escape or perhaps bargain for our release.

The man I'd labeled Toothless interacted with us more than the other men did. Even though he said few words, he made himself clear when he wanted us to do something. He would be the one I'd approach to ask about our fate—once I built up more courage, I'd figure out a way to outsmart him.

For now, I had to look after the other girls and maintain a brave face. But I was exhausted. I closed my eyes, hoping to fall asleep and then wake up to realize this was all a bad dream.

Chapter Nineteen

Hillsborough

Eager to get back to normal life, I looked forward to the next workday. I met Sarah as I walked into the office. "Mornin', Dr. Gil," she said through a stifled yawn. "How's Dutch?"

"A little skittish but getting better. And how are you? Late night?"

"Medic duty till midnight. Then, too pumped up to relax and fall asleep once I got home. Made two runs to Chapel Hill: an auto accident victim and the other a possible heart attack. Funny thing is, it wasn't his heart after all. Before we could get to the university hospital, he belched loudly, sat up on the stretcher, and said, 'I feel better now. Can I go back home?'" She held out her hands, palms up. "What more can I say?"

Sarah worked as a volunteer for the paramedic crew, hoping to embellish her resume before she finished her physician assistant program. She wanted to get her license and practice as a mid-level provider. I had every intention of helping her fulfill that dream in our office. She was a heck of a nurse and would be a great addition to our team.

"Dr. Gil, just a heads up. Miss Wainwright is, or was, first on your schedule. She called to cancel. Not really sure why. She didn't say."

I was pretty sure I knew why. Her X-ray had showed two nodules in the peripheral portion of the right lung, almost a sure sign of cancer—adenocarcinoma, to be more specific. Not what I wanted to see or have to share with her. When I called her over the weekend, her response was not unexpected.

"Young man, there must be some mistake. Lung cancer? I never smoked a day in my life, nor did anyone in my family, for that matter."

"I know, but lung cancer occurs in non-smokers too. It doesn't seem fair, but it happens. I'm so sorry, Miss Wainwright. I wanted to let you know as quickly as possible, but you need to come in so we can discuss what we're going to do."

"I might come in and listen, but I'm not planning on doing anything. That's a waste of my time and money. What will be, will be, I always say."

"Miss Wainwright, I'll respect your decision but please come in and hear me out."

I had no great expectations of convincing her to change her mind, but it was my duty to try. As a physician, I felt compelled to encourage my patients to be aggressive in seeking treatment. I always promised I'd be right there with them, pedal to the metal, at least until we saw proof the treatment wasn't working. Sometimes we had to recognize when it was time to stop treatment and let nature take its course. But I wasn't so sure Miss Wainwright would agree to give treatment a try.

Sarah checked later that day and told me Miss Wainwright had rescheduled for Wednesday. That day came and went with another cancelled appointment. When she wasn't on my schedule by Friday, I knew I had some work to do to get her in for a consultation. Or maybe I'd try something a little different. I'd chew on that a bit.

That Friday afternoon, George Owens was back. Despite our agreement for him to come in weekly, it'd been a few weeks since I'd last seen him. I'd checked in with the counselor, who told me he made an appointment but didn't keep it. He'd filled his prescription, but if he was taking it, it didn't seem to be helping much. He was still grieving over losing his son in the explosion. When he walked into my office, his appearance shocked me. He was thinner now, his face hollow-cheeked. He was more stooped, and his disheveled clothes hung loosely on him, like an outfit carelessly thrown over a coat rack.

"I've been worried about you, George. It's been a few weeks. Glad you're here today, though. How've you been?"

He looked up at me, his expressionless eyes two small mirrors reflecting the grief I'd seen in my mom's eyes when she and I talked about the choices she'd made. Emotions stirred that I'd suppressed for a long time.

"Not good, Doc. Don't know if I can make it. No joy in my life now. The wife and I aren't really speaking. Too hard to talk about anything, you know, 'cause it always circles back to Tyler."

I do know, more than you realize.

"It's hard, George, but you've got to give yourself time. Take it day by day and, when one day's too long, take things hour by hour. No one who's dealt with grief is going to judge you or think any less of you because you're struggling. When we lose someone we love so much, trouble dealing with it proves how much they meant to us."

"You're probably right, Doc. You usually are. Don't see any light at the end of this tunnel, though."

"Well, George, that light's a funny thing. It's there, whether you see it or not. You have to get back to seeing it or let it come to you. Have you seen the grief counselor?"

"No. I don't know 'bout doin' that. I'm a private person. Doubt I could share what's going through my head these days, especially when I can't even open up with the missus. I thought about talking to Rev. McElroy at the church, but I don't think that would help much. Don't really feel God's here for me in this mess. Besides, what can another person do, even if he is a preacher? It's my loss, my grief."

"I understand how you feel. I really do. But the weight of the burdens in our lives is lessened when we allow someone else to help us carry it. At least let me be that person for you, George. Come back regularly . . . please."

He shrugged, then nodded. "Okay. I'll try to be better about coming in, Doc."

"It's not about being better, George; it's about *being*, period. Right now, just be satisfied to exist, to let yourself feel whatever emotions run through you, and to give yourself time. You'll never get over this loss. Tyler doesn't deserve that, would he? But you'll find a place in your head where his life goes, and gradually, the good memories will overtake the painful ones, kind of like a healthy stand of grass kills the weeds."

George stood to leave. I shook his hand. Probably like his soul, his grip was weak and without much conviction.

George was my last patient that Friday. Fortunately, no late work-ins were added. I was mentally exhausted. Spending time with George took me back to those bleak months following my mother's death—a memory I was gradually squeezing from my brain's storage capacity but one that occasionally came storming back like a late summer afternoon thundershower. I'd done the best I could for George, but was it enough? Time would tell.

As I drove home, I mentally rehashed the week. My two most challenging patients, Eleanor Wainwright and George Owens, were both struggling . . . and hurting. I would have to call on all of my skills as a physician to meet their needs. I'd been here before, but it was always a challenge. As a physician, I was constantly learning and improving on my ability to provide for my patients, but I wasn't perfect. There's a reason it's called the *practice* of medicine.

Chapter Twenty

My decision to go into family medicine in Hillsborough had to do with family. If I were to pick the ideal practice, it would be full of families, with me providing care for the youngest, from birth to the oldest, until they slipped away from life as we know it on this earth. The dynamics within families can be fascinating but sometimes frustrating. That's why Eleanor Wainwright's decision to deal with her lung cancer alone and George Owens's choice to turn from his wife and handle grief by himself weighed on me like an albatross of sadness. They'd both inhabited an isolated island—one of them with no one in her life and the other about to lose the most important person left in his. I would deal with both, but I needed to call on the wisdom of Arnie Schmidt to help me navigate their medical and emotional journeys. This stuff wasn't taught in medical school, and Arnie had been around this block more than a few times.

As for Hillsborough, we weren't Mayberry but still a small town by big-city standards. That was fine by me. Everyone seemed to know everyone else, or at least pretended to. In a way, the town was like one big family. Maybe on a subconscious level, that's what I was looking for—something I'd never had.

Time and distance from the explosion seemed to help get the town back to normal. The furniture workers were back on the job in a deserted warehouse Hank Martin had rented and turned into a factory while his was being rebuilt. I didn't lose anyone with whom I was close. I was lucky, I guess. I'd been here two years and had melted into the community. But I wasn't from here—didn't bleed "Carolina blue," as Alex called it. I guess I was more of an in-law and here by God's grace, as Southerners liked to say. The only fatalities I experienced, and those only indirectly, were the deaths of Carlos and Tyler Owens. I knew neither of them personally. Once I decided to let the chief solve the mystery of Carlos's identity, only George Owens was left for me to try to put the pieces of his broken heart back together.

My days at the office were predictable. Most weeks were like the movie *Groundhog Day*—dealing with the same things repeatedly. Family medicine was a low acuity practice, with most patients dealing with chronic but not life-threatening illnesses: diabetes, hypertension, thyroid disease, and the like. My biggest professional enemy was the nefarious effects of age. Human bodies weren't designed to last forever.

Most of my free time was spent with Alex and Chrissy or on hikes with Dutch, unless I was on call. On this Thursday afternoon, I was already looking forward to the weekend. Alex and I were going with Bobby and Jill for a drive on the Blue Ridge Parkway and a hike in the Linville Falls area. A simple yet therapeutic few days. But everything changed with Alex's phone call.

"Gil, I need you over here."

"Alex, is everything okay? I've still got two patients on this morning's schedule. But if it's an emergency, someone can cover for me."

"It's my dad . . . he's had a stroke."

Her dad? Other than Alex briefly telling me that her parents' marriage failed when she was a teenager, she never spoke of them. She'd said her dad was on the road a lot with his job, her parents lost the magic, and they went their separate ways. After a trial apart, they legally separated and finally divorced. Alex lived with her dad until he fell for a woman far too young and way too soon after her parents' split. At least, that was Alex's opinion. The couple moved to Charlotte, leaving Alex in her aunt's care until she reached legal age. She never talked about her mom, and I didn't ask. I assumed her parents were either dead or completely out of her life. Turns out, I'd been wrong . . . sort of.

"Do you still talk to your dad?" I asked.

"No . . . well, yes, but rarely. It's usually brief and always awkward. But he listed me, not his gold-digging, floozy wife, as his next of kin, so the hospital called me. I've got to get down there, Gil. Will you go with me, please?"

Alex was maybe the nicest person I'd ever met, and she rarely spoke evil of someone. *Is there more to this story?*

"Alex, that's harsh. Why—"

"Save it, Sullivan. I'm not going into all that right now. Just help me."

I assured her I would. In fact, I'd call a friend and colleague of mine who trained in internal medicine with me at Chapel Hill, went on to do a neurology fellowship, and was now in a large practice in Charlotte. Maybe we'd get lucky and her dad would be a patient on his clinic's hospital service.

I grabbed Sarah, explained the situation, and asked her to have the front desk staff clear the rest of my day. She also agreed to pick up Dutch and keep him until I returned. Alex arranged for Chrissy to go home with a friend after school. I stopped by the house, changed, and made a thermos of coffee. Alex was outside pacing when I picked her up, and we were on our way not two hours after she'd called.

"Well?"

She cut her eyes at me. "Well, what?"

"Are you ready to give me more background and, what's more, ready to face your dad? You know, after all these years, it might be awkward. Especially if he's got residual deficits from his stroke."

"Residual deficits? English, please."

"Things like impaired consciousness, speech problems, weakness, or paralysis." I explained I'd talked to my buddy and, HIPAA notwithstanding, he'd updated me on her dad's condition. It was a cerebrovascular event in the left hemisphere, resulting in significant right-sided impairment. Fortunately, his speech was only partially affected, and his paralysis was improving.

Alex clenched her jaw and looked down. "Am I ready to see him in person? Guess we'll find out."

Chapter Twenty-One

Charlotte, NC

Alex

Gil was right. I had emotions about my parents boxed up and stored in the closet of my memories. Pulling them out and dusting them off was risky. Vulnerability scared me. A parent's job is to care for their child. My parents abandoned that responsibility when they went their separate ways. Now I was faced with caring about my father, or at least acting the part. But I had to try, so there was no choice but to be there for him.

The cavernous hospital halls seemed like an antiseptic-scented rat's maze. We passed various medical personnel and visitors who I assumed were all rushing to do their jobs or hurrying to find their loved ones' rooms. Nurses pushed medicine carts that clattered like train cars clicking on their tracks. Announcements occasionally came like a voice from Heaven, paging doctors to their next assignment. I was lost, but Gil casually navigated the way.

"Gil, you ever been in this hospital? You act like you know where you're going."

"Yeah, I did a rotation here during residency, but honestly, if you've been in one large hospital, you've been in them all. Pretty much the same layout. Steel yourself, babe. We're almost to your dad's room."

I wasn't prepared for what I saw when I walked in. My memory of the man was one of a tall, stout guy whose gregarious personality won the attention of everyone in the room. Now, a thinner version of that memory lay in front of me, in bed with an IV in one arm and a blood pressure cuff on the other. Wayward wisps of gray hair swirled over his scalp, and sad eyes sat recessed in a face marked by age spots and deep wrinkles. When his eyes found mine, I detected a slight but imperfect smile drooping on the right side.

"Hi, Daddy." The words caught in my throat. I noticed a slight nod.

I turned away to Gil and whispered, "He looks so much older."

Probably sensing my loss for what should come next, Gil said, "Mr. Campbell, I'm Gil Sullivan, a friend of Alex's. It's nice to meet you, sir."

My father nodded again, and then, with what seemed like an inordinate effort, looked from Gil to me and said with slurred words, "Thank you for coming."

I was floundering. "Gil, I don't know what to say," I whispered.

"Mr. Campbell, I'm actually a doctor, so I know how fatigued you must be after what you've gone through, so we're not going to stay long . . . but Carolina's defensive line couldn't have kept Alex away from here today." He glanced at me and smiled.

A nurse walked in and said, "Everything okay, Mr. Campbell? Looks like you've got company." She looked at us and then back at my father. "Physical therapy will be here soon."

Gil leaned in and said, "That's our cue to leave, babe."

"Are you feeling better, Daddy? Getting back your strength? Do you know how long you'll be in the hospital?" Firing questions was one way of hiding my emotions and masking the things I needed to say. Or maybe from having to say, "Goodbye."

He set his eyes on me and raised his eyebrows. I took that as a shrug. "Don't know," he finally uttered.

I took his left hand in mine. "Well, I know you're going to get better. And when you do, we need to visit you again. Things to catch up on, ya know? But for now, you need your rest, so we're gonna go." I kissed him on the cheek. As I pulled away, I felt a slight squeeze of my hand. Tears puddled in the hollows of those eyes trained on me.

My sobbing permeated the silence and filled the car. Finally, I spoke. "Gil, that was so much harder than I'd expected. I didn't think I had strong feelings for my father until I saw him. Then, oh my gosh, flashes of happiness, desertion, loneliness, and anger shot through my brain. I was at a loss for words."

"Yeah, I could tell. That's when I knew it hit you."

"What hit me?"

"A bond that can never be broken. The love parents and children share. I've seen it a thousand times in my training and practice. But I never personally . . ." He took a deep breath and ran his fingers through his hair.

"Sweets? You all right? Now you seem at a loss for words." I reached for his free hand, resting on the console.

"It's nothing." He shook his head. "Anyway, you handled yourself beautifully, Alex. I could tell your dad was touched. But are you sure you want to visit again and catch up on things?"

"I do . . . I think. That's how I feel now, at least. Maybe I just need to get back home and decompress."

He nodded and put both hands on the steering wheel. I closed my eyes and leaned back against the headrest. Gil had started to say something, but I wasn't sure what. I knew he'd lost his mom when he was younger but didn't know much more, and he didn't seem inclined to explain. I had enough parent issues to work through without worrying about what he was dealing with.

The streets of Hillsborough were empty when we arrived. Most houses' lights were off, reminding me it was past my bedtime. I suppressed my yawns, or so I thought.

"Am I boring you, Alex?"

"No, I'm usually in bed by now. I'm beat, physically and emotionally." We turned into my driveway. "Gil, I'd ask you in, but it's just too late. I apologize."

"No apology necessary. I need to get home too."

As he was about to drive away, I turned around, leaned through the window, and kissed him. "Thanks for dropping everything for me today, sweets. It means a lot."

As I walked into the house, I tossed my purse onto the couch, threw myself back in the recliner, and closed my eyes. The quick down and back from Charlotte was so overwhelming that I'd forgotten to even check my phone. Its screen illuminated the dark room, and my breath caught. It was a text from Suzie, sent three hours earlier.

Call me soon as possible. We need to talk

Chapter Twenty-Two

Chapel Hill

"I'm telling you, Bobby, it was pretty emotional. Didn't know if Alex would keep it together when she saw her dad."

We were sitting in Carolina's student center, two old guys with our mugs of coffee and a couple of sinful cinnamon raisin pastries. This was like coming home for Bobby and me. On this Friday, my last two patients canceled so, with no other commitments, I'd driven to the university hospital to visit a patient of mine who was recovering from kidney surgery. I called Bobby on the way and made plans to catch up with him while I was in town. Students were at tables piled with backpacks and coffee cups, far enough away that their animated discussions were mercifully nothing but quiet murmurings when they floated over to us. The aroma of caffeine concoctions wafted through the large dining area.

"I can't imagine. It's hard to put myself in that position since I've always had a good relationship with my parents. Well, for the most part, that is. We had our differences, as I've told you, mostly because of my teenage impulses. But my little dustups were nothing compared to what Alex has been through."

"The men in her life haven't exactly been role models. I guess that's why I'm taking it slow and trying to do the right thing by her," I said.

"Is that all, Gil?"

"Meaning?"

"Could it be that you haven't gotten past your mom's death? You've never told me much about your parents, but you did tell me that, near the end of her life, your mom said you needed to find happiness in yours. Maybe Alex can be the source of that happiness."

I had to admit, Bobby could always read me as easily as a Texas-sized billboard. And the reminder of what my mom had said to me near the end helped offset some of the negative things she'd said when I was a kid.

Bobby looked past me. "Well, look who's walking in."

I turned to see Jill rushing over. She gave me a hug and a kiss on the cheek.

"Hey, what about me?" Bobby asked. "And how'd you know we'd be here?"

"Called your office and they told me. Anyway, I see you all the time but getting to be with Gil's a real treat." She looked at me and winked.

"Jill, how've you been? Teaching going well?" I asked.

"Beginning of the year, you know. Kids still trying to decide if they like me or not."

"Oh, kids still do that, huh? Not that I'm saying I did." I shrugged.

"Fellas, I can't stay. I was nearby, getting some supplies for my classroom. Gotta be back for a teacher meeting but couldn't resist popping in to say hey. Bobby, be sure to talk about us getting together with Gil and Alex, especially since we missed our hiking weekend." She stood to leave.

I watched Jill as she left the Grind. "My friend, you're a lucky guy. She's quite a gal."

"Yep. That's what people are always telling me, anyway." He rolled his eyes. Bobby swirled what was left of his coffee and took the last bite of his bun. Then his eyes locked on mine as he leaned close. "I want you to be happy, Gil. If you think Alex is the one, go for it. But there I go again. I'm probably not the one to be giving courting advice." He shook his head and looked away.

"I'm working on it, Bobby, believe me. It's hard, but I'll get there." My finger traced the cup's raised university logo.

"I believe you. And I can see her as Mrs. Gilbert Sullivan." He winked. "Okay, well, good talk, but I've got to go back to the office before heading home. You take care."

Bobby stood to go, took a few steps, stopped and turned back. "By the way, Gil. This is totally random, but Jill and I might go to Machu Picchu over Spring Break to celebrate our anniversary. You know how she's into history. Personally, I'd rather go to Vegas—gambling, shows, and chorus girls." He laughed, gave me a thumbs up, and left the student center.

I stayed to finish my coffee, then got a refill. I stared into the cup as though I'd find answers there. Talks with Bobby always got me thinking—usually in a challenging but good way. Today was different. He seemed even more superficial than usual and had said some things that worried me. He was right about one thing, though—Alex was a special lady. The last thing she needed was another rip in her heart. If I were to fall in love with her, she'd deserve my full devotion. *I'll get there. I think.*

On the way home, I replayed my conversation with my friend. His trip to Peru got me thinking. Okay, wait. I needed to stop before going down that rabbit hole. There was enough going on here without the distraction of solving the Peru mystery. Besides, I needed to up my game with Alex and Chrissy. They deserved a dependable man in their lives. If that was to be me, I needed to be here for them.

Guess I'd driven the route so many times, my subconscious did the steering. I was almost home when my phone's chime startled me. Chief Riddick.

"Hey, Doc. Jasper Riddick here. There's been a break in the case, and I think you'll want to stop by the station as soon as you can."

"The case against Virgil?"

"No. Carlos."

"On my way, Chief. Thanks." As I re-routed the car, a fire truck screamed by, its siren blaring.

Chapter Twenty-Three

Hillsborough

Alex

"Suzie, you scared the daylights out of me with that text. It was all I could do not to call you when I got in, but it was too late. Now I'm glad I didn't bother you."

We were enjoying ice cream cones from nearby Big Dipper. We sat on the fringe of the town's park, beneath trees painted in hues of yellow, orange, and red. Birds rested on branches, chirping their approval of the crisp autumn air and high, Carolina blue skies. Unless I was in flip-flops, shorts, and a tank top and walking the beach on an early summer morning, this was my favorite time and place.

"Alex, I'm so sorry. When I sent that text, my head was spinning all around Cloud Nine. You know better than most how long it's been since I've been in a real relationship—not that an accidental meeting at the courthouse and one casual night out means this guy's the one. But who knows?"

"Stop apologizing and tell me about him, Suze. All the details." An errant Frisbee landed on our blanket, and I tossed it back to its sender.

"Well, it was right after court ended, and I bumped into him as I left the building. We made eye contact, smiled at each other, and then the magic happened. It was just like in the movies." She sighed.

"Go on."

"Turns out, he's a new grad from Wake Forest's law school. Grew up in little ole Morehead City and did undergrad at Elon. He's good-looking to die for and very sweet, but more importantly, he actually listens to me when I talk. How many guys can you say that about?"

"Can I give you a little advice? Tread carefully. I don't want your big, sweet heart to break again. What's his name?"

"Heath. Actually, Heathcote Jantzen. I know—his name makes him sound all fancy pants, but he's really down to earth . . . an enthusiastic young lawyer. But like I said, only one date so far. Don't want to get my hopes up." She picked up a leaf and twisted its stem back and forth. "You know, my past love life could be a country album. I figure my truck would break down and my dog would die if I had either one of those things. 'Course, the first track would feature the whole 'Todd' thing. But now—"

"You *are* sure you're not moving too fast, right?"

"I'm sure, Alex."

Maybe I was wrong to ask, but I had to be certain, given her history. When Suzie was a freshman, she'd fallen head over heels for another freshman. *Todd.* He wined and dined her until she was smitten before even knowing much about him. Turns out he was pledging a fraternity and had to win a girl's heart and then break it. He succeeded.

"Does he know you're a budding journalist?"

"Oh, yeah. I had to explain why I was in court. Didn't want him to think I was a defendant in some low-rent lawsuit or, even worse, headed for divorce court." Suzie laughed. "But what 'bout you and Gil?"

I looked away. *What about Gil and me?* I'd already explained to Suzie how reluctant we both were to let go of our pasts and move on. No need to rehash that. But I'd seen a certain look in his eyes lately—sort of a wistful gleam. Could he be coming around and, if so, how should I respond? Couldn't hurt that the tension of the explosion and its investigation, as well as the nonsense with Virgil, were now in our rear-view mirror. I loved being with him, and right now, that was enough.

"I've told you things are coming along, but it's slow, Suze. Neither of us is in a hurry. Maybe our relationship's just several dates ahead of you and Heath. I don't know. The way I figure it, though, having some of Gil's attention is better than none at all. Right now, I have to accept the fact that his medical practice is second only to God in his life. I'm third, but I think I'm gaining on the practice."

"Well, Heaven knows you oughta be right there, standing behind God. Leastways, that's my opinion. You're smart, funny, good-looking, and deep into a degree that will allow you to up your work game. Those are pretty good assets, girlfriend." She crossed her arms and hunched her shoulders to her neck as leaves tumbled over the manicured lawn.

"You're sweet, Suze. . . . Hey, this ice cream's making me cold. Let's walk over to the Scene for coffee."

"Sounds good to me. Guess summer's really over."

As we approached the coffee shop, I noticed a crowd outside its door and a fire truck parked nearby. People surrounded whatever was going on, some on their phones and some recording whatever it was.

"Gotta get inside that mob, Alex. It's the journalist in me, I guess," Suzie said, quickening her pace. I stayed on her heels as she elbowed and shoved her way through the crowd until we saw two firemen tending to a man lying on the street. His legs were awkwardly propped on the curb.

"Suzie, it's Tom Waters!" I screamed.

"Who's that?"

"The owner of Waters Pharmacy. An old friend of mine." I grabbed my phone and punched in the pharmacy's number. It went to voicemail. "Rich, it's your dad. Something's wrong. We're right outside Caffeine Scene. Get here as fast as you can."

A dog barked from inside the shop. *Scout.* I pushed my way past onlookers and ran into the shop. Scout's front legs were up on the big window facing the street. He was barking furiously, with his snout pressed on the glass. "What happened?" I asked the server closest to me.

"Tom was in here with Scout. As I brought him coffee, his phone rang. Reception was poor. Darn Wi-Fi comes and goes. He said he'd go outside to take the call and asked me to watch Scout. Next thing I knew, I heard a car horn and squealing brakes. I looked out and people were gathering. Scout was going crazy. Must have seen the whole thing, poor dog."

I wrapped my arms around Scout. "Hey, big fella. Everything's okay. Let's get you outside to your buddy."

Medic had arrived, and Tom was on a stretcher. Some kind of contraption was wrapped around his head. He squinted against the late afternoon sun. I got to his side and said, "Tom, it's Alexis. I've got Scout. He's fine, so don't worry about him. You're in good hands, and I've already called Rich." He managed a weak smile, and then his face went blank as his eyes closed. As the ambulance screamed its departure, the crowd slowly disbursed.

I grabbed my cell and hit Gil's name in Favorites. "Gil, Tom Waters was hit by a car. Medic's pulling away now. I spoke to him, but then he passed out or something. I don't even know if he's still alive."

"If he's been hit by a car, they'll take him to Chapel Hill for a major trauma evaluation. I'll check on him in a little bit and let you know what's going on. What about Scout?"

"I've got him. He was inside the coffee shop. Tom left him for a minute to take some stupid phone call."

"Okay. Take him to my house. He and Dutch get along great. Wait for me there. I've got to see Riddick about something before I come home—"

"I gotta go too. Rich just got here."

Tom's son was next to me in seconds. "Alex, what happened? Where's Dad?" Rich screamed between deep and labored breaths.

"Medic's got him. They're on the way to Chapel Hill. I spoke to him, Rich, and he responded. I'm praying he's gonna be okay, but you need to get to the hospital. Where's your car?"

"Back at the pharmacy. I ran over here fast as I could."

Suzie spoke up. "I'll take you to the hospital, Rich. I'm Suzie, Alex's friend. Going back that way myself."

I thanked Suzie and gave Rich a quick hug and a squeeze of his shoulder. I didn't tell him the whole story. He needed hope, not doubt, that his dad would be all right. Scout and I turned to go back to my car. As we walked, I prayed, and Scout kept glancing back at the accident scene.

Chapter Twenty-Four

Riddick was pushing papers around on his desk, a hopeless attempt to straighten a mess that'd been too long in the making and too much ignored. His hand bumped against an ashtray, some of its contents spilling onto the paperwork. A window unit air conditioner valiantly attempted to keep the stuffy room cool while doing nothing about the stagnant smell of cigarette smoke.

"You hear about Tom Waters getting hit by a car, Doc? Got one deputy still on duty, and he's trying to find the driver who hit him outside the coffee shop and then took off. Rest of them dumped their reports on my desk and left for the evening, while I'm stuck here figuring out things. Guess that's what I get for being the big—"

"I heard; Alex called me. Sorry to interrupt, but you said you had news about Carlos. What is it?"

"Oh, right. Yeah, we've been checking his mail since he died. Didn't see any harm in that, seeing as how he's dead and doesn't have anyone around here connected to him. Very sad, you know, to be all alone in a town—"

"Chief Riddick! The news, please?"

"Right. Well, a letter came from some place in Peru I can't even pronounce. I opened it, hoping we'd get some clue about who he is, or was. Is it 'is' or 'was'?"

"I don't know. Doesn't matter."

"Well, guess what? We got our clue. Here, read it for yourself."

He handed me a folded letter and then lit a cigarette. I opened the soiled sheet of paper and read a note that appeared to have been typed on a manual typewriter.

Dearest Carlos,

Greetings and God's blessings from Campoflores. Our people continue to hold you close in our hearts and pray for your safe return.

I am sad to report that not one of the missing girls has returned, and we have no further information on my sweet Luna and her fellow captives. We pray her intelligence and ability to speak English will protect her. Now one hundred villagers have been taken. Weeping has replaced the happy sound of children playing.

Our neighbors who travel report that some of our people have been spotted working, and some of the women and girls have been seen on the streets of Lima.

While our hearts are broken, we remain in faith that our Father God will watch over them and protect them, and some day return all of them to us.

May He continue to bless you as you earn money to continue the rescue mission.

Your partner in His service,

Elizabeth
2021-07-05

I looked up at Riddick and shook my head. "So Carlos *was* referring to children who'd been taken. Maybe the two children in that photo are his, and they're two of the missing?"

"Could be, Doc. Kinda reminds me of the movie, *Taken*. Love that Liam . . . what's his name?"

"Neeson. Liam Neeson, but that's Hollywood. This really happened, Chief, and it's tragic. Sounds like he was working here to finance a search for the missing kids. Pretty noble, if you ask me. Anyway, this gets us a little closer to identifying Carlos. We know he's got an associate, partner, or wife in Campoflores, and we know her name. There's gotta be a way to get to her. She deserves to know what happened to him."

"We're rocking on the same back porch on that one, Doc. This letter makes the case even more compelling. I'll check to see who has legal jurisdiction in that part of Peru, but I gotta admit I've never had to do something like this before."

Compelling indeed. Carlos likely had a family, possibly torn apart by whatever happened to those girls. I could relate to that. I couldn't do anything to put the pieces of my family back together, but I owed it to him to help his. I needed to rethink the situation, but right now, I had to check on Tom and get back to Alex. As I was leaving the station, I heard the call come in to Riddick with an update on the hit and run outside of Caffeine Scene.

———

On the way home, I called the emergency room at the university hospital. A buddy of mine from residency was on duty. One of the ER secretaries got him to the phone.

"Gil. Long time, my friend. What's the occasion?"

"Calling about someone brought in from Hillsborough. A hit-and-run victim named Tom Waters. I don't even know if he's there yet or, if he is, who saw him."

"They rolled him in a few minutes ago, and I triaged him. He's reasonably alert, and his vitals are stable, but he's going through evaluation in Major Trauma for any head injury or other internal trauma."

"Great. Keep me posted, please. He's a good friend."

I gave him my cell number before clicking off and hurried home to check on Alex and Scout.

Alex was sitting on my front porch, holding a glass of iced tea. Scout and Dutch were lying in the shade, up against a planter full of wilted impatiens spilling over the edge and cascading to the wooden planks. When they saw me, all three stood and met me at the top of the steps.

"Gil, did you call the hospital? Any news on Tom? Please tell me he's all right." When she mentioned his name, Scout's ears pricked up.

I recounted what I'd learned. "All we can do now is wait, but at least we know he made it to the hospital. We have your quick thinking to thank for that."

As I figured she would, Alex asked me why I saw the chief. I explained the details of the letter from the woman who identified herself as Elizabeth. The more I said, the wider her eyes seemed to get, especially when I told her I was rethinking my role in figuring out the mystery.

"Now, Gil—"

"I know. Stay in my lane. But I can't stand by and do nothing, Alex. That doesn't seem right to me or fair to Carlos."

"What are you gonna do? Go to Peru and track down a bunch of bad guys? Rescue stolen girls? You're a doctor, not a superhero."

"That's harsh, babe. Listen, I know I can't find these girls myself, but I can have a hand in seeing that every lead is followed and this Elizabeth person is contacted. By the way, and I know this sounds crazy, but how'd you like to take a trip to Peru?"

"What?" She put her hands on her hips and stared at me open-mouthed.

"Bobby and Jill are considering an anniversary trip to Peru. I got to thinking, maybe we could join them. I could go to Campoflores and find Elizabeth. She needs to know what Carlos was most concerned about in his final moments on this earth."

Alex took her hands off her hips, smiled, and reached for my hands. "Gil Sullivan, you're crazy, but you've got a heart of gold."

"And I'm a bit of a romantic, right?" I asked.

"All evidence to the contrary—at least so far."

"How's this, then?" I pulled her close, and we kissed, longer and harder than ever before.

Chapter Twenty-Five

Chapel Hill

I'd stepped outside my box and upped my game with that kiss, and I liked the way it had made me feel. I didn't see the proverbial fireworks, but at least I heard them in the distance. Anxious to keep the fires burning in our relationship, Alex and I were on our way to Chapel Hill for dinner that Saturday night. We had a table for two reserved at the Dome, an eatery landmark known for its elegance and, perhaps more importantly, its proximity to the Dean Dome, where Carolina hoops legends were born, and sometimes where hopes and dreams went to die. I wore my best sport coat and an open-collared shirt. Alex was stunning in a sleek, black dress cut low enough to be suggestive but still modest. In her heels, we saw eye to eye. Her hair was fixed in a way I'd never seen.

"I like your hair, babe. Never seen it in a bun before."

She rolled her eyes. "It's a *chignon*, Gil. Basically, a French twist."

"Well, I like your whatever it is you just called it."

She shook her head and thanked me. "Hey, I talked to my dad today. Still in the hospital but making progress. Still kinda hard to understand, though."

"Well, any progress is good." I felt an opening and took a deep breath. "Hey, Alex. You never talk about your mom. Did she just walk away from the family?"

She looked out the passenger window, sighed, and looked back at me. "Reckon now's as good a time as any, Gil." Another deep breath. "A long time ago, we were happy, and I thought everything was perfect. But I was a little kid. My daddy was on the road a lot with his work. I didn't think anything of it, but one day, I overheard Mama talking to close friends, telling them she thought something funny was going on. I had no idea what she meant. Anyway, things went sideways between them. They didn't talk to each other much, except when they fought and screamed. Sometimes, I heard noises that scared me. I think he hit her, but I never saw any proof of it. So, to answer your question, yeah, she walked away. Walked right out of my life."

"And she never came back or even contacted you?"

"I believe she would have if she'd had the time. Not long after she and Daddy divorced, she was with some friends at a small lake near the Virginia border. Within a few days, she came down with a fever, terrible headache, confusion, and then seizures. She was rushed to the university hospital and diagnosed with some kind of amoeba infection—"

"Oh, my goodness! Naegleria."

"Yeah, that's what they called it. I always think Nigeria, but I know that's a country. I was at summer camp at the time, and she was dead before I could get home."

I reached for her hand. "I'm so sorry, Alex. That's a terrible disease and an awful way to die."

"To make matters worse, before I could even process what happened, my dad hooked up with that gold digger—probably before the ink had a chance to dry on my mother's death certificate. Although she walked out on me, she was still my mother."

Now, it all made sense: why Alex had kept her married name, why her relationship with her dad was so strained, and why she disliked his new wife. Also, why she never talked about her mom until now. Some things are so painful the hurt never heals. I understood that as much as anyone.

"What about you, Gil?"

"What?"

"Your mom. You never talk about her."

"Later, Alex. We're almost to the Dome."

The restaurant reeked of style and privilege. It's where movers and shakers went to do business or privately meet special guests. Secluded tables were available if you knew the right people. Rumor had it there was even a private entrance for people who didn't want to be noticed. Lights were dimmed, soft music oozed from hidden ceiling speakers, and white linen cloths topped every table. The wait staff, both male and female, dressed in black slacks and white jackets, and all sported narrow, black bow ties.

Alex's mood seemed to have lifted. "This isn't our world, Sullivan, but it sure is nice to visit, right? Look around at the wait staff. They look like penguins!"

"This is where folks go when they're with someone very special, babe, and you're as special as they get." My face heated, and I must have blushed.

"That red clashes with your coat, sweets." She laughed. "I'm just messing with you. That's actually a very nice thing for you to say."

We both had starter salads, followed by beef tenderloin, asparagus, and mashed potatoes. Opting for that rare time when I'd have a drink, I ordered the bottle of expensive red wine Alex had selected. We topped it all off with crème brulee and coffee.

"Gil, you really overdid it, but this was yummy. Thank you."

I nodded. "Think about it; some people eat like this regularly. Hey, before we go, let me run to the bathroom."

I walked in and spotted Bobby washing his hands. "Bobby, imagine meeting you here!"

"Oh, Gil. Hello." He looked around as though he thought someone else he knew might walk in. "Jill and I are on our way out. Can't believe we didn't spot you. Alex here too?"

"Of course. Hey, stop by our table before you leave. We'd love to chat for a few minutes."

"Would love to, but Jill's already in the car. She's got one of her migraines, and I need to get her home. We'll catch you next time."

"Or, better yet, we'll make it a foursome," I said.

"Right, Gil. A foursome. Okay, good to see you." He patted me on the shoulder as he hurried by.

Alex was finishing her coffee as I got back to the table. "Something weird just happened, babe. I ran into Bobby, and he seemed off."

"Off?"

"Yeah, like something was bothering him. I don't know. Oh well, he said Jill has a headache and was waiting on him to take her home. Maybe that was it." I cocked my head and shrugged.

———

We were both quiet most of the way home. When we got to her house, Alex asked if I'd like to go for a walk.

"A walk . . . at this hour?"

"I think we'll be safe, Gil. It is Hillsborough, you know. Let's walk off dinner and enjoy the cool autumn air while it lasts."

Tree frogs sang and leaves crunched underfoot as we walked. My hand awkwardly found hers and held on.

"Uh, Gil. Is this a good time to tell me more about your mom? No pressure but we might as well both unpack our baggage on the same night."

I hesitated before starting the sad saga. My mom was from a poor family in Christiansburg, a town close to Blacksburg's Virginia Tech. She barely made it through high school, but after graduating, she got a job in the college cafeteria. There, she was spotted by my father, an upperclassman at Tech. He flirted with her and then convinced her to go to a movie on campus: *Hook*. Apparently, he'd been a Dustin Hoffman fan ever since *The Graduate*. Turns out it wasn't *Hook* after all. It was *Pirates of Penzance*, an old Gilbert and Sullivan production. After the show, one thing led to another, and my mom lost her innocence that night.

Alex's eyes were large as saucers. "Are you telling me—"

"Right. A one-nighter and she got pregnant—with me. Later, when she told my father, he freaked out. Said a kid would ruin his life and told her to get lost. My mother was crushed and confused. She had the baby, obviously, but didn't even know my father's last name, so she named me Gilbert and picked Sullivan for the last name." I shook my head. "Crazy story, but that's how it happened."

"Well, I'll give her credit for going through with the pregnancy. The alternative would have been easier . . . or maybe not."

As we walked back, I finished the story. My mom never recovered from my father's betrayal. With no education and too ashamed to go back to Blacksburg to work, she started cleaning houses in Christiansburg. She took me with her, avoiding the expense of child care. A few years later, she hurt her back at work. A doctor put her on pain pills, and she got addicted to them. Once the doctors wouldn't fill any more prescriptions and she couldn't afford to buy them on the street, she brought men into our house at night and used that money to buy her drugs.

"Men in the house? You mean, like one-night stands?"

"For a fact. You see, I walked in on her in her bedroom with . . . well, you know what I mean. Imagine a young kid seeing his mom like that. To make matters even worse, OxyContin became her drug of choice. One night, in a drunken stupor, she overdosed and never woke up."

Alex released my hand and took me in her arms. "Oh, Gil. I'm so sorry. Your poor mother."

"You see, Alex, my very existence was based on a relationship that never really existed, and then my mother's drug addiction and prostitution—more bad relationships. Guess that's why I wanted to go slowly and make sure I found the right woman . . . and I think I have."

We were back at Alex's place, at the walkway up to her front door. "Wanna come in?"

"Honestly, babe, I'm exhausted. Maybe next time."

"Okay, but know this: my door's always open, and I'm wide open to a deeper relationship with you. Even if it takes time."

After we kissed and said goodnight, I hugged her longer than usual, not wanting to let go. As I turned to head for the car, I felt my heart pounding in my chest. Maybe it was the romantic moment. But maybe it was what I didn't tell her. What still haunted me. What would have to wait for another day. Or maybe never.

"If you'd never been born, Gil, I wouldn't be in this mess." How many times did I hear her say that?

Some pages of our lives are not meant to be read out loud.

Chapter Twenty-Six

"My, my, Dr. Gil, you seem to have a pep in your step this morning," Sarah said as I bounded into the office on Monday morning. "Good weekend?"

"A great weekend, Sarah. How was yours?"

"Nothing special. Couple of medic shifts but, otherwise, took it easy and read a lot of the latest Nicholas Sparks novel. Oh, and I visited Ted's gravesite—just to check in and leave some fresh flowers."

Sarah's husband, Ted, had died of a cardiomyopathy several years earlier, leaving her a widow at too young of an age and before they could start a family. She always said he had the sick heart, but he left her with a broken one. I admired her courage and ability to smile while talking about him— not something I'm sure I had in me. She always attributed it to her faith and the passage of time that allowed her to put it in the right place in her brain.

"Well, I hate to burst your bubble, Doc, but Miss Wainwright's on your schedule today. Said she needed to check in with you. Not sure why, since she's not agreeing to any treatment."

"Actually, I called her and asked her to schedule an appointment. I told her I had something I wanted to talk to her about."

I was always anxious about patients who I knew would be a challenge, and Miss Wainwright fit that description to a tee. This time, I figured she would keep her appointment—out of curiosity, if for no other reason. I was preoccupied right up to when Sarah told me she'd arrived. I asked her to put her in my office. Sarah gave me a curious look and then shrugged.

Miss Wainwright cut her eyes at me and shifted in her seat when I walked in. Her perfume's odor permeated the room, otherwise filled with silence except for the classical music station playing softly on my desktop Bose.

"Thank you for coming in, Miss Wainwright. I have two things to talk to you about. First, your treatment."

"There'll be no treatment, young man. I've already told you that."

"Right, but I was hoping you'd change your mind and give it a try."

"I don't change my mind. Once I decide on something, I stick to it. Family trait, if you must know. That's how we built such a successful business."

"Okay. But please understand that you can call me anytime if you have a change of heart. Now, speaking of heart, I also wanted to talk to you about the homeless shelter for women and children. Unfortunately, the need for more beds is growing, and we're trying to expand the facility. I thought you might want to help with that—you know, as a way to give back to the community that helped your family's business be so successful."

She surprised me when she stood and reminded me she'd refused to even put a few coins in the collection jar at the front desk. "How can you possibly expect me to give you an even greater sum to build an addition? My family's business grew because we paid for it to expand as we became more and more successful. Didn't depend on the town to help pay for it. Never asked for a dime."

"But the shelter is a non-profit and really doesn't have much money in reserve," I countered.

"Well, young man, then I suggest you figure out a way to build your reserve without begging for money from people who have no sympathy for such a place and the people who use it."

"Yes, ma'am, but one more thing, please, before you go. We'd love to see you in church again. I'm told by some of the older members you used to attend regularly. Rev. McElroy's mighty good. Might bring you some peace as you . . . well, you know."

"Listen, I've spent enough time in church—probably more than you know—and I don't feel like that's where I want to spend what time I have left. After all, they're always asking for money too."

With that, she turned and left. I was stunned. Before I could mount a response, she was down the hall and headed for the front door. "Good talk," I mumbled to myself.

At the end of the day, after the staff left and only the providers lingered to finish their charting, I popped in on Arnie, our senior partner. I was frustrated and in need of some seasoned advice.

"Arnie, I need your help. What do you do when you've got patients who don't seem to respond to what you say or recommend?" I then explained my dilemmas with Miss Wainwright and George Owens.

"That's an easy one, Gil. You keep trying. You've got to be your patients' advocate, and you don't give up when they don't seem to comply. It's one of the challenges of our profession, but, boy oh boy, it's so sweet when one of them comes around and sees the light, so to speak. They're adults, Gil, and you've got to treat them like adults. Give them the best information you have and the best effort you can muster. That's really all you can do."

He made it sound so simple. I guess I knew it intuitively, but my frustration was clouding my judgment. I thanked him and stood to leave.

"Gil, wait a minute. I helped you, or at least, I hope I did. Now, you help me, please."

"What is it, Arnie?"

"I can't find my car keys—again. I swear someone must come in here and move them around. I've looked everywhere."

"Let me drive you home. Tomorrow, you can get the staff to help you look for them."

Arnie agreed, stood, slipped off his white lab coat, and reached for his jacket. We both heard the jangle and our eyes met.

"Found them, Gil. Must have put them in my pocket when I got to work." He sighed and shook his head. "Uh, Gil, can we keep this between us?"

I patted him on the arm. "Of course."

On the way home, I couldn't get my mind off Arnie. What had amused the staff when he began to act absentmindedly was now becoming a pattern. I'd seen him misplace his stethoscope or his computer and, a few times, walk into the wrong exam room. Sometimes, I'd see a patient for him on his day off, and his last encounter note was erratic or unfinished. Could these be early warning signs of something more ominous? The man had built this practice from the foundation up. He was a father figure to me, not just a partner. I and the other docs needed to help him in any way possible while still overseeing quality medical care. To see him struggle broke my heart.

Chapter Twenty-Seven

Tarapoto, Peru

Luna

For some reason, we were at a standstill, basically camping near Tarapoto. Our captors seemed in no hurry to continue. Two of the men would leave in the morning and not return until evening, sometimes with provisions for our captors and us. We were fed better and even given juice to drink. I overheard one man say they were working to earn enough money to keep going until they got paid for delivering us. Where that would be, I wasn't sure, but Lima seemed the logical destination.

Unfortunately, the men's appetites weren't sated with their improved diet. My heart broke for Andrea, who was their chief target for entertainment. They took her away from camp and out of earshot of us. Often, she was gone for hours with anywhere from one to three men. She returned to camp, shuffling along and whimpering, her clothes disheveled and often stained with dirt and blood. When Andrea seemed to no longer be the intrigue she had been, they took a second girl with them. She returned, as broken as Andrea.

These men were no better than wild animals, miscreants who succumbed to their vilest impulses. We had been taught in school about the dangers of such men and how to avoid satisfying their desires, but here, we were captives and totally at their mercy.

One small blessing was the location of our campsite, close to a river's tributary, with a brisk enough current that the water was visibly clean. They allowed us to bathe and crudely wash our clothes but always under the watchful eye of an armed guard. If any of the girls strayed too far from the others, the guard would grab her and prod her back to the human herd, using the barrel of his rifle to push her along.

At night, when we were all in the truck bed to sleep, we'd lie there and listen to the night sounds of cicadas and tree frogs. Save for the occasional lighting of a nearby guard's cigarette, we were in the black of the jungle. The moon occasionally illuminated the sky, and on a cloudless night, we'd see the Milky Way. These were our only vestiges of connection to the real world, assuring us there was life and a great universe still out there. I'd close my eyes and think about being at home, playing outdoors in the evening with my friends until that moon appeared. How careless were those times, all taken for granted . . . until now.

I attempted to keep the other girls' spirits up, encouraging them and talking in hushed tones about our life back in Campoflores. I promised them we would go back, that it wouldn't be long before men from our village would find and rescue us.

On one occasion, as I was talking, Toothless climbed into the bed of the truck and just stared at us. The stench of smoke and sweat was suffocating. Feeling particularly brazen, I dared to ask him why I'd been spared from abuse—why I seemed to be treated a little better than many of the other girls. His answer was an evil smile, absent three or four teeth, with a glimmer in his eyes, but nothing more. Finally, he must have grown bored with us, and he left.

I resumed my encouragement, reminding the girls of Bible verses we'd learned in school, particularly the twenty-third Psalm. If there was a valley of the shadow of death, we were in it or, at the very least, headed toward it. A few of the girls joined in the conversation. But not Andrea. She'd been reduced to a mute, whose whimpering and tears were the only emotions she could muster. I imagined evil could do that to a person, and these so-called men were evil personified.

Later, as Toothless escorted Andrea and me to relieve ourselves, he pulled me aside while cutting his eyes at Andrea. "You ask why we spare you? It is that we have special plan for you. We get big money for you." He threw his head back and laughed hideously, the sound bouncing from tree to tree. "You have nothing to say, chica?"

I stood between Andrea and him, a vain attempt to keep his eyes off of her. When we finished, I put my arm around her, and we walked back to our prison. Before climbing in, a hand clamped down on my arm. It was Notepad Man. He handed me a small sack and quickly ushered me onto the truck bed. Cautiously, I peeked in the bag, curious to see what it contained.

Pieces of hard candy.

Chapter Twenty-Eight

Hillsborough

Alex and I were at her house, eating popcorn and streaming episodes of *24*. Her idea, not mine. I'd wanted to go out, but she'd convinced me to hang out at her place. She said there was something we needed to discuss.

"Jack Bauer is such a bad . . . well, you know. I can't believe you've never watched this show, Gil. It's one of my all-time faves."

"I've got enough drama in my real life without having to go online looking for it. You know this is unrealistic, right?"

"All I know is it's fun to see the bad guys get what's coming to them, and Jack always sees to that."

"Yeah, I remember: guns, action, Spidey, Jack Bauer, whatever." I shook my head and reached for more popcorn.

She clicked off the monitor. "Your lack of interest is the perfect opening for me to get to what I wanted to discuss." She told me about her recent conversation with Suzie in the snack bar. Something apparently had her trouble antennae raised. "She and Heath were at the Dome last weekend—"

"The weekend we were there and I saw Bobby?"

"Yeah. Weird, huh? And she said they used a private door to enter and leave . . . 'all mysterious cloak and dagger stuff' were her exact words."

"Look, Alex, just because I told you some people use a separate entrance at the restaurant to be discreet, doesn't mean Suzie and Heath were up to anything. Maybe one of his partners pulled rank on a doorman to give the guy a chance to make an impression on her. Actually, sounds like it worked."

"You might be right, but something seemed off. Maybe I'm becoming paranoid, what with the bombing, Virgil's ridiculous behavior, and Dutch's injuries. Anyway, it sounded like they had such a good time that I suggested the four of us go out—if, that is, she continues to see Heath. We both know how quickly she falls for guys."

I seamlessly changed the subject. "Oh, Alex, I almost forgot to tell you. I talked to a friend at the university hospital today. Tom Waters is doing great. He should be home soon, but he won't be strutting around town with Scout leading the way, at least for a while. Dutch and I are sure gonna miss Scout when he goes back to Tom's place. That dog brings joy back to Dutch. . . . Maybe erasing some of his memories or shoving them to a quiet place or something. Who knows, maybe dogs' brains work a lot like humans' brains. We didn't exactly cover that in med school." I raised one corner of my mouth at my attempt at humor.

Alex didn't take the bait. "No surprise about Tom. He's like sour milk—hard to keep down."

I scooted closer to her and interlocked my arm in hers. She dropped her head to my shoulder. We were so close to each other that a whisper wouldn't have fit between us. Alex suddenly sat upright, pulled back from me, and then wrapped her arms around my trunk. We kissed. Several times. The scent of her body wash mesmerized me. My hands gently went to places they'd not previously been. It was probably the most intimate moment we'd shared. I was encouraged that we were both coming around in the emotions department. I closed my eyes and let the sweetness of the moment soak through my skin to my soul.

My beeper startled us awake. We'd been so relaxed, both of us had dozed off, right there on the couch.

"Sorry, babe, forgot to mention I'm on call tonight. Let me check with the answering service," I said as I stood and walked toward the kitchen. "Hopefully, this won't take long."

When I returned, she had *24* back on, enjoying watching Jack spoil some Russian knucklehead's assassination attempt on the US president.

"I'm back. Turns out it was nothing but a medication question."

"Great. Want me to back up the show to where we were earlier?"

"Uh, no, but thanks. I'm good."

Not five minutes later, I looked over, and she was sound asleep, head back and mouth wide open. I dozed off until sometime after the clock ran out on Jack's twenty-four hours. I sat up and nudged Alex awake. "I'm gonna head home, babe. We both obviously need some sleep."

Chapter Twenty-Nine

At the end of each day at work, I always peeked at the next day's schedule to see if there was anything I needed to review prior to the visit. Early on, Arnie taught me something they overlooked in residency training: Patients like to feel known—not only by their problems, but by their family members too. To walk into a room and stumble through a conversation about a health issue they expected me to be up to speed on was an awful way to start a visit.

Tomorrow was Friday and, per my instructions, George Owens was on the schedule in the day's last slot. I was already worried about Miss Wainwright, and now I had the added concern for Arnie Schmidt's well-being. Hopefully, George would be doing better.

I paced through the house, with Dutch on my heels and both our shadows trailing behind us. Either he sensed I was upset or he was hoping I'd beat a path to the pantry for his dog treats. I stopped, reached down, and patted his head. His coat was coming back nicely from where the vet had shaved him for his surgery.

"Hey, Dutchie. You're a good boy. I'm okay, so don't worry about me." He cocked his head, with his chocolate brown eyes laser-focused on mine.

"Yes, I'm fine . . . hey, I bet you're hungry!" Ears pricked skyward. "Okay, you win. Let me get you a rice cake." Pavlovian slobber trickled from his jowl.

He took the cake and retreated to his bed, where he was sure to break the cake into a million pieces of rice—maybe two million. I resumed my aimless patrol of the house, searching for clarity on how to help my patients.

I decided if George was still depressed, I'd push him even harder on getting professional help. Unfortunately, patients often pushed right back on that. They saw it as a sign of weakness. But the brain is like any other organ in the body. It can get sick, and when it does, it needs treatment, same as the clogged arteries of a heart or kidneys that no longer filter properly. But there's a stigma about mental health. If George wouldn't agree to see someone, it would fall on me to help him through this journey, and that might be slightly above my current pay grade.

Then I had a thought . . .

The last appointment of the week arrived. Hopefully, George didn't catch my look of disappointment when I walked into the exam room. Actually, shuffled might be more apropos. His expressionless face was longer and gaunter, his thin body lost in a bundle of sadness and desperation, covered with clothes now hanging even baggier from his lamp-post frame.

"Doc, I ain't cutting it. Every day's a replay of the previous day's misery. The missus and I hardly speak. I ain't been to see the counselor either. What's the point? Seems like my whole world's come apart. Don't see much reason to keep going, and I really don't feel like being here today."

I leaned toward him, eye to eye. "George, if you're talking about suicide, I can't let you leave this office without your solemn word you won't do that, or you'll call me if you even get an inkling to do it. I can't ignore that kind of thought and still honor my Hippocratic Oath."

"Yeah, well . . . okay."

"No, George. I'm serious. You must promise me—"

"Okay, I promise. I really do. Don't want you breaking that hypocritic oath, or whatever it's called. Reckon I've got enough misery in my life without adding more." He dropped his chin to his chest and slowly shook his head back and forth.

I'd said too much and gone too far, talking about what I had to do. I needed to focus on George, not me. A rookie mistake, but this was the wrong inning in the ball game to commit such a stupid error. I decided not to push the counseling referral today.

"Listen, George. Don't worry about me. Like I said, I trust you to call me if things get worse. But today, I'm going to check you over and get some bloodwork. I'm worried you might be anemic or vitamin-deficient, but we'll see what the labs show. Regardless, I want to see you next week. And I'll have Sarah call you Monday morning simply to touch base. Is that okay?"

"Yes, sir. I like Miss Sarah. Sure 'nough do. That'll give me something to look forward to. Appreciate your time today, Doc."

Sarah came in to escort him to the lab. She whispered to me, "Last patient of the day." I heard staff telling each other to have a good weekend and knew it was time to close up shop. I also knew my hunch from earlier was spot on—I needed to talk to Dunk.

I got lucky. The church assistant put me right through to him. He was wrapping up his day, too, but said he'd wait for me if it was that important. I guess preachers are like doctors—always available for a crisis.

———

Twenty minutes later, I sat next to my pastor in his office. "I can't tell you everything, Dunk, or I'll breach patient-physician confidentiality, but I've got a problem."

"With?" he asked.

"A patient. A patient I fear is so depressed he's got suicidal ideation. I need to help him, but I'm not getting through."

"Gil, I have trouble getting through to people every Sunday morning." We both chuckled.

"But seriously, I'm worried. He promised me he won't do anything rash, and he'll call me if he feels the urge to hurt himself, but I want to help him before it goes that far."

"Let me tell you about depression, Gil, it's caused—"

"No offense, Dunk, but I'm a doctor, and I know what causes it: genetic makeup, inciting event, a chemical imbalance with serotonin—"

"Those are medical reasons. But the real cause is the devil."

"Huh?"

He went on to tell me depression is the work of the devil. It's one of the spiritual battles we fight every day. And the ultimate victory for the devil is when a person becomes so despondent, he hurts himself or dies by suicide. Sure, all the medical things are real and contributory, but ultimately, it's the devil's victory.

"Gil, lots of people have family histories of depression and events in their lives that cause situational depression, but they don't all become suicidal, right?"

"Well, yeah. So what's the difference? What makes one person recover and another take his own life, or at least try to?"

"In part, the person's faith, or lack of it. Once the devil has you doubting your faith, mad at God, and believing life's so unfair, there's no reason to go on, the devil's won the battle. All that to ask, Gil, have you prayed with your patient?"

"Excuse me?" I shifted in my seat and caught myself massaging my temple.

"Have you prayed with this patient? You're a Christian. Even if your patient isn't, you can offer a prayer. Do you do that with your patients?"

"Well, no, actually. I haven't . . . and this patient is a Christian."

Dunk reached out and placed his hand on my shoulder. "You're missing a great opportunity to be God's voice. At least consider it, Gil. You've got nothing to lose, right?"

Nothing like being humbled by my pastor. I'd not thought about being a person of faith George could turn to. He wasn't ready to talk to the minister, but maybe I could reach him through prayer.

"Dunk, this has been helpful. Can't thank you enough."

"You can thank me by being in church this Sunday . . . and not falling asleep. You think I don't see you?" He raised his eyebrows and shrugged as I stood to leave. He chuckled as I walked out.

Dunk had given me a lot to think about on my drive home. If physical and mental healing were part of medicine, why not spiritual healing as well? Why should that only be something ministers do? Can't any Christian, including a physician, share their faith and use it in the routine practice of their job? No way was that taught in traditional medical schools. It would take some heavy lifting on my part to get comfortable using it in my practice. But for someone in trouble like George, neither he nor I had much to lose.

My phone's ringing broke my concentration. Alex. She cut to the chase with "Gil, we need to talk. Soon."

What now?

Chapter Thirty

"Gil Sullivan, you're not hearing me." Alex sighed and looked away. We were on the porch swing at her house. Chrissy was inside, and Alex said she didn't want her to hear us, especially if we started arguing. A chorus of cicadas sang in the background as dusk gave way to darkness and the air chilled.

"I hear every word, babe."

"Okay, fine. Then you're not listening."

"Now slow down . . . and calm down, for Pete's sake."

"Don't patronize me," she said, her voice rising an octave, or maybe two.

She seemed to gather herself and again explained how she'd suggested to Suzie that she and Heath have a double date with the two of us. A few days later, Suzie called back to say that Heath couldn't make that happen, at least not yet. No explanation. Just a flat-out no.

"What are you saying, Alex? Why would you think Heath's afraid to go out with us?"

"Because I think Heath's not Heath at all . . . Heath is Bobby!" Tears began to form.

"What in the world? You can't be serious! I know Bobby better than anyone, and he'd never do anything like that."

"If 'that' means cheat on Jill, I think you're sorely mistaken."

I handed her my handkerchief. "Alex, that's a serious allegation, and you can't assume you've added two plus two and gotten the right answer. Bobby's a good friend, and no way would I misjudge him. I think you're so worried about Suzie that you're looking for anything that would explain why—"

"Listen, Sullivan, are you anywhere close to making your point? And, by the way, I can do math just as well as you. Remember how you said he seemed a little off when you saw him at the restaurant? And how weird it was that he didn't at least stop by our table to say hello? I'm only saying it's worth looking into. Not sure how we can do that, but we need to figure it out."

"Okay, already. I'll talk to Bobby and just ask him, that's how. I'll figure out a good way to do it—or at least, I'll try."

"Listen, I got upset because Suzie's my best friend, and I don't want to see her hurt. Actually, devastated would be more like it. She thinks Heath, or whoever he really is, might be her forever guy. This could be a serious problem."

I put my arm around Alex and pulled her closer. I thought she was wrong, but I had to give her credit for worrying so much about her friend. Of course, I'd just volunteered to be the one to look into it—as though I needed another problem to add to my growing list. I'd keep that part to myself, as the last thing I needed was Alex thinking I was looking for a pity party. On the bright side, though, I'd probably find out Heath is Heath, not Bobby. That way, Bobby's off the hook; Heath's still in the picture as Suzie's 'forever guy,' or whatever, and, best of all, I'd score some points with Alex.

Alex nuzzled my ear and kissed me on the cheek. "Thanks."

Points scored.

———

Bobby agreed to meet me at the trailhead the following day for a run on one of our favorite courses. I figured having him out in the middle of the woods was the safest bet if things went south on me. Fifteen minutes into the run, I asked him to stop so I could catch my breath.

"Got a question, Bobby, but it's kind of a sensitive subject."

"Go for it. You can ask me anything." We stepped over into what little sunlight-dappled shade was available.

"The night we ran into each other in the bathroom at the Dome—"

"Yeah?"

"You were acting kind of strange, like you were worried about something. You were with Jill, right? I mean, neither I nor Alex saw her."

Bobby pulled his sleeve to his brow and wiped the sweat off. "I told you she'd gone to the car, Gil, and . . . oh, what's the use? I'm not gonna lie to my best friend." He looked around as though someone might be within earshot. "Uh, no, it wasn't Jill. I met a pretty young thing named Susannah and took her to the restaurant to impress her."

"What on earth's wrong with you? Cheating on Jill?"

"A simple fling, my man, and a few white lies about my background. Nothing serious. A guy gets bored sometimes, right? Needs to do something to prove he's still a man—you know, show he's still got it?"

"No, Bobby, I don't know, and what you don't know is Susannah happens to be Alex's best friend . . . and lies are wrong, no matter what color they are. Man, I can't believe this. The only thing you proved was you're an idiot and a cheater." My heart was pounding.

"Don't go getting all self-righteous on me, Gil! I wasn't cheating because I had no plans to get serious with her."

"That's a distinction without a difference, Bobby, and you know it." I wanted to punch him in the face. Instead, I grabbed my water bottle and took a long swallow, giving me a few seconds to calm down. I secured the bottle in my running belt, turned back to Bobby, and got right in his face. *Lord, give me at least a few of the fruits of the Spirit.* "It's no innocent fling to Suzie. You must have convinced her that you cared for her. I have no idea if she's in love with you, but she told Alex she thinks you're the one for her. This ends now, Bobby. You break it off with her immediately, as gently as you possibly can . . . and I do mean now."

"Who do you think you are, telling me what to do? I'm not your patient or your child, and now I'm not even sure I'm your friend. You have no business talking to me like that. All I want to know is which way you're running, 'cause I'm running in the opposite direction."

"Wait, Bobby, we've got more talking to do," I said, but I doubt he heard me. He'd already taken off the opposite way from the route we'd planned to run.

My stomach burned. How could I have misjudged such a close friend? What's this going to do to Suzie? Selfishly, I wondered how it would affect my and Alex's relationship. After all, I'd defended Bobby until now.

I jogged back to my car and toweled off. No sign of Bobby. He could take care of himself, and I had other things to worry about. Once I'd cooled off and stretched, I grabbed my phone from the car and called Alex. "Hey, babe. You busy? We need to talk, and I need to apologize."

Alex pushed open the screen door and met me on the front porch. She pointed to the porch swing. I didn't want to sit.

While she swung, I paced in front of her. Camouflaged birds chattered from a nearby cluster of oaks.

"Well, Gil?"

"I'm afraid you were right, Alex. Bobby admitted to the whole thing. What's more, he defended it as an innocent fling. Showed no remorse. I should have believed you, and I'm sorry I didn't."

She closed her eyes and slowly shook her head. "Listen, we've got something a lot bigger to worry about than you doubting me. Suzie's gonna be heartbroken. I can't believe this is happening. It's like something out of a soap opera, or from the lyrics of one of those cry-in-your-beer country music songs. How am I gonna break it to her?"

"Who says you have to, babe? Hopefully, Bobby will come to his senses and confess to her, apologize, and never contact her again."

"But she'll be heartbroken," Alex repeated. "She's such a sweetie, and I hate to see her hurt. The last thing she needs is betrayal . . . again."

"That's where you'll come in. Walk through it with her. Be her sounding board, or even the shoulder for her to cry on."

"And what if Bobby doesn't tell her and keeps up his Heath charade?" she asked.

"Then we'll just have to figure out a way to tell Suzie ourselves . . . but it would be a ton better if it came from him." I swatted at what was hopefully one of the season's last mosquitos.

"Let's go inside, Gil. I'll put on coffee and throw some leftovers together for dinner. Maybe caffeine and calories will help us figure this out."

Chapter Thirty-One

My patients' problems and the Bobby fiasco had distracted me from the matter of solving the questions that revolved around Carlos. A call from Chief Riddick the next day changed all that.

The stale stench of smoke hit me like August humidity when I walked into the dimly lit station, sending my mind back to the morning I hovered over a dying Carlos with smoke billowing from the plant. Jasper was leaning back in his chair, eyes closed, seemingly listening to the nearby scanner squawk one report after another from officers and medics in the region.

"Chief?"

He lurched forward and sat upright, scattering papers from his desk. "Doc! Good to see you."

"Did I wake you?" I asked as I retrieved his paperwork from the floor.

"Oh, Heavens to Betsy, no. I was focused on the scanner. We got some goings on 'round here but nothing like those big cities up north. I remember one time watching an episode of *Chicago PD* when the police captain got this emergency call over the radio—"

"Chief, you called me. About Carlos, right?"

"Oh, yeah. Carlos."

"Have you learned anything?"

"Matter of fact, I sure have. Called one of the Raleigh boys I know from way back. Works in the State Bureau of Investigation. Pretty highfalutin, if you ask me. Not that I couldn't work there. Scored pretty high at the police academy, if I say so myself. In fact—"

"What'd he say, Chief?"

Riddick's SBI contact told him there is a problem with trafficking in South America. Ironically, it's not as bad in Peru, but it does happen. The perpetrators try to avoid the national police by going into the back country to kidnap their victims—mostly women and children—where the national police don't normally patrol. These remote areas are hard to get to, and the people rarely venture away from their village, even when a crime has occurred. They're so fearful of retribution, they don't report it.

"So, what do we have to do to look into it?" I asked.

"My buddy said our best bet is to contact the State Department and use them to get through to the US Embassy in Peru. Our people over there apparently assist the Peruvian police in training programs to help them combat criminal activity." The chief stopped and chuckled. "Or, I reckon you could go over there and try to reach the village yourself to, you know, get the lay of the land and talk to this Elizabeth gal. Sounds like some kind of CIA operation, if you ask me."

"Yeah, Chief, imagine me trying to do that. But at least we have somewhere to start."

"Well, good luck getting through to someone at the State Department. You know how the feds work—when they work at all." He shook his head and laughed again.

"Actually, Chief, I have an idea of exactly where to start. If there's nothing else, I'll be on my way. Thanks for the update."

He cocked his head and squinted his eyes. Maybe he was confused, but he said nothing.

———————

My foot in the door at the State Department was Representative Trey Culpeper, Bobby's dad. Surely, Bobby would get him to reach out to someone who could help me. First, I'd have to repair the damage done to our relationship when I confronted Bobby on the trail. I'd be willing to meet him halfway. After all, we'd been good friends, and it wasn't my right to throw stones. I remember Dunk preaching something to the effect of pointing out a speck in someone's eye while missing a log in your own. *Sometimes, the Bible sure makes self-righteousness difficult.*

I called out Alex's number to my car's Bluetooth. She picked up on the second ring.

"Hey, Alex. How's everything?"

"Well, things were goin' great. I took Scout back to Tom Waters this afternoon and visited with him for a while. He's doing so much better. Kept thanking me for calling his son and for taking care of Scout. He's so sweet, but it was embarrassing."

"Someday I'm going to ask you more about your history with Tom. But what do you mean things *were* going well? Did something happen at Tom's place?"

"No. I was driving home from his house when Suzie called. She was really upset—so much so, she could hardly talk. When I calmed her down, she told me Heath had called and broken things off. Something about his career and the devotion it required making it hard for him to be in a serious relationship. She was so embarrassed, Gil, because she was sure she'd finally found her guy. Now she's back home in Charleston. Said she needed a few days, but it sounds like she's just licking her wounds. Can't really blame her."

"Sounds like Bobby came through after all. He's probably learned his lesson."

"That might be the greatest leap of faith you've ever taken, Gil."

I changed the subject. "Jasper Riddick called me today and gave me a big update on the Carlos puzzle."

"What'd you find out?"

"All of this probably has to do with child trafficking in Peru. I need to look into it further, but I do want to kick the tires with you on some thoughts I have. Right now, I need to get home and take Dutch out and then review some charts for tomorrow's patients. Can you meet me for dinner after work tomorrow?"

"Of course I can! You've got me intrigued now. Call or text me tomorrow and tell me when and where."

Dutch was at the window, paws on the sill, before I even got out of my car. Amazing I could be gone all day with him left alone, and all he wanted was to say hello when I returned. After the requisite ear scratching he loved, I changed into my running clothes and we went out the door. My neighborhood reflected the coming change in seasons. Cooler and less humid air, leaves beginning to fall, and seasonal flowers of summer no longer brilliantly colored. As I ran, Dutch loped nonchalantly, his tongue lolling from the side of a mouth I swear was smiling.

I thought about Alex. If there was a silver lining to Bobby's escapade with Suzie, it was that it highlighted how special my relationship was with her. She was always there for me and willing to help me, even if it was just to be a sounding board. I was lucky to have her in my world. But just thinking that wasn't enough. I needed to get on with it and tell her. No question about it, when it came to courtship, love, and everything that circled around a close relationship, my game needed a serious upgrade.

Chapter Thirty-Two

Luna

We were now just south of Tarapoto but stalled. The truck's engine sputtered, drew its last breath, and finally died. As two of the men prepared to go into Tarapoto in search of engine parts, they grabbed one of the girls and threw her into the Jeep and sped away. Our captors allowed the rest of us to sit in the tall grass on the side of the dusty road. I was the only girl not crying. A tropical storm, typical for this time of year, pelted us, temporarily cleansing us but then leaving us in mud that caked our legs and stained our clothes. With it came cooler air, albeit briefly. Back home, the men called these storms "work chasers," as they would run in from the fields during the heavy downpours, seeking dry purchase.

Once the rain stopped, the sticky heat pressed us further into submission. Our clothes clung to us like heavy, wet blankets. Such weather was so different from that of my native country, where my mum and I had experienced slow drizzle and fog on our rare visits there.

Guards stood close by, guns in place. Notepad Man strolled by, his back to us. Suited me. The less eye contact, the better. His gift of candy was probably a bribe for something more.

Once they told me they had special plans for me, I felt emboldened and found my voice. After all, with our situation becoming desperate, I had nothing to lose. When I caught Toothless alone, I said, "Please, the girls are scared to death. They know what your friends do to Andrea. Take me, if you must, but please leave her alone." I swatted at a fly, likely attracted by my filth and sweat.

"So, my *chica*, you can speak. *Bueno.* As I told you, we save you for special reason. For now, you must keep all girls calm. They do what we tell them."

"But they're tired, hungry, and scared."

"I will see what I can do for food and water. But other men? I have no control over them. Men have their urges, yes?"

I narrowed my eyes and took a step back. "You and your friends aren't real men. You're disgusting pigs."

He threw his head back and laughed, displaying what stained and yellow teeth he had left. "You, *chica*, I like. You have fight in you. Be careful what you say. Some of other men might not like hear that." He spit into the grass and walked away. Any thoughts I had of outwitting him now seemed futile.

A few hours later, the two men returned. They jumped from the Jeep and ran over to Scarface. He turned red in the face and stomped around like a bull cornered in a pen. All three men were waving their arms, pointing, and yelling—although I couldn't hear what they said.

When the yelling stopped, Scarface called someone on his cell. Toothless walked over to me and told me to get the girls back into the truck.

"Once engine fixed, we move. Worry about feeding you later," he said.

"What was all the yelling about?"

"No time now. Get girls in truck. *Vamonos!*" He stomped off.

The girls stood and tried to get into the truck quickly, but they were stiff from sitting so long and weak from a lack of nourishment. The younger girls struggled to climb in. Suddenly, Notepad Man appeared and helped them up. When I looked at him, he turned and walked away.

We sat in the truck, trying to wipe dirt and mud from our faces and hands. The men cursed as they worked on the engine. I climbed down to keep watch on what they were doing. Dusk quickly yielded to darkness. Lanterns hung from the truck's bonnet, illuminating the engine and sending piercing beams of light into the jungle, where howler monkeys screeched and frogs sang in monotonous cadence. The girls huddled together, as though closeness might grant them security. I tried to hear what the men were saying, but too many were talking and the chorus was chaotic and non-sensical. Finally, the engine roared to life.

Toothless walked to the back of the truck to tell me we were leaving.

"We've never traveled during the night. Why tonight?"

"When men in Tarapoto, they overheard *policia* discuss young girl who was rescued and being sent back to village."

Ava was rescued.

"And the girl they took with them today?"

"They deliver her to buyer outside Tarapoto. The *policia* never had clue." He laughed.

I climbed onto the bed of the truck just before it rumbled off. Some of the girls smiled when I told them Ava had been saved. Others stared off and were soon sound asleep, lulled by the gentle jostling of the truck's slow progress.

But Ava was saved, so there was hope for us too. I smiled at that thought as I closed my eyes and fell asleep.

Chapter Thirty-Three

Hillsborough

"First patient's roomed and ready, Dr. Gil," Sarah said. "Should be a simple one. Sore throat and what looks to me like a strep rash."

"You making diagnoses already, Dr. Sarah?" I smiled.

"No, and I'm not a doctor, nor do I want to be. Too old for that. I'll settle for getting through PA school. Only seven more months." She sighed.

"My sources tell me you're doing a lot better than getting through. More like the star of the class."

Her cheeks turned a crimson red. "Please go see your patient."

Sarah was a gem of a nurse, and I looked forward to having her work with me as my PA, if she'd have me. Like Alex, she made my world better—not only at work but as a friend. I could count on her, and having people like her in my life was important.

Once again, Sarah was right. The kid had strep. A simple fix. It set the tone for what was an easy day, with no difficult encounters but punctuated with another sad episode with Arnie Schmidt. At lunch, he came into the breakroom and rummaged through the fridge, frantically searching for what he'd brought to eat. Then one of the nurses reminded him it was his half day. No office lunch, as he always made it a point to finish the morning on time and be home for lunch with the love of his life, his wife Ruth. He attempted to laugh it off and shook his head slowly. One of the nurses jumped up and walked him back to his office to gather his belongings.

I glanced at Jim Greer, my partner, who looked up from his plate of leftover chicken penne pasta. I raised my eyebrows and hoped my expression conveyed to him a "we need to talk about this sometime soon" message.

That evening, I was a few minutes early, but Alex was waiting on the porch. She stepped down, looking stunning in her white blouse, black leggings, and prized Tory Burch sandals. Her blonde hair was pulled back in a ponytail, and she wore soft pink lipstick. "Where to, my good doctor?" she asked as she hopped into the car.

"You know, you never let me do the gentlemanly thing."

"I can open my own door, but thanks."

"You good with Vino & Vittles? Been a while since we've been there." This was the area's best attempt at combining good wines with great Southern food and excellent service, all in a casual atmosphere.

"Sounds good. I'm starved."

"Hey, a couple of things to discuss on the way, but first, any update from Suzie?"

"She texted to say she was feeling a little better and expected to be back in a few days. My guess is she'll be fine. I'm not sure we should tell her Heath is actually our friend Bobby . . . well, actually, Gil, he's more your friend than mine." I felt her eyes cut toward me like two daggers.

"I don't think she has to know. What good would it do? I confronted him as soon as you told me what you suspected. It didn't go well but, to his credit, he did break it off. We should avoid the subject when we're out with Bobby and Jill, unless he confesses to her."

"Sullivan, there won't be any Bobby, Jill, and us. No way. I know it's not very Christian, but I don't think I can forgive him for what he did to my best friend, and I'm sure I'll never forget."

A quick glance told me Alex's mood had changed. She looked at me, but the smile was gone.

"Okay, I get it. Well, if and when Suzie finds another guy—"

"Oh, she'll find another guy. Are you kidding me? She's bright, sweet as she can be, and drop-dead gorgeous. No worries about her rebounding from the whole 'Heath' thing. Now, what were you going to say?"

"Uh, I don't remember—must not have been important." Mercifully, we'd arrived at the restaurant.

Dinner held less friction. "Great idea to come here, Gil. Nice wine, comfort food, and a laid-back ambience. I love its vibe." She sat back from the table and cradled a glass of wine in both hands.

"Agreed. I'm stuffed, but it was delicious. No room for dessert but always for more coffee."

As if on cue, our waiter came over and refilled my cup. Alex waited for him to walk away. "Okay, what's the second thing?"

"Excuse me?"

"You said you had a couple things to discuss, right?" She wrinkled her forehead, eyes narrowed.

"Right. I talked to Riddick earlier and learned a lot. It's likely Carlos was referring to stolen children—possibly trafficked, based on what the chief's contact at the SBI said. But since it's Peru, we have to go through the State Department to reach the US Embassy there. They're the ones who work directly with Peruvian law enforcement." I paused and took a sip of coffee. "The only thing I've come up with is having Bobby ask his dad to make a connection for us."

"Good luck with that. Sounds like you and Bobby aren't exactly on great terms right now."

"I know. But I think I can make it happen. Worth a try, anyway." I paused again and took a deep breath. "There is one more little thing, babe." She arched her eyebrows. "This probably sounds weird, but I'm going to Peru, to Carlos's village so I can find and talk to Elizabeth. This is possibly a family now destroyed, so I need to do what I can. I couldn't fix my family, but maybe I can help hers. Anyway, she deserves to know what happened and to know the authorities are looking for the children."

"But Gil, that sounds kinda dangerous. Let the experts handle it. They know what they're doing."

"I can't get those kids out of my head. What if it was Chrissy? Wouldn't you pull out all the stops to find her?"

"But it's not Chrissy, or anyone else we know. You don't know these kids, Gil. Why would you put yourself at such risk?" She put her wineglass down and locked her eyes on mine. "I can think of a dozen reasons it makes no sense for you to do this: this is way out of your area of expertise; you'll put yourself and anyone who goes with you at risk; you have patients to take care of, and you have people important to you right here in Hillsborough. Do I need to go on?"

I leaned in and answered in a low voice. "No, I get it. Those are all valid reasons to stay. But two reasons I should go trump them all."

"Oh, yeah. What are they?"

"I was there, babe. With Carlos. He asked me to find the kids, and I have to honor his request."

"Yeah, I can kinda understand that. And the other reason?"

"Because there's only one thing worse than being lost, Alex. It's being lost and thinking nobody's out there looking for you."

Chapter Thirty-Four

Alex

I was at Stately Raven, pulling a half-day shift and restocking books. The coffee brewing in the breakroom filled the store with a rousing aroma, masking the odor of musty books, all of it occasionally diminished by a rush of cold, fresh air when a customer entered. But my focus was on Gil and a country some three thousand miles away. I couldn't get out of my head the notion he planned to traipse all the way to Peru on some kind of wild mission. It worried me and tested my faith.

Maybe my faith wasn't strong enough. Rev. Dunk would likely be disappointed if he heard me say that. I'd tried to push back on Gil's decision, but clearly, he'd made up his mind. If he was anything, he was a determined man. I knew how he'd set his sights on medicine and, once he accomplished that, was so dedicated to every patient. Now, his goal was to go to Peru and do what he could to honor Carlos's memory and help the missing children. The tinkling of the entry bell brought me back to Hillsborough.

"Is that one of my favorite people? Alexis Morgan?"

I turned to the clicking of claws on the bookstore's weathered hardwood floor. Tom Waters and, of course, Scout.

"In the flesh, Tom. Gosh, it's so good to see you. Hey there, Scout." He nuzzled against my leg and pushed his head under my hand until I scratched his ears. "Good boy. Glad to see you've got your old buddy out and about. Tom, watcha up to? Can I help you find a book for someone?"

"No, thanks. Not really shopping for books today."

"Well, if you came by just to say hi, I really appreciate it. You look so good. Now that I know you're fine, I want you to know how worried I was about you."

"I was lucky, Miss Alexis, or as lucky as a fella can be who gets hit by a car. Guess I didn't see it coming, no pun intended." He slowly shook his head.

"Next time, please take Scout with you wherever you go. If he'd been there—"

"I know. I know. He'd have never let me step into the street. Learned my lesson the hard way, that's for darn sure. I'm lucky to be here talking about it."

"We all feel the same way."

"Miss Alexis, can we talk privately?"

"Sure. Let me grab a couple coffees and some cookies from the break-room." I gently grabbed his elbow with one hand, pushed the book cart with the other, and helped him into a chair. Scout obliged by plopping beneath the table. "Okay, we're alone, Tom. What's on your mind?"

"Well, you know your dad and I go back a long way. Grew up here, played baseball together on the high school team, double dated some—all that kinda stuff kids do."

"Yes, I know. And I know you're still friends, even though he no longer lives here."

"That's right. I've called him a couple times at the rehab facility to let him know I was thinking of him."

"Very thoughtful of you. Thanks."

Tom explained he'd filled my dad's prescriptions when he lived in Hillsborough, including his anti-depressant—something I didn't know he ever took. Tom said he'd get depressed and then become very impulsive.

Maybe that explained why he hooked up with his trophy wife so soon after mom was out of the picture.

Tom stopped and took a deep breath, looking around as if he could see if anyone else was within earshot of us.

"It's still just us, Tom."

"Well, Miss Alexis, seems his hook-ups started way before his current wife."

"What?"

"All that time on the road and away from home, he got lonely. He met some gal at a truck stop over in Tennessee and had a pretty serious relationship with her—over a long period of time, I should add."

"How serious?"

"Uh, very serious, Alexis. Matter of fact, your mom found out. That's a big part of why she divorced him. There's another thing too . . . You have a brother."

I choked on a piece of cookie and coughed. "I have a brother? What on earth are you talking about?"

"He got this gal pregnant, and she had a baby boy. Your dad eventually ended the relationship, but he never stopped supporting his son. Visited him whenever he was on the road. I've known it forever, but your dad swore me to secrecy. Anyway, he grew up to be a fine young man. He's a state policeman in Tennessee."

I was in disbelief. "Tom, why are you telling me all this?"

"Your dad wants you to meet him."

I stared at him for several seconds. "I am not going to Tennessee to meet a brother I never knew I had. Sorry, but I won't."

Tom bit at his lower lip. "You don't have to, Alexis. He's here."

"You mean 'here' like here in Hillsborough?"

"Yes, ma'am. He was in Charlotte, visiting your dad—been mighty good about that, if I must say. Your dad suggested he come to Hillsborough and meet you."

"Why now, after all these years?"

"Best I can tell, Alexis, your dad almost met his Maker and now realizes we aren't even promised tomorrow, much less a long future. Probably figures it's high time the two of you met."

I sat silent for several more long seconds. "Okay, then. I guess I'll do it—for my father. What kind of daughter would I be if I didn't at least try to honor his request? Is this something you promised my dad you'd set up, and, if so, when will I meet him?"

"He's actually over at the Scene, waiting on us. That is, if you're ready to meet him."

"Tom, five minutes ago, I didn't even know I had a brother, and now you're asking me to go have coffee with him? I don't know if I'm up to it."

"No, ma'am, I'm not asking. Your dad is. And listen, you handled Virgil when you went through all that mess with him. I think you can handle meeting a fine young man like Chris."

———

When my shift ended, the three of us walked over to Caffeine Scene, Scout patiently at Tom's left side, with me on the right. His arm, interlocked with mine, tensed when we stepped off the curb. We entered the Scene and a young man sitting alone stood up, unfolding his long legs from beneath the table. One glance and I knew it was him—my dad from about twenty years ago.

Scout stopped at the table, and Tom followed his lead. He reached out, shook the guy's hand, and then turned in my direction. "Chris, this is Alexis. Folks here know her as Alex."

He extended his hand. "Chris Campbell. And most friends call me Soup—you know, like the soup brand? Please, you two have a seat. The waitress should be right back with my Americano, and we'll get the two of you something—my treat. Goodness, this is so surreal, seeing a sister I didn't even know I had until a week ago."

His smile was pleasant enough, but his deep-set green eyes and square face crowned with a flattop intimidated me. "Well, that's almost seven days longer than I've known about you!" I attempted a smile.

"Alex, I suppose the elephant in the room is the question of what kind of double life our father led. As for me, he's always been good to me, at least during his infrequent visits. When I was a kid, he wasn't around very often, which confused me. My mom blamed it on his job—you know, being on the road so much." He shrugged.

Chris went on to say their dad had come clean when he visited him in rehab. He was ashamed he'd led two different lives with two families, and it was time to own what he'd done and try to get his daughter and son together.

I explained he wasn't much of a dad and husband for me and my mother, either. When he was home, he was cold, distant—something I'd held against him for years. That made it hard to visit him in the hospital after his stroke, but I'd made myself go.

"And now, I'm glad I did. I really need to get back and visit him in rehab, but it's hard to know what to do or say."

"Yeah, I get it. I think he appreciates the company, but he has a hard time saying so." A waitress came by with Chris's coffee and took orders for Tom and me. Tom asked for his to go.

The more we talked, the more we understood our experience as kids was pretty similar. Somewhat of a connection, albeit a small one.

Finally, Tom stood, as did Scout. "I reckon I'll mosey on and leave you two to finish getting acquainted. Y'all have a lot of catching up to do. C'mon, Scout." He grabbed his leash firmly in one hand and his cup of coffee in the other.

"Please be careful, Tom," I said.

"I'll be fine, Miss Alexis, but thanks. Scout, heel."

"Chris—"

"Soup. Please."

"Right. Soup, tell me about yourself. Tom says you're a policeman." The beep of a car horn distracted me, but through the window, I could see that Tom had safely navigated the street crossing.

"That's right. I work for the Tennessee State Patrol, out of the Nashville office. Pretty much patrol Interstate 40 all night long. So the very highway that brought our dad to my mom is now the one I work. Pretty ironic, huh?"

I nodded. "Third shift?"

"Yep, graveyard shift. I like it, and I'm single with no kids, so I don't mind being away from home at night. Plus, once I get a few hours of sleep, I've got more time to do what I love."

"Which is?"

"Skeet shooting."

I almost spit out a sip of coffee. "You shoot?"

"Yep. Pretty good too, if I do say so myself. I recently reached the AA level."

"Well, it must be a genetic thing, because I shoot too. I'm nowhere near AA classification, but I love guns and stuff like shoot 'em ups on TV. Kinda freaks Gil out."

"Gil?"

"Oh, yeah. Gil Sullivan. He's my boyfriend."

"Cool. I'd love to meet him . . . By the way, what's your shotgun of choice?"

"Perazzi MX 2000. Feels good snuggled against my shoulder, plus it sounds so sexy," I said.

"Good choice. I shoot with a Beretta A400. Makes me feel tough."

"Oh, like Robert Blake in the old TV series?

"No. I shoot with a Beretta, not a Baretta. They're spelled differently."

"They're homonyms."

"Whatever."

I grinned. He reminded me of Gil, and he seemed like a really nice guy. I incorrectly assumed this would be an awkward meeting. Stories of family members discovering each other weren't unusual, and I'd often wondered if they were authentic or made for television. Now I knew. I guess blood *is* thicker than water.

Before leaving the Scene, Soup and I exchanged contact information on our cells. "Let me talk to Gil about dinner out for the three of us. I'll call you." He nodded. I turned toward the door, stopped, and turned around. Soup was right behind me. We shared a brief and awkward hug.

Chapter Thirty-Five

I was anxious to see Alex. It was one thing to think about how lucky I was to have her in my life but a big leap to tell her. I'd stood guard over my emotions for so long; it was difficult to release them from my soul and share my heart. Yeah, we'd both been patient with our reluctance to move any faster in our relationship, but how long could that last? Any guy would be lucky to have Alex, so why wait and risk losing her to someone else? I was doubly blessed with her support of my decision to find Elizabeth. For me, there really was no other option. Could it be dangerous? Sure, but danger had come to our little town, proving no one's totally safe anywhere. But first, I had to see Alex. Feeling like a teenager calling a girl for a first date, I took a deep breath and made the call from the office.

She spoke before I could. "Hey, sweets. Boy, do I have a story to tell you that you'll find hard to believe."

"Actually, I was calling to see if I could come over tomorrow after work. We can talk then. And I've got something to tell you too."

"Bet my story is better." She laughed. "See you tomorrow."

Well, that was easier than I'd expected, but it was just the first step. The face-to-face conversation would be more challenging.

Through the sheets of rain and the last light of day, Alex was a cloudy image, swinging on her front porch, her favorite perch. Perfect. Outside, where Chrissy wouldn't hear our discussion. I pulled up the hood of my rain jacket and ducked my head as though that would keep me dry. Clusters of musty-smelling leaves dotted the walkway.

"Hey, Gil." She patted the space beside her. "Have a seat. It's finally fleece pullover weather, but I still want you snuggled up against me. Don't you love this weather? Crisp air, the sound of rain hitting the roof like corn popping in the microwave, and leaves blowing off the trees—kinda like a scene from a Nicholas Sparks movie, right?"

A romantic mood. Perfect. "Yeah, Alex. It's nice, but I could do without my clothes getting soaked."

"They'll dry, and I don't think you'll melt!" She kissed me on the cheek.

"You seem mighty happy. I wanted to—"

"Gil, let me go first. I've got to tell you who I met yesterday."

She went on to tell me about Chris, or "Soup," as she said he liked to be called. Discovering a sibling in her life and her father's shameful double life had to have jarred her, but she seemed none the worse for it.

"Good grief, Alex. That must have been difficult to hear. I wish Tom had read me in on it. I could've been there when you found out."

Alex planted her feet on the porch. The swing stopped; her smile disappeared, and she looked at me with narrowed eyes. "Tom had no reason to include you. He knows I'm a big girl, and I can take care of myself. And please, don't go judging Tom."

"Hold on. I didn't mean anything by it. Don't be so defensive. What's the deal with you two? Just because he gave you and your friends free milkshakes back in the day doesn't make him a saint. Correct?"

"Now you're stepping in it, Sullivan. If you've got a few hours, I'll tell you all about it."

I rubbed my right temple. *Oh, boy. Here we go.*

Alex told me her dad was absent from her life so much when she was young that she became resentful. Started acting out and misbehaving—nothing major but enough to worry her mom and Tom. Having been such a good friend of Alex's dad, he'd kept a close eye on her. He'd stop by the house to visit with Alex and her mom, take Alex to ball games or the movies, or take her by the store for a milkshake. In such a small town, no one gave it a second thought. Especially since it was Tom.

Her eyes puddled with tears, and she stared off, as though trying to once again see those now-distant memories. She stopped and sighed deeply.

"Tom and I were like two puzzle pieces that fit together perfectly. He singled me out as the one he would help when he had no obligation to do so—actually treated me like I was his daughter. He saved me, Gil. Turned my life around through simple acts of kindness. And he's never asked for anything in return, not even a thank you. How many people can you say that about?" She arched her eyebrows. "Not many, I bet. Oh, I do love that man."

The one. *There it is again.*

"Okay, I'm busted. And I have even greater respect for Tom now, not only as a pharmacist but, more importantly, as a person." I slowly shook my head. "I really had no idea, Alex."

"Well, in all fairness, you had no way to know, but now you do. Okay, enough of that. What'd you want to talk about? . . . Gil? You're doing it again. Where are you right now?"

I cleared my throat. "I'm here, trying to figure out how to say what I want to say."

"Well, say it, for Pete's sake."

"Okay, but it's not easy. You see, I've been thinking. I really haven't been fair to you."

"Meaning?"

"I mean I've been holding back, not really telling you or showing you how I feel about, you know, *us*. When I was a kid, my parents weren't exactly the greatest role models in my life and, turns out, yours weren't either. But you've been so open with me and so giving. And I need to give back to you and not let my past dictate my life. Truth is, Alexis Morgan, I love you."

She looked down, her chin nearly to her chest. A sniffle. Then a sob. She looked up and smiled through tears.

"Sure, Sullivan. I bet you say that to all the girls." Her arms were suddenly around my neck, her face against mine. We kissed in a moment I wished could last forever.

"But you've never told me you love me, Alex."

"Wanted you to go first, and you did. You finally said it." She threw back her head and laughed. "You've made my day, sweets."

I pulled a small box from my rain jacket pocket. It slipped from my hands, and I kneeled to get it. I looked up at Alex. "Babe, I want you to wear this." She took the box. Her face turned red, and her lower lip quivered.

"Open it," I said.

"Okay, gimme a moment." She took about as deep a breath as possible, opened the box, and pulled out a delicate silver cross necklace. Shaking her head and laughing, she said, "Gil, it's beautiful. I love it." She pulled her hair up from her neck, and I slipped it on and fastened it.

Alex stood and grabbed my hand, leading me inside the house. She pushed me onto the couch and sat on me, her legs straddling mine. My hands found the gentle curves of her back as she pushed herself closer. Her breath warmed my neck.

I pulled back. "Alex?"

"Yeah, sweets?"

"I could sure use some coffee."

"Well, that was about five minutes of romance, Gil, but probably a record for you. I'll go put it on." She raised her eyebrows and cut her eyes at me. "And don't you dare go anywhere. We're not finished here."

She returned with two mugs. "Coffee, as ordered. Hope Keurig's okay."

"Of course. Thanks, babe."

She sat beside me, threw an arm across my shoulders, and said, "So I was thinking maybe we could go out to dinner with Soup. You know, nothing fancy, more of a get-to-know-you type of thing. Maybe El Capitan Loco. Whadda ya think?"

"Sure, because you know how much I loved that place last time we went, right?" I winked.

"Soup's a Tennessee boy. He'll love its ambience."

"'Ambience' might be a bit too fancy a term for that restaurant, babe."

Chrissy walked in from her room. "Hey, Dr. Gil," she said.

"Hey, Chrissy. How ya doin'?"

"Chrissy, your homework finished?" Alex asked.

"Yeah, Mom. I'm going to bed. Just wanted to tell Dr. Gil hi. Oh, and Mom, I saw Miss Jill the other day after school. Said she hadn't seen you in a while and wanted to catch up with you soon. Anyway, goodnight."

We looked at each other. "Alex—"

"I know. I need to figure this out without lying to Jill or telling her the full truth about Bobby. At some point, I'm bound to bump into her. Actually, she comes into the bookstore fairly often."

"How 'bout this? Tell her you've got a lot of balls in the air right now, what with your dad's health issues, the news about Soup, working, and finishing school. Just put her off."

"I guess you're right. Better than being fully honest and potentially destroying her marriage."

We both nodded.

Chapter Thirty-Six

My load was lighter. The monkey was off my back. Pick any metaphor you'd like, but bottom line, telling Alex I loved her was a huge relief for me. Scary but a relief. A commitment I never planned to walk back. Sharing that moment with Alex was something I'd always remember. Just one thing bothered me: She didn't come right out and say she loved me.

I bounced into the office, my feet barely touching the floor. The day's visits hadn't started, but the phones up front were already ringing, staff members were bustling about, and Sarah was sitting at her desk, hunched over her computer.

She looked up. "Oh, morning, Dr. Gil. Schedule's pretty full already but looks like it's gonna be a good day. No troublemakers, far as I can tell. But before you go in with your first patient, Dr. Greer wants to see you."

I knocked once on Jim Greer's door frame, stuck my head in, and saw him pacing back and forth in front of his desk, a massive oak structure I'm sure rivaled in size and weight the Resolute desk in the White House Oval Office. No exaggeration.

"Gil, thank goodness you're here."

"What's up?"

"It's Arnie. When he came in this morning, he started roaming around. When I asked him if everything was okay, he became irate and said he couldn't find his office. I escorted him there, where he sat down and started crying. He told me he just couldn't do this any longer. His memory's shot, and he's afraid he'll make a mistake and hurt a patient." Jim took a seat, bent over, placed his elbows on his knees, and cupped his face in his hands. "We've got to get him home, Gil. In fact, Mrs. Schmidt is on her way now to pick him up."

I didn't know what to say. We'd all seen some decline in Arnie's mental state—but mostly harmless forgetfulness. Now he was lost—in the very office and practice he'd started and grown to what it is now. Today was the day I planned to tell Arnie, Jim, and Sarah of my plans to go to Peru. That would probably have to wait.

Arnie commanded respect and appreciation, not only for his clinical skills but also for creating a practice that gave all of us employment. He was a tough old bird, but he was well-respected and loved. I'd take the affection he enjoyed when I got to that point in my career in a New York minute. I remembered asking Arnie about retirement several times, and he just brushed it off. Said he'd know when it was time, and he wanted to be sure to exit the stage on his own terms. Now, that wasn't likely in the cards.

At the end of the day's schedule, Jim and I were sitting in the break-room, talking about Arnie's situation and how we'd handle it. Sarah walked in and grabbed her jacket from her locker.

"Sarah, have you got a minute? I've got something to tell you and Jim."

"Dr. Gil, I don't like the sound of that. If you're leaving, please don't dump that on us now."

I laughed. "No. I'm not leaving. No way I'm letting you off that easy. Please, sit down."

Before I recounted everything, starting with the explosion and continuing through what Chief Riddick and I had learned about Carlos and the missing children, I apologized for bringing this up on such a tough day. Then I mentioned how Carlos, for some reason, ended up in our little town, presumably to earn enough money to go back to Peru to carry out his heartfelt mission. I told them about the letter from Elizabeth and how I felt obliged to go to Peru and visit their village. After all, she deserved to know the truth about Carlos's fate, and the children deserved our every effort to find them, or to enlist the people who could. When I finished, they both stared at me.

"Well?" I asked.

"Gil, I admire you," Jim said. "What an adventure! Dangerous, in some ways, but so honorable. I say you should go, with no hesitation. I'll get some third-year residents to help out here—might even be a way to screen them for possible employment. After all, Arnie's not . . . well, you know."

Sarah's eyes were puddled in tears. "Dr. Gil, this is such a beautiful thing for you to do. I need to give it some thought, but do you think I could go with you? Maybe we could do a medical clinic in . . ."

"It's Campoflores, and that's an intriguing idea, Sarah. Let me think about it, and you do the same. After all, we'd be in a pretty remote part of Peru."

"You think I'm not tough? I work with you." She shrugged and then grinned.

I left for home feeling almost as good as I'd felt when I got to work that morning. Arnie's situation was still heavy on my heart, but I knew we'd all look out for him and do the right thing. I was actually getting pretty excited about the prospect of going to Peru. But there was someone I needed to talk to. I pulled up Dunk McElroy in my "Favorites" and clicked on his name.

After working my half day, I met Dunk at the local pizza joint the next afternoon. The enticing odors of cheese, pepperoni, and onions smacked me in the nose when I walked in. An iconic eighties hit, Billy Joel's "Uptown Girl," was blaring from an old-fashioned jukebox sitting in the corner. Dunk waved me over to his table and greeted me with a man hug.

"Thanks for meeting me, Dunk. Got some news to share—and a request."

"Of course. What's up?"

I explained how I came to be interested in a trip to Peru and what I planned to do while there. As I talked, he leaned in, focused on every word. When my name was called, I got up to grab our slices and sodas.

When I returned with our food, Dunk was shaking his head. "Fascinating, Gil. I didn't realize Carlos was a pastor and had no idea he was here as part of a greater mission."

"We didn't know, either—not until Chief Riddick read a letter to him that arrived after he died. But Dunk, I've got an ulterior motive for telling you this." I shifted in my chair.

"Which is?"

"Just wondering—and it's totally okay if you're not on board—could I give a mission minute about Peru during an upcoming service? I want people to understand the situation, but I'd also like to ask them to contribute financially to the cause."

"I see. Well, Gil—"

"Like I said, Dunk, if it's out of line, no worries."

"Actually, I was going to say it sounds like a fine idea to me—long as you're certain you're committed to the trip. How about this Sunday?"

"Yep. I'm committed, and Sunday's great. Thanks."

The rest of lunch was punctuated with small talk, mostly Dunk talking about the Heels/Blue Devils basketball rivalry. It was basketball season, but truthfully, it's always college basketball season in North Carolina. He also asked me about my patient who'd lost his son. It'd been a while since George's last office visit, and it was a good reminder I needed to get him on the schedule before I left for Peru.

Chapter Thirty-Seven

El Capitan Loco was just as chaotic as it was when Alex and I last visited. Luckily, one of the few tables left was far from the loud music and wild dancing. I took a seat and massaged my temples, trying to stave off a headache I sensed coming. Alex and Soup ran out on the dance floor to join in on what looked to me like a bunch of chickens prancing around. They laughed as they swung from one partner to another, somehow always ending up with each other again. I wasn't interested, but if Alex was happy, I was happy.

They finally returned to the table, arm in arm. Soup whispered in her ear, and she giggled.

"Well, that looked like fun," I said.

"Gil, you're such an old soul. After we eat, you're going out on the floor with me. Want you to show me your moves."

"I'll take a hard pass, but thanks. Now look at the menu so we can order."

After taking our orders, the waitress returned shortly with drinks—beer for the siblings and a pitcher of Coke Zero for me. The band took a break, and the decibel level notched downward.

"So, Chris, Alex tells me you're a state patrolman."

"Yep. And it's Soup, by the way. Love nicknames. In fact, when I look at you, I think 'Sully.' Okay if I call you that, Gil?"

I cut my eyes at Alex, who was stifling a giggle, and then looked at Chris. "Yeah, sure. No problem, Soup."

"And you're a doctor, right?"

I nodded. "Guess that means we're both kinda in the people business, right?"

"That's right," he said. "But I bet you get a lot more respect than I do. People love their doctors. They may complain about the cost of health care and how long it takes to get an appointment, but once they're in the office, they're happy. Now don't get me wrong. I'm not complaining. I love my job. But life's about more than work, right? What do you do for fun when you're not doctoring?"

"I run or I play with my dog Dutch. Sometimes he and I run together. Do a little fishing. Guess that's about it. Alex told me you have a love for guns and shooting like she does."

"That's right. We plan to go shooting while I'm in town. Would you like to come out and shoot some pigeons?"

"Thanks, but I'm not really the shooting type. Plus, I can't see myself trying to kill innocent birds."

Alex and Soup looked at each other and broke out laughing.

"No, sweets, clay pigeons, not real birds. It's simply target practice. One pigeon, or a pair of them, is released, and we try to hit them. Loads of fun."

"I'll think about it," I said.

Mercifully, our tacos and salad arrived. Discussion ended as we polished off our dinners. Without mercy, however, the band members climbed onto the stage and resumed their crazy Tex-Mex songs. After dinner, Alex and Soup ordered two more beers. I leaned into Soup, my voice raised, and asked how long he was planning to stay in town.

"I've got three days of vacation left. Plan to go back to Charlotte to see our dad before heading home." He turned to Alex. "And that reminds me, sis. I had a thought. Why don't you ride with me down to Charlotte?"

"You know, I do need to see Daddy, and it would bless his heart to see us together. No classes or work tomorrow. I'm supposed to be in court, but I think I can change that."

"Court?" Soup asked.

Alex shook her head and said, "Not what you're probably thinking. I'll be in court but only to observe. It's part of my social work degree requirement."

"Oh, okay. See what you can do, and I'll call you in the morning."

———

I was driving Alex home from the restaurant, and I guess I was quieter than usual.

"Well, sweets, what'd you think of Soup? Isn't he great? It's amazing how much we have in common and how comfortable we are with each other."

"Yeah, he's great. Nice guy."

"Well, try to curb your enthusiasm, why don't you?"

"No, really. I do like him. He's just different from me. You know, a little rough around the edges. Seems kind of wild. Not sure our Venn diagrams intersect much, if at all."

I could almost feel her eyes burning through me. "Oh, you mean he likes to have fun, like dancing? And he shoots guns? He's my half-brother, for Pete's sake, so if you and I are a thing now, and he's part of my family, I want you to like him."

I nodded.

"Hmm. Know what? He's single, good-looking, and a really nice guy. Maybe I could hook him up with Suzie. Whadda ya think?"

I had a feeling this conversation was headed south. "Listen, Alex. I know you mean well, but Suzie's coming off of a major disappointment. Might be a little too soon to expect her to rebound."

"Who are you suddenly? Dear Abby?" She looked out the passenger window.

"Don't ask my opinion if you don't want it," I said.

Neither of us spoke for the last few minutes before we got to her place. "Alex, I know it's not late, but I'm beat. I'm going to drop you off and go home. Dutch needs a walk, and I have some chart work to do. But . . . are we good?"

She sighed. "Sure, we're good. You can drop me off here."

She opened the door and put out one leg. Suddenly, she turned back to me, leaned over, and kissed me on the cheek. "I know tonight wasn't your cup of tea, so thanks for going."

"I loved it, babe . . . and for the record, I really do like Soup."

———

Like usual, I'd forgotten it would be dark when I got home and had failed to leave a lamp on for Dutch. No matter. From the light of the street lamp, I could see him through the front window, paws on the sill and tail wagging like a clock's pendulum. That's my boy.

As soon as I walked in, Dutch jumped up and grabbed my thigh with both of his front legs. I swear he was hugging me. I rubbed his ears. "Hey, Dutch boy. How ya doing? Let's go get you something to eat." He followed me to the pantry, mouth open and tongue hanging out. Suddenly, he froze.

"Dutch? You all right?"

He turned, growled, and took off for the front door before either of us even heard the doorbell. He jumped up on the door, baring his teeth and growling like I'd never heard before. I looked through the peephole. It was Virgil.

Either for fear of my own safety or having Dutch push his way out the door, I spoke without opening it. "Virgil, what are you doing here?"

"I need to talk to you. Please."

"Then talk."

"I'm wanting to apologize for what I done. For hurting your dog. See, I love dogs. Most of all, I'm tore up 'cause I hurt Alex and Chrissy."

Virgil sounded genuinely remorseful. "Hold on, let me leash him." I got Dutch on his lead and cracked open the door. "Let me grab a seat and get Dutch to sit beside me."

He stepped in, removed his ball cap, and sat opposite me. "Like I said, Dr. Sullivan, I'm wanting to apologize to you and—did you say his name's Dutch?"

"That's right. Listen, Virgil, what you did was not only against the law, it was plain dumb. And to hurt my dog? Truthfully, forgiving you is a tough pill to swallow."

He nodded, and went on to say he wanted to reach out to Alex, but the sheriff had ordered him not to get within one hundred feet of her or Chrissy. He paused and dropped his chin to his chest, shaking his head slowly. The house was so quiet, I could almost hear Dutch's apprehension. He had both eyes trained on Virgil.

Virgil looked up and said, "See, Dr. Sullivan, I ain't had much education and no way was I ready to be a daddy—or a husband, for that matter. I should've just walked away from Alex and Chrissy, paid what support I could, and visited when they'd have me. Once I lost them, it wasn't long before I knew what I'd thrown away. But Alex wouldn't have me back, and I reckon I don't much blame her. Seein' her with you—that jest drove me crazy mad, and I ended up doin' something really stupid. That's right. Stupid, even for me." Tears mounted in his eyes, poised to overflow like foam at the top of a glass of Coke Zero.

His words touched me, and I believed him. "Listen, Virgil, it had to be hard for you to come here tonight. And I can forgive you, but you've got to earn my trust—and Alex's, if that's even possible. But I can't speak for her, Chrissy, or even Dutch."

"Leastways, can you tell her I'm sorry for what I done, please?" See, I got me a court date comin' up. Reckon I'm lookin' at jail time that I sure 'nough deserve. But I'd feel a bunch better if I could make amends for what I did to y'all."

"Of course. I'll let her know."

He stood to leave, and Dutch pulled toward him, straining against the taut leash. I forced him to sit. "Virgil." He stopped and looked back. "I appreciate you coming by. That took courage."

"Thanks, Dr. Sullivan."

"Please, call me Gil."

Chapter Thirty-Eight

Alex

S uzie was back from Charleston. She texted that she was anxious for us to meet and talk. It was important to see my best friend, but the timing was bad. Soup and I were preparing to head down to Charlotte to see our dad. *Our dad. Sounds weird.* I called Soup, and he agreed to put off the trip until the afternoon. Said he could use the free time to hit the range for a little target practice.

"Target practice? Where in the world will you—"

"Sully called me first thing this morning. Said he'd talked to the police chief, and I could stop by the station and he'd get me to the range."

"Gil did that?"

I beat Suzie to Shorty's Diner, grabbed a table, and waited. I'd worked there part-time in high school and was still such a frequent visitor that they let me in through the private entrance. I was greeted with the rich aroma of coffee, an assortment of pastries, and bacon crackling on the grill. Cartons of eggs stood by, waiting to be cooked to order and served steaming hot. The owner and cook, Jeff, walked in, ducking his head to get his tall and lanky body safely through the kitchen doorway. Ironically, his nickname was Shorty, taken from his role as short-order cook.

"Howdy, Alex. How's the Baroness of Breakfast today?" he asked in his usually gregarious way.

"Ready to roll, and how's the Earl of the Egg?" I said, attempting to match his alliterative game. "Looks like you've been busy."

"Yep, getting ready for the cravers of caffeine, as well as other culinary creature comforts."

I laughed. Shorty was not one to be outperformed.

He followed me out to the booth, where I sat. Suzie walked in, and I stood to give her a hug. "So good to see you, Suze. And this is my friend, Shorty. Shorty, meet Suzie."

"At your service, Suzie. Let me conjure up some coffee and croissants for you chicks."

Shorty walked away, and I leaned in. "Yeah, he talks like that. Sort of a verbal game he and I play. Anyway, how're you doing?"

"You know, I'm okay, I guess. Still not over getting dumped by Heath, but I figure I've got to trust God. If Heath's not the one, He has someone else in mind for me. Least I hope so, anyway."

"Sugar, you know He does. When one door slams, another swings open."

"Well, it'd sure be nice if Mr. Right walked right through that open door," she said, pointing to the diner's door.

I assured her it would happen, and then I took a deep breath. "I've got a couple of news items for you."

First, the news that Gil had told me he loves me. Then I told her about the gift box and how I thought it was an engagement ring. "Boy, was I relieved when it was a necklace instead!"

Suzie threw her head back and laughed. "That's priceless. Wish I'd been a fly on the wall. So what's your other news?"

As I gave her the short version of the back story on discovering I had a brother, her eyes widened. She plopped her coffee cup on the table, and some of it splashed out.

"But he's fun and totally cool. I really like him. Both of us are kinda victims of our dad's indiscretions, so we share that, and we're trying to forgive him. In fact, we've decided to head down to Charlotte to see him."

"So this whole 'brother news' is a good thing?"

"I think so. At least, the notion's growing on me." I put a hand on Suzie's forearm. "Suze, I'd like you to meet Soup. I think you'd really like him. What about a casual dinner with me, Gil, and him?"

"I don't know, Alex. Not sure I'm ready to date again."

"Don't think of it as a date. You know, simply a night out so my best friend can meet my newest family member."

Thirty minutes later, we finished our brunch and stood to leave. "Just think about meeting Soup, Suze, and I'll give you a call later today. We don't have much time 'cause he's heading back to Tennessee soon."

"Hey, girlfriend?"

"Yeah?"

She tilted her head and arched one eyebrow. "Did you tell Gil you love him too?"

"Gotta go, Suze."

On the way to my car, Soup called. He sounded out of breath.

"Alex, where are you? I need to see you—now."

"I'm leaving the diner. Meet me at Caffeine Scene. We'll grab some coffee."

Soup was pacing back and forth in front of the Scene. We took a seat on an outdoor bench. I noticed his eyes were red. "Soup, is everything all right?" A dog barked and a car horn blared in the distance, mingling with the noisy conversations of passers-by.

He turned to face me fully. "Alex, I got a call from the rehab facility. Dad died early this morning."

The world stopped spinning for a moment, and there was dead silence. Then, somewhere off in the distance, I heard Soup speaking again. He explained our dad had some kind of blood clot that formed in his leg. Slowly, Soup's words registered. "They think it moved to his lungs and killed him."

He put his arm around my shoulders and pulled me close. "If it helps, Alex, they said he probably died in his sleep, instantly and without pain."

"I . . . I don't know what to say, Soup. A few months ago, I didn't even have a relationship with my dad. His stroke made him vulnerable—more human, you know? And I was trying to repair our broken mess. I thought we could make up for lost time and be a family . . . or at least—"

"I know what you're trying to say, Alex."

A woman strolled by, so pregnant she looked like she was going to pop. "Look at that, Soup. It's like people leave this world as new lives enter."

"Circle of life, right?"

I looked away and nodded. "We've got to get down there to make arrangements. You know, get his body back home and talk to Rev. McElroy about a service."

Soup stared down and slowly shook his head. He looked up at me and took me by the hand. "No, we don't, Alex. I got a second call, this one from his wife. She said she'd take care of everything and didn't need our help. All of it would be done in Charlotte—privately."

My fists clenched. "I hate her," I said. "She stole our dad, and now she's stealing our ability to honor his memory. Can she do that?"

"Yes. Whether we like it or not, she is his wife."

"Yeah, some wife." I knew that was a nasty comment, but it was hard to be a loving Christian in the emotion of the moment.

"Alex, let me drive you home. We can get your car later."

"I need some air, so I'll walk home and worry about the car later."

"You good with being alone?"

"Gil's finishing early today. I'll call him and ask him to stop by. I don't want to tell him over the phone."

I gave Soup a hug and walked away.

Wind whipped the post office flag. I pulled my collar higher and pressed my crossed arms to my chest. The seasons were changing—in the air and in my life.

Chapter Thirty-Nine

I had a free afternoon, with no commitments. Pretty unusual for me. I walked out of the house with Dutch. The last of the leaves were blowing from the trees, with Dutch trying his best to snap at the ones that floated by him. Empty beds lay dormant, waiting for their winter plantings. I scrunched my shoulders and shoved my one free hand into my fleece pocket. A few blocks into our walk, my phone chirped. Alex.

"Hey, babe. Dutch and I are out on a walk. You on the road to Charlotte?"

Her voice broke. "Gil, I'm home, not on the road. I need to see you right away. Please."

"I'll be there as quickly as possible. What's going—"

She disconnected.

What in the world?

I hurried home and jumped in the car, lowering the back window partway so Dutch could stick his head out. Immediately, his nose pointed to the sky, his eyes squinting against the sun and cool airstream—Heaven for him.

Alex met us at the door and threw her arms around my neck, sobbing as she tried to speak.

"Hey, babe, let's get inside so we can sit and talk."

Dutch lay beside the couch as we sat. "Now, talk to me," I whispered in her ear. "Why didn't you go see your dad?"

"He died, Gil."

"He died?"

"Yes. Before we could even leave for Charlotte, Soup got a call from the center. Some kind of blood clot in his lung that killed him instantly. At least, that's what they said."

"A pulmonary embolus."

"Yeah, I think that's what they called it."

"Alex, they were right. If it was an embolus, he would have died pain-lessly and quickly." I wanted to say there were worse ways to go, especially at his age, or that maybe it was a blessing, but I held my tongue. I'd learned James was right in his book when he said we should be quick to listen and slow to speak. Especially with acute grief, people simply need an ear . . . and a shoulder. "Tell you what. I'll cancel tomorrow's schedule so you, Soup, and I can go down and handle the details."

Alex's crying intensified. Dutch cocked his head and looked up at her. "There are no details. That wife of his said she'll handle it all, and we don't need to be involved." I pulled her close and let her cry.

"What about Chrissy, Alex? Does she know?"

She shook her head. "Not home yet. Soccer practice." Her crying eased, and she sat up straight and looked at me. "But she didn't even know him, Gil. He was never in her life and barely in mine until recently. Like I told Soup, just as we were trying to reconnect, he's gone. We lost whatever chance we had." She stared out the window.

"You are a family, babe. You've got Chrissy and now Soup. I'm not exactly family, but I'm not going anywhere." She settled back against me. The last hint of sunshine filtered through trees, peeked through the windowpanes, and cast long shadows that danced against the far wall.

"You're right. But it's so hard."

"I get it. He was your dad. Not a perfect man but still your dad."

After a minute of silence, Alex went to her room for a sweater while I made coffee and put on water for tea. She walked in and reached her arms around my waist and held me tightly, her head squeezed between my shoul-der blades. I gently grasped one of her arms.

"Your water's almost boiling. Is green okay?"

"Let's go with chamomile. It might calm me." When I turned around, she rested her head on my chest.

We sat in the near darkness of her kitchen. Dutch joined us when Alex asked him if he wanted a treat. Cheerios. Like me, his tastes were simple.

"Gil, I know this is random, but Soup's only here for one more day. Can we go out to dinner somewhere quiet tomorrow evening?"

"Sure."

"There's something else, but I don't want you to be mad at me or think I'm stupid."

"Alex, please."

"I had brunch with Suzie. She's doing okay, but she's still hurting. Girls can tell things like that. Anyway, I told her about Soup; one thing led to another, and before I could catch myself, I suggested the four of us go out tomorrow."

"And?"

"She said she'd think about it. I've got to call her back this evening. I know you think that was a mistake—"

"It's fine, Alex. In fact, it might be exactly what all four of us need." Dutch sat at attention, waiting for more Cheerios. "Guess I have to get this boy home for some supper."

"You leaving?"

"Not yet. I'm waiting until Chrissy gets in and you tell her about her granddad. If that goes okay, then Dutch and I'll head home."

Chapter Forty

Chrissy took the news well, so with no further drama to tackle that night, I went home, fed Dutch, and went to bed early. Today promised to be a less emotional one . . . I hoped. The day's schedule was unremarkable—the usual number of Medicare well checks with sick visits mixed in. With winter approaching, we were seeing the seasonal infections: influenza, respiratory syncytial virus, and lots of common colds leading to sore throats and ear infections. No call or text from Alex about dinner tonight, but I figured she'd contact me during my lunch hour. *Lunch hour. What a misnomer. When, if ever, does that happen?*

The text came at lunch, as I expected. Was predicting each other's behavior a sign that Alex and I were growing closer?

> Dinner's on. All four. Pick me up at 630 please. Going to Dome

Alex was right. Suzie was ready to stick her toe in the water. I should've known to trust her intuition over mine. A female thing, I suppose. Before I left work to go home and get ready for dinner, Sarah poked her head into my office and asked to speak to me.

"Dr. Gil, I've given it some thought. I'd really like to go with you to Peru. Who knows what kind of medical care those poor people get? Maybe we could do a clinic. It'd be a great experience, and it wouldn't hurt to have it on my resume."

"You don't need to worry about your resume—at least, if you're going to work here with me. Tell you what . . . let me give it some thought. I want to make sure I'll have time to hold a clinic, given everything else I'm planning to do."

"Like what, if I may ask?"

"Making sure those kids are found and returned home." Saying it out loud gave it a reality that hadn't sunk in.

"Okay. Well, let me know as soon as you make a decision. Thanks, Dr. Gil."

———

A car I didn't recognize was parked in Alex's driveway. I was greeted at the door by Soup.

"Hi, Sully. Have a seat. Alex is almost ready." He paused. "Say, you don't mind if I ride with the two of you, do you? I don't know my way around these parts, but I'm happy to follow you if you'd like."

"Don't be silly. I doubt Alex would settle for anything else."

"I'm ready, boys." Alex was stunning. Her hair was in a French braid, and she wore just a hint of makeup. Her white blouse and gray slacks were set off by low black heels. She handed me her black peacoat, turned and slipped into it. "Let's roll."

The ride to Chapel Hill was short and punctuated with small talk between Soup and Alex. She filled him in on Suzie, hitting the high spots but avoiding any talk about Bobby. Finally, she reminded him this was a dinner among friends and family, not really a date. Soup snuck a peek at me and rolled his eyes.

The Dome was busy, as usual. Our reserved table was ready, but we stood inside the door until Suzie arrived. She walked in and greeted Alex with a hug.

"Suzie, this is my brother, Chris."

"Nice to meet you, Suzie—and please, call me Soup. Everybody does."

"Then Soup it is!" She glanced at me. "Hi, Gil. It's been a while." I nodded.

Alex's smile was a mile wide as she looked back and forth from Suzie to Soup. "Okay, let's grab our table."

She and I led the way. I leaned in and whispered, "Babe, I saw that look on your face. Remember, it's just dinner, right?"

She cocked her head and shrugged. "Sure, sweets."

We kept the conversation comfortable. When Soup learned Suzie was a journalism major and wanted to be a reporter, he told her he hoped she'd be fair to cops. Everyone but Soup laughed.

Alex stopped the conversation and said, "Gil, tell them your news."

I went through the entire story from the explosion and Carlos to learning about the trafficked children. I could recite it in my sleep. Suzie's gaze was riveted on me, slack-jawed. Soup's eyes narrowed, complemented by a slight furrow in his brow.

"Gil, it sounds too dangerous to me. We've had a few encounters with adults and children in Tennessee who were labor- or sex-trafficked. The few traffickers we caught were a pretty tough crowd. You might want to leave the trafficker hunting to professionals."

"You mean the Peruvian authorities, right?"

"Yes, and the American staffers who support them. Are you familiar with INES?"

"Never heard of it," I said.

"INES is a non-profit headquartered in Maryland that works undercover in other countries to help the authorities find and rescue traffic victims. Not only do they have resources and skills they share, they're also on the ground to assist in the mission. And they have associates who provide after-rescue care to make sure victims become survivors."

"How do you know so much about it, Soup?" Alex asked.

"They have a domestic division, and they've helped us find victims and their traffickers in Tennessee."

Suzie leaned in to Soup. "People are trafficked right here in America?"

"More than you or anyone else would realize. And not just sex trafficking. Labor trafficking too."

"What does that mean?" I asked.

"Traffickers bring in adults and children who can pass for adults to fill jobs in places desperate for help. Areas that have gone through the devastation of a hurricane, for instance. Those construction contractors just want warm bodies to do the work. No questions asked."

Alex set her glass down quickly and sat back in her chair. "So are you saying that our country's complicit in trafficking?"

"Not the country, Alex, but some companies that employ laborers. What's worse, any child in America with a screen is vulnerable to traffickers who dwell on the dark web. Kids respond to a seemingly innocent message, and before they know it, they're entangled in that trap."

Alex gasped. "You mean kids like Chrissy?"

"Unfortunately, yes."

I was intrigued. "So what does INES stand for, Soup?"

"It's not an acronym, it's a name. A girl's name."

I guess I looked puzzled. Soup then launched into the organization's origin. Two former special-ops military men were working private security for a rich New York international businessman. One of his French associates, also extremely wealthy, lost the one thing money couldn't buy: his daughter, Ines. She was kidnapped when the family was on vacation in the French Riviera and held for a twenty-million-dollar ransom—more money than even this guy had. The man's New York colleague sent his two ex-military security men to France to track her down.

"And?" Suzie asked.

"They found her . . . but too late. The failed mission devastated them. With initial funding from their boss, they began the organization and vowed to do all they could never to lose another child. Both of them had gone to the Naval Academy, so they set up shop in Annapolis and named the organization INES. The name's a little confusing, which helps keep them under the radar—exactly where they like to stay."

My mind was racing. "I had no idea, Soup, but it sounds perfect for what we need in Peru. How do I contact them?"

"I've got contacts in INES through my work. I'll put you in touch with someone who can get the ball rolling in Peru."

"Perfect."

Not only had I learned something that could give my trip a greater chance for success, but dinner went well too. Our meal was peppered with small talk. As I'd admit later to Alex, Soup and Suzie really seemed to hit it off. She seemed genuinely disappointed that he would have to go back home the next day.

As we walked Suzie to her car, she looked up at Soup and said, "Really great to meet you, Soup. Hope to see you again."

"Don't worry, you will." He looked at Alex and grinned. "I've got family here to come back and see."

As we drove back to Hillsborough, Alex asked Soup what he thought of Suzie.

"Well, she's smart, cute, and fun to be with."

I glanced in the rear-view mirror. "Does that mean you want to see her again?"

"You can bet the ranch I do."

I think I heard Alex grinning.

"Oh, totally unrelated, but there's something I forgot to tell you at dinner," I said. I'm doing a mission minute at church this Sunday. Just trying to make people aware of the phenomenon of trafficking and, if I'm being honest, trying to get some funding for the trip. If we can get INES working on behalf of the children, I can focus on a medical mission and trying to meet with Carlos's friend."

Alex put her hand on my forearm and looked back at her brother. "See why I like him so much, Soup?"

Chapter Forty-One

Put me in an exam room, give me a patient with a medical problem, and I can talk comfortably one-on-one all day long. That's my turf. But public speaking? Not so much. Even if I didn't appear to be nervous, I always felt I had that "deer in the headlights" look. Normally, I relaxed in church—sometimes even fell asleep, as Alex would readily attest to. But with my name in the bulletin as a speaker, I was as nervous as a fly in a room full of swatters. Seriously.

Alex elbowed me in the ribs. "Unless you've got a headache, stop rubbing your temple. It's annoying."

"Sorry." I sat on my hands until Dunk called me up.

I walked to the lectern, mentally replaying my mission minute one last time. Everyone knew the backstory of the explosion, but they didn't know the specifics of Carlos's case. I reviewed those details, explained I felt called to travel to Peru and visit his people, and gave an overview of how a domestic organization could assist in the rescue of traffic victims. It was the ending I struggled with.

"Finally, my friends, traveling to Peru and conducting a medical clinic will take money. I can fund it partially, but I'll need help, especially if other volunteers go with me. I ask you to prayerfully consider supporting what I believe is an important mission." As I looked over the congregation, I spotted her on the back pew. Fortunately, I was at the end of my spiel because seeing Eleanor Wainwright sitting there rendered me speechless. When our eyes met, I swear she was sporting a slight grin.

When the service ended, I hurried to the back to catch Ms. Wainwright, but she was nowhere to be found.

Alex caught up to me and slipped her arm in mine. "Proud of you, sweets."

At the exit, Dunk greeted us and thanked me for my little talk. He leaned in and said, "Gil, either call me or come by the office in the next day or so. I'd like to talk to you about something."

———

That evening, my partner Jim Greer called and asked me to meet him at the office an hour early the next morning.

I arrived the following morning to find him and Ruth Schmidt, Arnie's wife, sitting in Jim's office. He motioned for me to take a seat.

"Gil, Ruth's here to talk to us about Arnie."

I looked over at her. "Morning, Mrs. Schmidt." She was fashionably dressed in corduroy slacks and a turtleneck pullover. Her silver hair fell gracefully to just below her ears, framing a thin, lined face.

"It's Ruth, please. And good morning to you, Gilbert. As I explained briefly to Jim this weekend, Arnie wants to return to work, at least on a part-time basis." She cleared her throat and shifted in her chair. "He believes he got confused from fatigue and some dehydration, maybe from working outside the evening before that awful morning in the office. I just don't know, but he does seem sharper and less forgetful now."

I glanced at Jim. He was biting at his lower lip. "Ruth, you and Jim know Arnie much better than I do, but we all know he would never want to put a patient in harm's way. He might think he's ready to come back, but I'm not—"

"Maybe on a very part-time basis, Ruth," Jim said. "We could even have the girls lighten his schedule and select encounters that wouldn't be too challenging. You know, just to see how things go. Is that what you were going to suggest, Gil?"

I swallowed hard. "Absolutely."

Ruth seemed pleased. She looked at Jim, and then, at me, she smiled and said, "Thank you, gentlemen. Getting back to the office in any fashion will mean the world to Arnie." With that, she stood, thanked us again, and showed herself out.

Jim and I sat there and looked at each other. He slowly shook his head. "Gil, I hope this is the right thing to do. We're going to have to keep a close eye on Arnie. Pat's been his nurse forever and probably knows him almost as well as Ruth does. I think we can trust her to let us know if she sees any problems."

"Sounds good. We can also take turns looking over his notes at the end of each day."

I met Sarah as I walked out of Jim's office. "Morning," I said. "Hey, I want to talk with you about Peru when you have a few minutes."

"It's early, and your first patient won't be here for thirty minutes. How 'bout now? Oh, and speaking of patients, George Owens is on your schedule at the end of the afternoon. I know you prefer those visits on Friday, but he had a conflict, and I figured you'd want to see him rather than put it off."

"Good call. Thanks. Let's go to my office."

Sarah sat across from me, leaned forward, and rested her hands on the desk as I spoke. I explained what I'd learned about INES and how their work would free me up to do a medical clinic. "Of course, I couldn't do it alone, and no one would be better at helping me than you—if you're still interested in going, that is."

She broke out in a big smile. "Of course, I'm interested. By the way, I heard most of this in church on Sunday."

I narrowed my eyes. "You were there? I didn't see you."

"I knew you'd be nervous, so I kinda hid behind some big fella in the pew ahead of me. You did a great job."

"Well, thanks. So you heard me make an appeal for some financial support—"

"Dr. Gil, I fully intend to pay my way."

"I wasn't implying you wouldn't. What I was going to say, though, is we'll need to see how much money's donated and how far it gets us in medications and supplies."

She nodded. "I understand. But I don't want money to be an issue." She glanced at her watch. "Your first appointment might be here now. I need to get to work."

"Okay. We'll talk more later."

My schedule went well, with no major issues until I saw George Owens. His face was long and drawn, with downcast eyes showing no expression. When he extended his grease-stained hand to meet mine, his arm veins coursed like tendrils through a once-muscled forearm that was now thinner and pale.

"Afternoon, George. Thanks for coming in. I'll be out of town over the holidays and wanted to see you before I leave. Good news: Your bloodwork was normal. But how're things going?"

"I'd say not too good, Doc. Still working at the body shop. Helps keep my mind off things. But home's kinda fallen apart. The missus and I have split up. We were both miserable, and it seemed worse when we sat around at home without much to say. Matter of fact, just seeing other people goin' 'bout their lives all happy and stuff while we're sufferin' is hard too. Don't get me wrong, I don't fault nobody, but it don't seem right while we're sufferin'."

"I get it, George. I don't think what you're going through is all that unusual for someone grieving. I'm sorry, though, that you and your wife separated. I mentioned counseling at an earlier visit. There's the option of couples counseling too. And, of course, you can always consult with your minister."

"Doubt either would work, Doc. Reckon the counselor person would be the only one talkin', and I'd just be angry with God if I talked to a preacher."

"That'd be okay, George. God can handle it. Give it some thought. Now, I want to see you when I'm back at work. Between now and then, promise me you'll do your best to eat and sleep adequately. More important, if you get so sad you consider hurting yourself, you must either call the office or go to the emergency room. Can you guarantee that?"

He nodded. "Reckon so, Doc. Thanks."

———

The steam had evaporated from my anticipation of the Peru trip by the time I got to the church office. So far, I'd failed George. All I knew to do was to keep seeing him; encouraging him. He'd be on my mind until I saw him again.

Dunk pushed away from his desk and stood to greet me. We both took seats in two easy chairs that bookended a low, round glass table. Two ceramic coasters and a wooden sculpture of praying hands sat on the table.

"Thanks for coming by, Gil. Let me get you some coffee." He walked over to the Keurig and then turned to me. "You're probably wondering why I needed to see you, right?"

"Well, Dunk, it's kind of like getting called into the principal's office."

He chuckled. "Nothing to worry about, and I'm glad you're here because I have some news that was just confirmed this afternoon. But first things first . . ." He leaned against the counter, with a wall of Bibles, commentaries, and concordances as his backdrop.

Dunk explained he'd been praying about my trip to Peru. For my safety, for the children's safe rescue, and for God to provide all that I needed. Then God nudged him and told him he should go with me. He resisted, thinking he was needed here more.

"Then I decided Father Jose could step in and preach the couple of Sundays we'd be gone. Wouldn't hurt good Presbyterians to get a little dose of Catholic medicine, right? After all, we're all Christians." He held out his hands and shrugged.

"Dunk, I hadn't even considered having you go on the trip, but I'd love it. You might even be able to conduct services in Campoflores. Soon as we see how much money comes in, we'll know how much it'll cost each of us."

"That's the news I wanted to share. Got a call today from a lady who wouldn't identify herself. She wants to underwrite the mission trip—and I mean the whole thing. Wouldn't give me her name but said you'd probably be able to guess."

Ms. Wainwright, maybe? I was stunned. "To be clear, Dunk, you *do* mean the entire package?"

"That's right. 'Whatever it takes' were her exact words."

After a prayer of praise, our conversation morphed into a review of how the Carolina basketball season was going. When I stood to leave, I had a smile on my face. We'd have no out-of-pocket expenses on the trip, but more importantly, I think I might've finally cracked a tough old gal's veneer. With the trip fully funded and with Dunk and Sarah on board, it was time to do some logistical planning. First on the list was reaching out to INES. I'd need help from Washington, DC. Time to talk to Bobby.

Chapter Forty-Two

Bobby reluctantly agreed to see me the following day at his office, right after we finished work. Given the way we left things on our last run, I really couldn't blame his caution. I caught myself rubbing my temple as I sat in his reception area and thumbed through an outdated issue of *Our State* magazine. Finally, his assistant walked me back to his office.

He waved me in, shook my hand, and we both took a seat. "What can I do for you that was so important we couldn't just talk about it over the phone?"

"Listen, Bobby. First, let's clear the air. You've got to understand where I was coming from with our last conversation. It's Alex's best friend, for crying out loud."

"Yeah, I get that, and I'm sorry. I was being stupid, but I felt like you attacked me from some moral perch . . . and I thought we were good friends."

"There was no easy way. We still are good friends. Consider this, Bobby. Do you really want to risk the prospect of a scandal if you plan to run for office?" He raised his eyebrows and screwed up his lips. *Had he never considered that?*

"No, I don't, and just so you know, I've sworn off all boorish behavior. I'm focused on my marriage. But I'm also on pins and needles just waiting to see who tells Jill first: you or Alex."

"Neither of us, Bobby. We decided to leave it alone. I did my part by bringing it up. Far as I'm concerned, it's past history, and I'm pretty sure Alex feels the same way."

Bobby's grip on the chair's arms seemed to ease. He slipped off his glasses, looked down, and ran his fingers through his cropped hair. "I'm ashamed, Gil. With a beautiful wife who's devoted to me and the prospects of a political career, I had nothing to prove. Maybe with the current success of my law practice, I figured I could get away with anything. Maybe being the son of a United States congressman went to my head."

Bobby had just tossed me the perfect segue. I explained I was there not only for reconciliation but also to talk about his dad. After updating him on my plans, I told him I needed a contact in Washington to reach out to the US Embassy in Peru to set in motion INES's operation.

"INES?"

"Sorry. Yes, INES. Learned about it from Alex's brother, and I think they're the answer to actually finding these children."

"I didn't know Alex had a brother, and I've never heard of INES. Let me make us some coffee. We've got a lot of catching up to do." A hint of a smile crossed his lips.

We had a good conversation. Bobby was receptive to the notion of getting his dad to help me. In fact, he said it would be a very easy thing for him to do. All I had to do was let Bobby know once I'd talked to the people at INES and then he'd contact his dad. When I stood to leave, he grabbed me and gave me a quick hug.

"Thanks for stopping by today, Gil. But more importantly, thanks for setting me straight. I'm far from perfect, and I needed that."

"Well, get in line with the rest of us, Bobby. There was only One who was perfect."

———

I needed to update Alex on several things. I left Bobby's office and pulled out my cell.

> Last minute, but can u meet me for pizza?
> Need to talk

> Sure. Give me 30 min. C u there

"Hey, sweets. Hope you don't mind the leggings and no makeup. I didn't exactly get a lot of notice." Alex kissed me quickly, and we walked into the pizzeria. "What's up?"

"Bunch of stuff I need to tell you about." We ordered and took a seat.

She leaned in as I told her I'd just come from seeing Bobby, and he'd promised he would get his dad to help me.

"But there's more, babe. Bobby is making a real effort to change. You know, less of that sophomoric behavior and more focus on his marriage."

"If he really means it, that's good news."

"Seemed sincere to me, and I can read him like a book."

"Yeah, right. Just like you knew it couldn't have been him duping Suzie into believing he was somebody he wasn't."

"Fair point. Hey, I also talked to Dunk yesterday. He wants to go on the trip to Peru and get this; he told me someone anonymously funded the entire trip."

"Gil, that's wonderful! Wonder who it was?"

I shrugged. "Like I said, anonymous." I took a deep breath and gently grabbed Alex's hands. "There's something else I need to tell you. Should've told you earlier, but when your dad died, I didn't want to stress you out."

Alex cocked her head and squinted. "Go on."

"Virgil came by the house to see me."

"Virgil? Your house? With Dutch there?"

"Yes . . . to all three. He was remorseful, babe. Pitifully so, actually. After apologizing to me, he asked me to do something for him."

"What was that?"

"Well, since he has that restraining order and can't get near you and Chrissy, he wanted me to tell you how sorry he is." She opened her mouth but stopped long enough for the waitress to set our pizza and drinks on the table.

"He's sorry all right. The nerve of—"

"Alex, you're not hearing me. He's truly sorry. I believe him. And I forgave him."

"You're saying you forgave him for hurting Dutch?"

"I can forgive without forgetting, and I told him that. Listen babe, what good is it to carry around hate and resentment for him? That only burdens us, right? Pretty sure forgiveness is biblical."

She pushed her chair back from the table and crossed her arms. "Biblical or not, I'm not sure I can bring myself to forgive him, Gil. That's a big ask. Maybe you're just a better Christian than I am."

"Oh, c'mon, babe. It's not about who's a better Christian. You know that. Just give it some thought. I promised him I'd pass along his message. What you do with it is completely up to you."

We ate our pizza in silence.

On our way out, Alex turned to me and said, "If you don't have any more surprises to spring on me, I've got something to tell you. Soup talked to his INES contact in Tennessee, and they'd love to be involved in the rescue. He said all we'd have to do is get the proper authorities to invite them into Peru, and they'd use their tactical skills to search for the girls."

I took her by the hand and pulled her close. "Man, that's great news. Everything's falling into place . . . but are we good?"

"Yes, we're good. You know we are."

"What about Virgil?"

"Don't push your luck, Sullivan."

Chapter Forty-Three

Luna

Nights were easier. I'd peek through the holes in the tarp and see the moon and stars, reminding me that God was still looking over us. I'd point that out to the other girls but got little reaction. Finally, we'd all fall into a restless sleep. But the days? Each day seemed to grow longer than the previous one. We tried to nap as we huddled in the back of the truck as it bounced along. The girls said very little and seemed to become more withdrawn. This was so different from our days back home—a happy time that now seemed so distant.

Ava's pleas for me to come outside drew my attention away from my books. After the school day ended, my mum usually had extra studies for me, as Spanish was not my first language and I had much to learn. My friends' laughter and chatter disrupted my concentration, but Ava's calls were impossible to resist.

"Mother, may I go outside to play? Just for a little while, please?"

"Luna, you know how important it is for you to learn this language. Study a bit longer and then you can go."

"But being with my chums will help me just as much. They always speak Spanish."

"Nice try, but do as I say."

Once my mum was satisfied I'd studied enough, I ran into the large lot just beyond our little house. The girls were kicking a soccer ball up and down the field, usually missing our makeshift goal. I laughed as they chased the ball rolling toward the woods. We didn't share a common language, but their love for soccer was as strong as it was for my chums back in England.

Ava left the group, ran to me, and gave me a big hug. Silently, she grasped my skirt and stayed close as we mingled with the others. Our voices merged with those of the sparrows and tanagers clustered in nearby trees.

Once we tired of running, the girls sat together, happily talking about the next time we'd all gather to go to the market in Moyobamba. For many of them, that was as far as they'd traveled from the village. The bigger world I knew was foreign to them, and no amount of explaining made them understand how different Europe was from South America.

The sun dropped in the sky, casting longer shadows from the trees. I heard my mum's voice calling, "Luna? It's time to come in, Luna!"

———————

"Luna . . ."

I startled awake and realized the voice I'd heard was in my head, and the children playing was just a memory.

Sometimes, memories are all we have to hold on to.

Chapter Forty-Four

Sarah stood there, her mouth gaping. "You mean the whole trip's paid for, Dr. Gil? I won't have any out-of-pocket expenses?"

"Well, maybe the souvenir T-shirt you buy in the airport. Never been to Peru, but I'm sure they'll have them."

"Oh, my goodness. This is so exciting." The sparkle in her eyes made my day.

"This will be like an off-site externship, Sarah. You'll almost be finished with school, so there's no reason you can't see patients alongside me. Might as well get used to that." I winked.

"I wonder who our benefactor is?"

"I think it's Miss Wainwright."

She furrowed her brow. "No way. That dear old lady's as tight as a tick."

"Well, I've been talking to her, and who knows, maybe something finally registered. She was in church Sunday when I gave my mission minute. Although she's resigned to finish out her life without any medical intervention, maybe she's choosing to intervene financially in others' lives—you know, to make a difference."

"Maybe. I didn't see her in church, and I'm kinda surprised she was there."

"We'll just keep all this to ourselves for now. It was given anonymously, so I don't want to risk upsetting her if I ask her about it before we go. If she really is our benefactor, won't it be fun to thank her and tell her all about our trip when we return?"

It was one of those good days at the office. Both Sarah and I were in excellent moods, and no patients threw us any curveballs. "Routine" and "uneventful" were terms I was coming to cherish as descriptions of a day at work.

Sarah got busy checking online with the Peruvian Ministry of Health regarding medications most needed in the rural areas. She placed orders for antibiotics, analgesics, and the anti-parasitics we could use to address the routine problems we'd encounter. Chronic problems like hypertension and arthritis would need to be referred to the closest medical facility, likely in Tarapoto, a nearby town. Health care was free in Peru, so expense wasn't the issue. It was getting people from remote villages the help they needed. We learned cars were few and far between, and nothing like Uber existed outside of large cities like Lima.

While at lunch, I called Soup to update him and get the contact information for his guy at INES. I'd need to pass that along to Congressman Culpeper, who'd agreed to make the necessary arrangements. All he needed was a name at INES to connect with his people at the embassy in Lima. I owed Bobby for making that happen.

"Name's Don Calvin," Soup said. "I'll send you his contact info. Sounds like you're making good progress, Sully. Keep it up. And remember, anything that comes up domestically, I'm in. Say the word and I can coordinate with Don and the stateside team to rain fire down on these heathens."

"Appreciate it, Soup."

"One more thing. I haven't even told Alex yet, so don't spill the beans. I'll have some time off soon, and I plan to spend some of it in Hillsborough with her and Chrissy. Maybe see Suzie again, too, if she's in town. I guess I'll miss you."

"I suspect they'll like that . . . all three of them."

We made a lot of progress that day. I decided to stop by Alex's and surprise her on my way home. The police chief's car sat parked in the driveway.

I knocked but walked in without waiting for a response. Alex and Riddick stood outside the door to Chrissy's room. A mixture of shouting and crying came from within the room.

"Stay away, Mom, and just leave me alone. If you don't, I might hurt myself."

Alex looked at me and grabbed my arm. "Gil, Chrissy's upset about something and won't come out of her room. When she threatened to hurt herself, I called Chief Riddick, thinking his presence might persuade her to open the door."

"Thanks for coming, Chief," I said. Riddick looked at me and nodded.

He leaned in and said, "Doc, we got us a situation here. Nothing I've said's made a speck of difference. Just not as easy as those TV negotiators make it look. Reckon she'll listen to you?"

"Keep talking to her as calmly as possible. I'll be right back."

I rushed home, grabbed Dutch, and drove back to Alex's. I figured Dutch had as good a chance of reaching Chrissy as any of us.

"Chrissy, this is Dr. Gil. I've got Dutch with me, and he's pretty upset hearing you cry and scream. Can we come in and talk with you, please?"

"Just the two of you?"

"Promise."

Chrissy cracked open the door, one eye peering right at me. "Come in, but just you and Dutch."

Her backpack was on the floor, with books strewn across the area rug. The bed covers were in a pile. Chrissy took a seat amid crumpled facial tissues scattered over the sheet. She rocked slowly, her knees pulled to her chest, with both arms wrapped around her legs.

"Chrissy, I'll just sit with you, and Dutch will sit beside the bed, okay? Now, tell me what's wrong."

"School. My parents. Everything in my life."

"Meaning?"

"We were rehearsing for the school's fall play today. The teacher began talking about our parents and siblings coming to the show, and some kids started teasing me about my dad. Said there was no way a criminal would be welcome, even if he were around. I got so angry, Dr. Gil; I didn't know what to do, so I left school and ran home."

A fatherless home. "I understand . . . and I don't blame you."

She cut her eyes at me. "You don't?"

"Listen. My father walked out on my mom before I was even born. Never knew him. Don't even know if he's dead or alive. My mom tried hard to be a good mother, but she came up short. But look at your mom. She loves you, Chrissy, and she's working hard to make a good life for the two of you. A life that I'm now a part of. Just think, are you really mad at her or is it the kids and your dad you're upset with? I know your mom, and I bet if you walk out that door and go to her, she'll be relieved, not mad."

Chrissy looked up at me and slowly nodded. She reached down and patted Dutch's muzzle and then wiped her eyes with her shirt sleeve, caught her breath, and went to the door. When she opened it, she folded into her mom's arms. Riddick looked at me, smiled, and gave me a thumbs up. After a few minutes, Alex turned to me.

"Chrissy and I are going for a walk. Mind if Dutch goes too?"

"I doubt he'd settle for anything less. Go ahead."

Riddick and I watched them walk out the front door. He stood there, shaking his head. "Good job, Doc. Glad you came along when you did. Reminded me of this movie I saw where a crazy person barricaded himself in a storage room, and all the talking in the world wasn't—"

"Chrissy's not crazy, Chief. She's upset and confused, and I don't blame her. But I think she's going to be fine."

"Didn't mean no harm, Doc. Well, since the dust has settled, reckon I'll be on my way."

I sat and thought about what Chrissy had said. Kids need their parents—both parents—in their lives, even if they aren't perfect. Neither I nor Alex had that growing up, but it wasn't too late for Chrissy.

I looked up as they walked in, hand in hand, with Dutch trailing. "Chrissy, I bet Dutch could use a little playtime. Do you mind taking him out and throwing him the ball?"

"Well?" I asked Alex after Chrissy went outside.

"She's okay, for now. Just needed to vent."

"No, babe, what she needs is to have her father back in her life. Virgil's not perfect, but she loves him, no matter how you feel. I don't know about you, but I sure wish I'd had my dad around as—"

"Gil, stop. We talked about her father. I realize now she needs to have a relationship with him. But I'm not there—at least, not yet. He'll have to wait on me, and I'm not making any promises." She peeked out the back window and looked back at me. "By the way, what caused you to stop by?"

"It was a good day, and I felt like topping it off by surprising you. When I saw Riddick's car, I was the one who was surprised."

"Well, sweets, I'm glad you came by . . . and brought Dutch over too."

Chapter Forty-Five

Work got busier as cooler weather settled in for the fall. Preparations for the trip made things even more hectic, but it was an exciting busyness. Neither I nor Sarah had ever been outside the US, but having passports in hand made us feel like world-class travelers on the verge of a huge adventure. Dunk had lived in Scotland but had never been to South America. Preparations were in order, with just one more thing I needed to do before leaving.

Alex and I had talked extensively since Chrissy's meltdown, and we agreed we needed to stop by and see Chief Riddick. When we got there, he was alone at his desk, leaning back in his chair with his feet propped on his desk. Buttons strained to keep his shirt anchored over his ample girth. As I took off my coat, I noticed Alex fanning the air in front of her face. Riddick sat up quickly, put out a half-smoked cigarette, and stood to greet us.

"Gil, Miss Alexis. Good to see y'all. Sorry 'bout the smoke. Little company's a welcome change for me. My deputies take off for home as soon as their shifts end. Can't say I blame them. I'd do the same thing if I had a family to go home to. And those families? Goodness, Deputy Clark's young'uns are a handful, I'd say. It's like a circus at that house. Speaking of circuses, that Barnum and Bailey Circus used to come right down the interstate, near our little town, when it headed for Charlotte. Heck of a note to see those elephants on the highway—"

"Chief, can we cut to the chase? It's been a long day."

"Of course. Sorry. Please sit a spell and tell me what I can do ya for."

We sat back in chairs with arm supports that felt smooth and oily from heaven only knows how many years of use. I looked at Alex and nodded.

"We want to talk to you about Virgil, Chief Riddick," Alex said.

"That rascal. Just sayin', and I don't mean to talk ugly about your ex, but he did some pretty stupid stuff."

"We couldn't agree more, Chief," I said. "But he came and talked to me and seemed genuinely remorseful. Actually, the reason we're here is to drop all charges."

"Drop the charges? You mean all of them?"

"That's what we mean, Chief," Alex said, nodding. "And we'd like you to rescind the restraining order too."

"Well, dang if that don't beat all. Can't say I ever had somebody do that. You sure?"

Alex glanced at me and then back at the chief. "Yes sir, we're sure."

"Okey dokey. I'll put it all into play. Gotta contact Virgil's lawyer and do the necessary paperwork. And if I ever do something stupid, I hope the person I hurt's as forgivin' as the two of you." He shook his head.

As we left and leaned into a headwind, Alex hunched her shoulders and pulled her coat tight to her neck. "You know, Gil, I always feel like I need to wash my clothes and take a shower after I'm in that building."

"Yep. Nasty smell but a small price to pay for what we accomplished. Feels pretty good to let go of the past and forgive. Right?"

Leaves dropped from their perches, floating shadows in the near darkness. Alex looked up at the dusky sky and shrugged. "Right, I suppose."

"So, what now, babe? You hungry? 'Cause I'm starved."

"Yes, but I need to get home."

"Why don't I drop you off and pick up some carryout for us?"

"Thanks, sweets, but no. I've got to let Chrissy know she can see her dad now. Also, since he won't be charged with anything, technically he's not a criminal. She'll be relieved to hear that, but I better do this alone."

"Understood and agreed. Hop in. Let's get you home."

———————

If I could count on my fingers, I could count on Dutch patiently waiting for me. Tonight, he was at the window again, his tail wagging like a metronome at one hundred twenty tempo. He danced around me as I walked in and then nuzzled into my cupped hands.

"Let's get us both something to eat, buddy. I've got some good news for you. Soon, you'll be spending time with Alex and Chrissy. Bet you won't even miss me, will you?" He cocked his head as though he was considering what I was saying and then launched into his bowl of dog food. I was lucky Alex had agreed to keep him, as I hated to board him about as much as he seemed to hate being there. *I bet that tail won't miss a beat.*

While I was eating leftovers, I checked my emails. One from Dunk, saying he had our mystery funds in hand, and we could proceed with paying for our supplies and plane tickets. I emailed Congressman Culpeper to share Don Calvin's contact information and to ask him to send me confirmation once he put Calvin in touch with the embassy. Everything was falling into place. As Dunk had assured me, God seemed to have His hand in this.

Chapter Forty-Six

Luna

We woke up hungry. The morning sun worked its way into our mobile prison, seeping in through the tarp's rips from overhanging tree branches along our route. The girls stirred, sat up, and rubbed the sleep from their eyes. They looked around, probably desperate to find our situation nothing more than a bad dream. If Lima was our destination, we'd probably covered half the remaining distance overnight. Soon after, the truck came to a stop. Toothless pulled back the tarp and looked around until his eyes locked on mine.

"Get them out of truck. We have food. The men will take everyone to woods to do business; then you eat."

They sent us in threesomes, with a guard close by. Notepad Man walked the perimeter of the woods, keeping his head turned toward the truck except for an occasional glance our way.

Before my threesome made it back, a car from the other direction pulled up and stopped. The driver got out and walked toward the truck. I heard girls start to cry, apparently afraid another one of them would be carried off. The car's driver pulled out an envelope I presumed was full of cash. He reached inside, however, and pulled out a map, spread it over the bonnet of his car, and conferred with Scarface and Notepad Man. I heard their muffled conversation and saw heads nodding. Finally, the man folded the map, stuck it in the envelope, and shoved it into his back pocket. He walked to the car and grabbed another envelope—this one stuffed with money he handed to Scarface as Notepad Man looked on. Toothless then walked him to where I stood at the back of the truck, reached in, and pulled Andrea out by her hair. She fell to the ground. Map Man grabbed her by the arm and pulled her to his car. Her screams pierced the quiet of the morning, causing the other girls to scream too.

The guards hurried us back to the side of the road, where Juanes and plantains were laid out beside the water jug—the best breakfast we'd had since we were taken. The eggs and chicken would give us much-needed protein, and the rice and plantains would fill us up. I suspected the food had been purchased in Tarapoto and we'd be fed better now. If our destiny was to be what I feared, our captors would want us as healthy-appearing as possible. To my surprise, the jug now held diluted papaya juice, another new treat.

When Toothless walked up, I confirmed my suspicion. "Why good food now? Is our journey almost over?" I asked.

He smiled hideously. "We want you be fat and happy when we get to Lima. Easier to sell you. More money for us. Hurry, *mis chicas*. We have much more miles to travel. Tomorrow, we be there."

"First, they're not 'your girls.' They're the girls of the village. Second, this is the first decent meal since we were taken. Let them eat."

"And you?"

"I will eat when they're done. Besides, you said I would be looked after, so I should have plenty of food when we get to Lima."

"Who said we go to Lima?"

"You did, you idiot."

He raised the butt end of his rifle over me. I crouched and put my arms over my head. Then Scarface stopped him. "Leave her. She has injury, cost us money." Toothless lifted both arms and backed away.

"Eat. Finish soon. Then we go. Understand?"

"I understand."

The improvement in our diet did little to lift the girls' spirits. They were tired, dirty, scared, and still malnourished. No one asked me where we were going or what the kidnappers would do with us. Maybe they didn't want answers that would only make things seem worse.

I bit my lower lip and wiped my eyes. Right before climbing into the truck, I noticed Notepad Man on the side of the road, his pad and pencil in hand.

Chapter Forty-Seven

Thirty-two thousand feet above the Caribbean

I heard the *thunk* of the plane's landing gear stowing as we pulled away from the Miami airport and increased our altitude. Dunk had the aisle seat, where he could stretch his legs. I was at the window, and Sarah was sandwiched between us. I inserted my earbuds and hit Elton John's "Rocket Man" on my playlist. It seemed appropriate. We'd flown out of Raleigh, with a connection and short layover in south Florida. From there, we'd fly over the Caribbean Sea and finally touch down in Lima.

Alex had taken us to the Raleigh airport. It was hard telling her goodbye. It wasn't exactly Bogart and Bergman on the tarmac in the closing scene of *Casablanca*, as "We'll always have Hillsborough" didn't have quite the romantic flair of "We'll always have Paris," but we had a moment. I wrapped Alex in my arms and breathed in one last exhilarating blast of Chanel Eau de Something, which I'd learned she wore only on special occasions.

"You be safe down there, Gil," Alex whispered in my ear.

"I'll be fine. Got a nurse and a preacher with me. What can go wrong?" I shrugged.

She pulled back from me and locked in on my eyes. "Just be careful. If you come back dead, Sullivan, I'm gonna kill you."

"But I'd already be—"

"Go. Get out of here." She smiled through her tears.

I grabbed her one last time. "Remember, I love you."

"You're sweet, Gil."

"Stop playing hard to get."

She leaned in and said, "Who's playing?" She smiled again and arched her eyebrows.

I released her and turned to walk to the gate, regretting my last state-ment. I didn't want to leave like this.

"Gil."

I looked back at Alex.

"You come back, you hear?"

Okay, so I did mean more to her than perhaps she was letting on. If so, I was a lucky man. After the men in her life had disappointed her, she'd still found a place in her heart for me. Maybe even love, but I'd have to wait for confirmation on that. Chrissy was coming around too. While I'd never be her father, I could be a stabilizing male influence in her life—something she desperately needed, especially if Virgil's attempt at reconciliation fell through. As much as I looked forward to getting to Campoflores and meet-ing Elizabeth, Carlos's mystery woman, I was already looking forward to getting back home to the warm-couch comfort of Alex, my friends, and my practice. As my playlist progressed from Sir Elton to Billy Joel, Elvis, and others, I drifted off to sleep.

I startled awake and sat upright. Sarah grasped my forearm. "Just air turbulence, Dr. Gil. Nothing to worry about."

"Man, I was really out of it."

"Yeah, the attendant came by with drinks, and I grabbed you a Coke Zero."

"Thanks. I'm parched."

"I guess so. Your mouth was wide open . . . you're quite the snorer."

"Sorry. Where are we, anyway?"

"About an hour from Lima."

Almost there.

━━━━━

We deplaned onto a tarmac, leaving us with a short walk to the airport. Dunk led interference through the crowd and got us to the baggage carou-sel. We were happy to see that our personal bags and six boxes of supplies had arrived safely. After loading them onto a luggage carrier, we made our way to Immigration and Customs, thinking we'd breeze through as mission-aries. A uniformed man looking very official stood at the entrance. As we approached, he offered his hand. When I reached out to shake, he pulled it back and then extended it again, rubbing his thumb back and forth over his index and middle fingers. Then I understood. I handed him a twenty that he shoved into his pocket. He extended his hand again. Another twenty did the trick.

We had just enough time in the airport to use the restroom and get a bite to eat before catching our next flight. While Dunk and Sarah finished eating, I walked over to a bench at one of the windows. In the distance, beyond the children playing soccer on a concrete slab, I saw Lima's buildings, crammed together and protected with bars on the windows. Not a confidence booster.

A quick call to the US Embassy confirmed Don Calvin had contacted them. "Yes, sir. Mr. Calvin gave us everything we needed, as well as your contact information. We've vouched for INES with Peruvian law enforcement officials. Our understanding is they're already in the field."

"Very good. Thank you so much."

"One more thing, Dr. Sullivan. Be advised that you'll lose cell service pretty much once you get north of Tarapoto. We actually left a package for you at the airport's security office. It's a satellite phone. The INES team will also have one, just in case they need to reach you, or you them."

"Never thought of that. Thanks again." Such a simple thing, but I'd overlooked it. I sent a brief text to Alex, reassuring her we'd made it safely to Lima.

The three of us trekked out to the regional carrier that would get us to Tarapoto. Sarah and I looked at each other. "A real puddle hopper, Dr. Gil."

"Puddle hopper?" Dunk said.

I nodded. "A name for a smaller plane that makes short flights. No worries, but be sure you keep your head down when we board, Dunk."

"If it gets us out of Lima, I don't care how small it is." Dunk hiked his eyebrows.

"Well, it'll be cramped, but our flight's only about ninety minutes," Sarah said.

Fortunately, the flight wasn't full, and Dunk could stretch out over two seats on one side of the aisle. Sarah and I took the other side. As we climbed to altitude and turned clockwise to head north to Tarapoto, we saw the gleaming waters of the South Pacific slowly disappearing from view. Too excited to rest, I pulled out the newest in Baldacci's *Memory Man* series and lost myself in Amos Decker's latest adventure.

We descended over a brilliantly verdant canopy of trees that yielded to the landing strip's concrete expanse. An uneventful touch down left us just outside what appeared to be the airport's main building, probably no larger than my house in Hillsborough. With one bar of service, I checked messages and calls for what would likely be the last time until we were headed home. I'd missed a call from INES when the cell was in airplane mode, but my voicemail held great news. The team already had a lead on one of the girls. They were in pursuit and someone would contact me once they had more information. Dunk and Sarah were thrilled.

"Answered prayers, chum," Dunk said.

Sarah said, "Good news, Dr. Gil. Clearly, they must know what they're doing."

A young man approached us. He was short and wiry, with straight, jet-black hair peeking out from under a baseball cap. "*Hola.* You go to Campoflores?"

"Yes. I'm Gil, and my friends are Sarah and Dunk. Are you our driver?"

"*Si.* Call me Johnny. I get your bags, and we be on our way." The corners of his mouth turned upward in what I soon learned was their constant position.

"How long of a drive is it, Johnny?" Sarah asked.

"Too long today. We stop in Moyobamba, eat, stay tonight, and finish trip tomorrow."

I looked at Dunk and Sarah and shrugged. What choice did we have?

It was an old VW model, decked out in multiple colors of paint and sporting several dings and dents. I figured we'd have better odds of winning in Vegas than having that bus get us to our final stop. "You own the van, Johnny?"

"No, Mr. Gil. Van owned by my *iglesia.* I drive, it gets money. Americans give us van. Said it came from festival long time ago. Maybe, Wood Stick?"

I laughed. "Yep. That fits. Everybody, climb in, and Dunk, say a prayer that Woodstock gets us there safely."

We lost pavement not far outside the airport. The ride got so bumpy that reading wasn't an option, so I took in the landscape. Trees stood in the distance, coming closer as the road took us into the jungle. Flashes of afternoon sunlight worked their way through the van's open windows. I looked over at Sarah and Dunk, both of whom had drifted off, likely aided by the gentle jostling and the warm afternoon air.

The three of us startled as the van came to a sudden stop. Men approached us wielding machetes and carrying burlap sacks.

"Johnny, what's happening?" Sarah asked.

He turned to us and smiled. "No worries. Coconuts."

The men came up to the side of the van and pulled out coconuts, offering to slice off the tops of them and sell them to us with straws to suck the juice. Not wanting to disappoint them, or perhaps hoping to keep them happy, I bought three. The men smiled and turned away, disappearing into a copse of trees.

"Gil, you think these are safe?" Dunk asked.

"Safe?"

"Yes. Did you see those machetes? Wonder what else they've been used on?"

We agreed to set the coconuts aside and give them to Johnny when we got to Moyobamba.

Our journey resumed. As we bumped down the road, we engaged in small talk with Johnny.

"Johnny, do you drive for a living?" I asked.

"No. I janitor for *mi iglesia* in Moyobamba. Drive van, how do you say . . . some of time."

"Part-time?"

"*Sí.* Part of time."

We seemed to be chasing the sun as it gradually sank from view beneath the trees. Finally, the noise of a nearby town seeped into the van. Civilization.

"We almost to my home," Johnny said. I take you to motel and show you where to eat."

Sarah leaned forward. "Aren't you eating with us?"

"No. Go home to family and to feed animals. See you in morning."

Trees slowly disappeared as small stucco structures began to populate the roadside. Some appeared to be houses, while others were clearly marked as businesses. Companies offering cell phones with minute plans seemed popular. We arrived at what looked like the main drag, with buildings lining both sides of the road. Johnny stopped at an adobe-style motel and took us inside to check in. We passed a couple of tables for four as we walked to the desk, a large sheet of plywood colorfully painted and supported by four wobbly legs. The clerk, a woman with beautiful gray hair put up in a bun, handed us keys for two rooms. We stowed our bags and then followed Johnny outside.

"Down street. Arizona Chicken. *Muy buena.* You like it. I see you in *manana. Ocho en punto.*"

As we headed down the street, every local eye seemed to watch us. "I guess it's pretty easy to spot a gringo, right?"

Dunk looked over and wrinkled his brow. "Gringo?"

"It's a term used down here for foreigners, especially Americans, Rev. Dunk," Sarah said.

"But I'm Scottish."

I laughed. "Trust me, Dunk, down here, you're a gringo."

"Well, chum, call me a gringo or anything else—just call me on time for dinner. I'm starving."

"That's not quite the way it goes, Dunk."

Sarah laughed. "I'm hungry too. Those power bars and apples we bought at the Lima airport are long gone."

Strange for a food joint in the deep bosom of Peru to look like Americana, but Arizona Chicken checked the proverbial boxes. Formica-topped tables, each populated with four metal chairs, sat on a black-and-white checkered floor. A smiling, middle-aged man stood behind an imposing metal counter, waiting to take our order. A rack of hot sauces sat near the end.

Johnny was right. The fried chicken and sliced potatoes were delicious. We washed it down with some kind of red juice that was as sweet and delicious as anything I'd ever tasted. As dinner wrapped up, Dunk pushed back from our table and patted his stomach. "I'm stuffed."

"Me too," Sarah said. "Crazy we came all this way and found a fried chicken joint, huh?"

As we approached the exit, metal scraped loudly across the linoleum. I turned to see a man bolt out of his chair. He grabbed his throat and leaned forward, his face turning from red to an ugly blue. I ran over and stood behind him, wrapped my arms around his mid-section, and forcefully pushed in and up—the Heimlich maneuver. A piece of chicken shot from his mouth and landed on the side of his dinner companion's plate. She jerked back and covered her mouth with both hands. He shook all over, but his color slowly improved. As I walked away, he grabbed my arm, looked up at me, and said, "*Gracias.*" I nodded and patted him on the shoulder.

Sarah looked at me with wide eyes. "Oh my gosh, Dr. Gil. You just saved that man's life."

"I don't know about that, Sarah. I just saw him before you did and beat you to the punch—no pun intended."

"Regardless, Gil, well done," Dunk said. He gently squeezed my shoulder.

Sarah wouldn't let it go. "But what if we hadn't been here, and no one here knew what to do?"

"Who knows?" I said. "That's life, I guess. Probably a God thing, but you'd have to ask Dunk. Sometimes we're put in the right place at the right time, and we're the one person someone needs."

The one. There it is again.

Dunk looked from Sarah to me. "Sounds about right, Gil—biblical, in fact."

———

We walked in silence, soaking in the ambience of this little third-world town. "Doubt Campoflores will be anything like this place," Sarah said.

"And I'm pretty sure all our meals aren't going to be this yummy . . . or end as exciting!"

I shook my head. "Let's hope not."

We agreed we were all beat and ready for bed. I checked my phone. No service, but I set an alarm for six. I grabbed my book and climbed into bed, figuring even Amos Decker's latest quest wouldn't keep me awake for long. I was right. In the middle of the night, I woke up with the book on my lap and my nightstand lamp still on. A warm breeze had the window curtains dancing. Dunk was curled up on the other bed, seemingly undisturbed by the light. I switched it off, rolled over, and, just before I fell back to sleep, thought of Alex, Chrissy, and all the folks back home.

I miss them already.

Chapter Forty-Eight

Moyobamba, Peru

Morning sun streamed through our window, waking me well before my alarm sounded. Dunk was already showering. Roosters crowed nearby, their chorus mingling with vehicle engines and voices—people apparently getting an early start on their day.

"Morning, pal," Dunk said cheerfully as he walked into the room toweling his thick, red hair.

"Way too upbeat for me, Dunk. Dial it down a notch, please."

He laughed. "Grab a shower and then we'll meet up with Sarah and catch some breakfast. Spotted a bodega a block or two from here."

"What, no Starbucks?" I extended my hands, palms up. "And what's with *bodega*? Now you're speaking Spanish?"

"Funny. Actually, I do fancy myself somewhat of a Renaissance Man." He laughed. Again, too much joy before six in the morning.

Once showered and dressed, I joined Dunk as we left our room. Down the hall, Sarah sat in the lobby, waiting.

"Morning, fellas, and a beautiful one it is! Hungry?"

Another cheery morning person.

We headed to the bodega. No disappointments. They served, of all things, Charleston Coffee Roasters Organic Peruvian and had an array of bagels behind the counter. Given the feast from the night before, continental would work fine this morning. We each got a coffee to go, and I grabbed an extra for Johnny.

"Gotta say, I wouldn't mind hanging out here a while longer if we didn't have more pressing matters," I said. "And I'm pretty sure Johnny wants to leave at eight o'clock."

"I went for a walk before you gents made it out of your room. There's a medical clinic a block off the main drag. Wasn't open yet, but it seemed inviting from the outside."

"Hmmm," Dunk said. "Maybe a medical mission trip in the future?"

"I'm in," I said. "And Sarah, we might be able to refer patients here from Campoflores."

Johnny was leaning against what was left of the front quarter panel of Woodstock, waiting on us at the motel. "I get bags. Almost time to go."

"Here, Johnny." Sarah handed him his coffee. "You like coffee?"

"This what we call 'gringo coffee,' but *gracias*. Mr. Gil, I ask why you go to Campoflores, *por favor*?"

I took a deep breath and decided honesty was the best policy. "Johnny, do you know a man in Campoflores named Carlos?"

"*Sí*! Padre Carlos. But he not there. He in America."

"Well, that's why we're here. I met him in America, and I need to talk to his wife, or maybe friend . . . Elizabeth?"

"Miss Elizabeth? *Sí*. She *amiga* of Carlos. Nice lady."

We all climbed aboard, and Woodstock reluctantly came to life after a couple of cranks. As we neared the last of the town's buildings, it caught my eye.

"Johnny, stop the van." I jumped out and ran around the back of Woodstock, just in time to get a glimpse of a guy wearing a hoodie. It had the same dragon on the back that the bomber had worn in Hillsborough. I ran after him, but he vanished. Not sure what I'd have done if I caught up to him, anyway. I jogged back to the van and climbed in, out of breath.

"What was that all about?" Dunk asked.

"Probably nothing."

Before long, we were on what looked like a trail cut through the woods, with exposed tree roots and rain-washed ruts marking the way.

"You see not much now. Trees. We be in Campoflores in about three hours, or four."

An hour into the trip, I heard my phone ring. Unable to hear over Woodstock's engine noise, I asked Johnny to stop.

Johnny looked around at me and said, "You go to chase man again?"

I shook my head, climbed out, and walked to the edge of the woods.

"Dr. Sullivan. This is Kevin Morris from INES. Want you to know we got one of the girls. Found a young teen near Tarapoto, locked in a room in some old geezer's house. All we've got is her name, and that was from him, so who knows? She won't speak—just hugs her legs to her chest and rocks."

"Praise the Lord . . . and, please, call me Gil. Thanks for letting me know. So what now?"

"A couple of us will get her back to Campoflores."

"Great. Maybe we'll see you there. By the way, Kevin, what's her name?"

"Name's Andrea. Leastways, that's what the old man said. He was so scared, he started singing like a choirboy in church, so I think he's telling the truth."

"Got it. Thanks again."

"One more thing, Gil."

"What's that?"

"They won't all be this easy. Got a little lucky here in Tarapoto, but barring a miracle, the others might be a lot harder to find."

"Then we'll pray for a miracle."

One of the few happy days of my early childhood was Christmas. I woke up bursting with excitement about what I'd find under the tree. Today, I felt that same emotion as I climbed back into Woodstock. It was a high, like a balloon filled with the helium of gratitude and joy.

"Well?" Sarah said.

"Great news. They found one of the girls. Her name's Andrea, and she'll soon be on her way back home."

Sarah put her palms together, looked up, and said, "Thank you, Lord . . . but is she all right?"

"She's being evaluated by a doctor, per INES protocol. But emotionally, it doesn't sound too good." I told them about her refusal to speak.

"Well, Gil, Andrea just went on my prayer list, along with all the others whose names we don't know yet," Dunk said.

Now I was so wired, I couldn't nap, and the ride was too bumpy for me to read. I stared out the open window as we passed tree after tree. The monotony of it lulled me into thoughts about Alex, my partners, and all my friends back home. I forced my attention to the task at hand. I still had a clinic to run and a long discussion with Elizabeth once we got to Campo-flores.

Woodstock's sudden deceleration brought me to life. I sat up and asked Johnny what was going on.

"We stop. Bathroom. Have lunch."

Sarah turned her head from left to right. "Uh, Johnny, I don't see a bathroom."

"Bathroom everywhere, Miss Sarah." He pointed to the trees and chuck-led.

We settled under the stingy shade of a roadside tree. Johnny grabbed a sack from the passenger seat. "*Mi esposa* make lunch for us." He pulled out a jug of water, plantains, and rice wrapped in pita bread. "We share."

While we were eating, Johnny caught my attention, and I followed his gaze toward the vivid blue sky dotted with gray wisps of clouds. He looked over at the three of us and said, "We eat fast. Get in van. Big rain come soon."

You live in a place long enough, I suppose its patterns, rhythm, and nature get into your DNA. It gives you an intuitive sense of what's right, wrong, or about to happen. A tingling of the skin or a sniff of the nose. I'm not really sure, but Johnny was right. Before I could finish my sentence arguing how beautiful the sky was, the first raindrops fell.

We gathered what was left of lunch and hurried back to Woodstock. As he drove away, Johnny turned to us, nodding. "We make good time today. Be there in about one hour."

The back-and-forth monotony of the wipers made me sleepy. Without knowing what was in store for us for the rest of that day, a nap would prob-ably be a good thing. I rested my head against the window and fell asleep.

Chapter Forty-Nine

Campoflores, Peru

Stray goats, scrawny chickens, and bare-boned dogs gathered in number as we drove into an area where the tree line was well off the road and wild grasses grew in clumps around the remaining tree stumps and flowers that dotted the fields. Happy sounds of children laughing and talking in the distance grew louder as we approached what I presumed to be Campoflores. Scattered, small, cinderblock structures sat along the road's edge.

"We here now," Johnny said. He blew Woodstock's horn, a weak bleat, effectively announcing our arrival. Children came out of the woods and spilled onto the road, running along and laughing, beating on the sides of the van, and yelling, "*Senor Johnny, Senor Johnny.*"

A makeshift soccer field sat in the center of an area bordered by small block buildings and wooden shacks. At opposing ends were netless goals crudely fashioned from bamboo poles. Children kicked a partially inflated ball from one end to the other and then back again. Had I closed my eyes, the sounds could have been those from Hillsborough's community park. One larger cinderblock house with flowers growing in the front yard sat at the road's end. Set back from it was a stucco building with a large, white cross mounted on its red-tiled roof.

Women peeked out the windows of homes. While some came out, grabbed their children, and took them inside, others slowly ventured our way. They all seemed to know Johnny and greeted him warmly in a dialect I knew was Spanish but, beyond that, I had no clue. They quickly looked our way, probably wondering who we were and why we were there.

The three of us walked around, taking in this little village secluded deep in the midst of this South American country. A woman stepped out of the cinderblock house and headed toward us. She walked confidently, with perfect posture and a purposeful gait. Her brown hair was gathered in a single braid and knotted down her neck. But what stood out the most was her complexion—a pale white, in contrast to the other villagers, and marked only by worry creases at the corners of her eyes.

As she neared us, she extended her right hand, firmly grasping mine. "Hi. I'm Elizabeth. You must be the team from the States . . . North Carolina?"

We introduced ourselves. "So nice to finally get here." Then I asked, "But how'd you know we were coming?"

"I got word through our sister church in Moyobamba that Johnny was bringing some Americans to our village. I knew Carlos was in your state, so I hoped you were from there. Come inside, please, and I'll get us all some tea."

As we followed her, I whispered to Dunk and Sarah, "Stay with me when I give her the news. She might need the heart of a minister and the shoulder of another woman."

We followed her into a house furnished sparsely and neat as a pin. Outside a back window, I heard the noise of what had to be a generator. She must have noticed me looking that way.

"We have a generator that runs when we have petrol Johnny delivers from Tarapoto. Only a few of our houses and, of course, our church, have power. Most of our citizens cook on an open fire." She pulled the kettle from the stove burner, poured steaming water into four mugs, and handed each of us an Earl Grey bag. "Sorry, no other options. I happily accept whatever I can get from back home."

"Which is where?" Dunk said.

"London, and I can tell by your accent you're not a North Carolinian."

"Scottish."

"Oh, well, we'll get along famously." She smiled as she took a seat in a worn wooden chair. Elizabeth looked at each of us and then focused on me. "I've been so worried about Carlos. He hasn't written in response to any of my mail. I assume the post delivered them."

I took a deep breath before speaking. "Actually, Elizabeth, that's why we're here."

As I explained the bombing and its victims, my encounter with Carlos, and his dying request, tears welled in Elizabeth's eyes. She pulled a handkerchief from a side pocket of her dress and dabbed her eyes. Sarah moved her chair over and put an arm around her shoulders.

"Elizabeth, you and Carlos must have been close."

"Oh, yes . . . a very good mate and colleague. We worked together in the church. He was our father, or what you'd call 'minister.' I'm a missionary of sorts."

Dunk sat up straight and wrinkled his brow.

"Let me explain." She got up, walked to a side window, and stared outside as though she were hunting for words. Then she took her seat and began her story. Elizabeth was the head librarian at a Church of England seminary, where she met her future husband, Manuel. He was a brilliant student from Tarapoto who scored so well on his high school exams, he was admitted to the University of Cambridge. From there, he enrolled in seminary. They met, fell in love, and married right before he graduated. When he decided to take the job as the minister of the Protestant church in his hometown, they moved to Tarapoto. It was a small mission that didn't pay much, so Manuel supplemented his income by working in the growing fields. While at work one day, an eyelash viper bit him and, before his co-workers could get him to adequate medical care, he died.

"That's so sad, and I'm terribly sorry, Elizabeth," Sarah said.

Dunk nodded, and softly asked, "So where does Carlos come in?"

"Carlos was Manuel's classmate in seminary and his best friend. When we left for Tarapoto, he went to Campoflores to form a sister church. Their dream was to one day grow their congregations to a size that would justify construction of a larger building where they could co-pastor. Once Manuel died, their dream died with him. But Carlos remained here to serve the congregation."

"And you?" I asked. "Did you come to Campoflores then?"

"No, no. I was pregnant at the time of Manuel's death, and I had returned to London for prenatal care and to stay with my parents. I never saw my husband again." She looked down and slowly shook her head. "My daughter Luna was born and raised in London until she finished primary education at age ten. I'd kept in touch with Carlos, and six years ago, we moved to Campoflores to join him in his work at the church. I teach the village children in the little church school. Luna spent so much time with Carlos that she grew very close to him—almost considered him her second father."

"Luna's such a beautiful name," Sarah said. "Is there a story?"

Elizabeth sighed. "She was born the night of a beautiful full moon."

I smiled. "Luna—Spanish for moon."

"Right. And her Spanish name also honors the memory of her father." Elizabeth wiped away a tear.

I pulled out the weathered photo. "I found this in Carlos's shirt pocket."

She gasped and covered her mouth with her hand. "That's my Luna."

Chapter Fifty

Lima

Luna

We'd arrived. I'd been here before but only to the airport several years earlier. The noises of Lima reached us, somehow pricking our skin and alerting our senses to an experience soon to come—and unlike anything we'd ever imagined. The bumps and rolls of the dirt road gave way to a paved highway, and I realized we were now moving faster. The girls were looking at each other and softly murmuring concerns. We turned off the road to a smaller, graveled one and traveled for several minutes until the truck came to a stop. Scarface walked around to the back, pulled back the tarp, and ordered us to get out.

The truck was parked next to a flat-roofed, large, metal structure, marred by dents, rust, and graffiti. In the distance, the city's buildings rose from the ground like a phoenix, taller than anything we'd ever seen. Scarface's men marched us into the building, where we were ordered to undress completely. They handed each of us a bar of soap, a small bottle of shampoo, and a washcloth and towel and sent us into a shower room. I scrubbed until I thought my skin would wash off, grateful for the chance to remove weeks of grime and the salty residue of sweat. The men leered at us the entire time, pointing and laughing. After toweling off, we were given underwear, simple dresses, and shoes to wear.

Our captors led us into a room where several rectangular tables sat end to end. Hot food was brought in from an adjacent kitchen, and we were told to eat as much as we wanted.

Some of the girls relaxed and even started talking, perhaps thinking all of this was a sign that better treatment lay ahead. The few who realized we were being prepped for something awful hardly touched the food.

Toothless walked over to me. "Some girls no eat. Need to eat. Need to be strong and pretty. Men come soon."

It wasn't a statement worthy of a response.

Just as the men back home herded their goats home for the night, we were poked and prodded into a small room where we sat on the floor, nearly as cramped as we'd been on our journey. One screened window allowed us a wisp of fresh air. A black bug crawled near the screen, trying unsuccessfully to get through the window. It bumped into one corner of the screen, backed away, crawled to the other end, and repeated its effort to escape. It was trapped. For some reason, the bug's frantic attempts at freedom mesmerized me. Then it hit me. *We're that bug.*

Soon, we heard gravel crunching under the weight of tires, car doors slamming, and unfamiliar voices. Toothless came into the room and ordered me to have the girls follow him. We marched outside, where we were met by Scarface, Notepad Man, and men we didn't know walking toward us from expensive looking cars like I remembered from my years in London. Toothless lined us up in a single row and the men walked back and forth, looking us over from head to toe. Once he settled on a choice, each man would grab one of the girls and pull her away, hand an envelope to Scarface, and take her to his car. Notepad Man kept his head down and recorded every transaction. Then he watched each car speed away and made additional notes.

One of the men grabbed me by the arm, but Toothless interceded. "She not for sale. We have plan for her." He reluctantly released me, stroking me across the chest as he did so. My skin crawled.

I glared at Toothless. "What's going on?"

"Payoff. You think we travel this far and not make money? You the big payoff." He arched one eyebrow. "You worth *mucho dinero*."

"But where are my friends going, and why?"

"To new home. Different places. You no worry."

We both turned to the sound of an approaching car—the largest and shiniest black car I'd ever seen. An overweight, middle-aged man with balding, black hair accented by gray at the temples, bushy eyebrows, and strong facial features stepped out of the back seat. He grinned as he lumbered toward me but then turned and went to Scarface, where another envelope exchanged hands and Notepad Man quietly recorded the sale.

The visitor turned back to me and spoke with no obvious accent. "Hello, Luna. I'm your new owner. Call me Grandfather."

I spit on the ground and locked my eyes on his. "You don't own me, mister. I belong only to my mum and my God."

He looked at Toothless and laughed. "Oh, she's a feisty one, isn't she? All the more exciting, if you ask me."

He gripped my arm tightly. I pulled back but wasn't able to free myself as his grasp tightened. He pulled me toward the car where his driver stood at the open back door. I was forced inside with my new captor. The door slammed shut.

"Where are you taking me, mister?"

"First, as I said, you're to call me Grandfather, not mister. Second, we're going for a little ride. Be patient."

We left the gravel drive for a paved stretch that led to a larger road. The night sky brightened as we approached a place that jumped from the recesses of my brain. It looked familiar. I suddenly remembered it from when my mum and I had arrived years earlier in route to our new life in Campoflores. The words on the tallest building came into focus: Jorge Chavez International Airport.

That's when I realized I was leaving Peru.

Chapter Fifty-One

Campoflores

Elizabeth gently touched the image of the larger girl. "That's my daughter. May I hold it, please?" She took the photo and clutched it to her chest before giving it back. "The little one is Ava."

"Ava?" Sarah said.

Elizabeth nodded. "Ava is Luna's little chum." I looked at Dunk and winked. "Almost inseparable. At least, until they were taken."

"Are you saying Luna was one of the children stolen from the village?" I asked.

"I'm afraid so. The last group—Luna's group—made it a total of one hundred villagers who've been stolen from us." She looked out the window again, seemingly searching for an answer that wasn't there. "Some have been returned, including Ava, praise God."

"Returned to Campoflores?" Dunk asked.

"Yes. Several weeks ago. Our regional police officers found her on the streets of Lima and brought her back to us, but she can't bring herself to talk about what was done to her and the other girls."

Now, Sarah's eyes were moist. "I'm so sorry, Elizabeth. I can't imagine what you're going through."

"There are no words. I wake up in the morning, and I'm fine. Then, with my first blink, I remember. I think of Luna and how much I miss her."

Sarah shook her head. "But there's hope."

"Hope? I'm a strong Christian, and I know in God's providence there's always hope, but with every week that passes, I'm feeling less hopeful."

Dunk walked over to Elizabeth and put her slender, pale hand in his massive one. "When we feel defeated and maybe wonder why God's allowed something awful to happen, we're letting the devil work on us. But we can't let him beat us. That's when our faith has to be its strongest, Elizabeth."

She lowered her head, stood, and paced the floor. "I know, but it's so hard." Her gait was now just a shuffle.

I cleared my throat. "Elizabeth, we do have some news that might give you hope. Another one of the girls, Andrea, was found, and—"

"She was found? Where, and how?"

I explained the role INES was playing in the rescue. Working with Peruvian authorities, they'd tracked Andrea down outside Tarapoto. Emotionally spent but physically healthy. INES planned to work Andrea's captor for information on any of the other children, or what he saw when he bought her. I saved the best news for last.

"She's on her way home, Elizabeth. Someone from INES is escorting her back to Campoflores as we speak. We're out of range for the sat phone, but I expect to hear from the men bringing her home as soon as they get closer. She should arrive any day."

Elizabeth dropped her head and sobbed. Finally, she was able to look up and say, "Andrea was taken with Luna, Ava, and the other girls. Maybe there is hope for the other girls after all . . . for my Luna."

Dunk turned toward me. "Sarah and I will get our bags and supplies from Johnny. Why don't you and Elizabeth talk while we do that?"

"There are two small guest rooms in the back of our church. You can take your bags there. It's the building back of my house with the cross—"

"Oh, I know where it is. I can spot a house of worship from a mile away," Dunk said.

I looked at Elizabeth and grinned. "Back home, Dunk's our minister."

"Marvelous. Maybe you'll be our guest for a Sunday service. I've been filling in for Carlos, but it's not the same."

"I'd love to," Dunk said.

Once they left, I explained Sarah's and my work in the medical field and asked her about holding a clinic. I described the supplies we brought and what I thought we could accomplish.

"That would be wonderful. Our people have to travel to Moyobamba or Tarapoto for health care, and they usually only go when Johnny happens to be in our village. It's too far for most of them to travel on foot." When she got up and walked over to heat more water for tea, her head was erect and her steps were purposeful, confident even.

"Well, we'll do what we can."

"This is such good news. A medical clinic, an actual minister preaching in our little church again, and now, Andrea's rescue. You've lifted my spirits. Thank you, Dr. Sullivan."

"You're welcome, and it's Gil, please."

Sarah and Dunk returned. "That's a lovely little chapel, Elizabeth, and our rooms are so cozy and neat," Sarah said.

Dunk nodded. "I'm looking forward to being in the pulpit, but I'm worried the villagers won't understand me."

I shook my head and said, "No worries, Dunk—sometimes North Carolinians don't even understand you."

"Our people use a dialect of Spanish but not the Queen's Spanish, so to speak. I learned it when Luna and I moved here. I'll be your interpreter."

"All right then," I said. "It's all falling into place."

Elizabeth suggested we go to our rooms and get some rest. She'd come and get us when dinner was ready.

Chapter Fifty-Two

Atlanta, Georgia

Luna

s our flight descended and we broke through the final layer of clouds,
a city appeared that looked almost as big as how I remembered London. I didn't know where we were going, but I wanted to get off
that airplane. My "grandfather's" waistline spilled over the armrest between
us, and the combination of his sweat and cologne violated my nostrils and
sickened me. I nicknamed him "Beast" and chuckled to myself despite my
predicament. Whenever a flight attendant walked by, he grabbed my hand
but then quickly cut his eyes at me after she passed, his forced smile replaced
with a glare. I pretended to sleep for most of the flight.

We entered the airport and walked toward a sign labeled "Baggage
Claim." My captor guided me with his hand, firmly squeezing my shoulder. The weight of that big arm was nothing compared to his very presence
weighing heavily on my soul. A mural on the wall showed an overhead view
of the city, similar to what I'd seen from the air. In the lower corner of the
photo was the word "Atlanta," with a peach logo beside it. I recalled my
friend, who had traveled to the US from London and then back, talking
about the Peachtree State. We were in Georgia. The United States—perhaps
my destination. As for my destiny, I had no clue but figured I'd know soon.

Beast walked me out of the airport, and we climbed into a large car with
tinted windows. Our driver sported a thin mustache, was dressed in black,
and wore a short-brimmed black hat. The traffic rivaled that of London's
Oxford Street, barely moving as he darted from one lane to another, in
and out of traffic, onto a morass of roads that merged and split until they

finally came into a single, large highway identified as Interstate 85. Dense rows of buildings bordering the road slowly gave way to a more open and greener view, with clusters of houses in the distance. Our driver took an exit that led us into a neighborhood with houses bigger than any I'd ever seen. Manicured lawns landscaped with well-trimmed shrubs, leaf-laden trees, and summer flowers reached down to the road. We pulled into a winding driveway with a large door ahead of us. The driver reached up, pushed a button, and the door slowly opened. Before we could get out of the car, the door closed.

The house was ornately decorated with furniture and paintings as fancy as those in London's nicest museums. A neatly dressed young woman walked in from another room. Her dark hair, streaked with gray strands, was pulled back into a tight ponytail that fell shoulder length, revealing her long neck and soft facial features . . . except for her eyes. They silently spoke evil.

"Take her. The other one is ready and waiting for me, right?" Beast said.

"Yes, sir. As always."

She turned back to me, and we walked to a room furnished with two single beds and a wooden dresser. A comb and brush sat on one end. No pictures or creature comforts like I'd known in my earliest years.

"This will be your room, young lady." She pointed to a pink stuffed bear on one of the beds. "That's for you. Grandfather likes to see his little girls with their gifts. He thinks it's cute when they lie there naked, clutching their stuffed animal."

There was a purple stuffed dog on the other bed. "That's Maria's. Don't touch it."

"Who's Maria?"

"No questions. By the way, what's your name?"

"Luna," I said.

"Well, Luna. Do as you're told, and you'll have no trouble from me or from Grandfather."

"He's not—" I stopped myself and simply nodded.

"You stink." She pointed to a door adjacent to the dresser. Take a shower, and I'll have some clothes laid out for you when you get back. And another thing, you must keep your bathroom clean. I'm not going in there to clean your filth."

Another nod.

I showered and dressed quickly. Nakedness made me feel more vulnerable, if that was even possible. As I slipped on my shoes, another girl about my age walked in. Her pitch-black eyes were bloodshot and tears streaked her cheeks. Her dress was disheveled and dotted with moist red spots. She quickly crawled under the covers of her bed and pulled them over her head, covering her straight black hair.

"I'm Luna. Are you okay?"

The silence was awkward.

"I'm scared. Are you? Can we talk?"

She pulled the blanket back from her head. Our eyes met. "My name's Maria."

"Where are you from?"

"Mexico."

"Were you . . . taken?"

She got out of bed and quietly closed the door. "My family was visiting my father's parents in Texas. As we came back over the border, agents stopped our car. But they weren't agents; they were kidnappers. Both my parents were shot, and I was rushed to a waiting truck. I don't even know if my parents are—"

"I'm so sorry, Maria. I was taken, too, with my friends from my little village in Peru. How long have you been here?"

"Weeks." She shrugged. "Months, maybe. I've shut out the world and tried to sleep as much as possible, except when Grandfather takes me to the special room."

"You mean to—"

"Yes. It's awful. He has his fun with me and then kicks me out of the room, where that woman waits to bring me back here."

"When I was a young girl in London, my mum and I loved a movie called *Beauty and the Beast*. The beast was big, hairy, and ugly. He was also mean, at least at first. I know this man's not your grandfather. He told me to call him that, too, but I refused. Actually, I call him Beast, but not to his face . . . even though I know he'll never become nice like the one in the movie."

A hint of a grin.

"I know it's been hard for you being here alone, but now I'm here."

"No. There were others. They just disappeared." Maria's hand tremored as she rubbed at bruises and red marks on her wrist.

"I will not leave you, Maria. We must be strong together. We must have faith we will be rescued—that God will take care of us."

"If God was going to take care of us, why would He let this happen?"

I had no answer.

Chapter Fifty-Three

Campoflores

Our makeshift clinic was the side porch of Elizabeth's house, our only privacy a row of bamboo and clusters of Amazon lilies outside and a sheet hung from a rope pulled taut across the porch's inside width. Screens kept bugs out while allowing what little breeze there was to drift in. When Sarah and I had ended our work the previous day, a line of people still waited in the evening's dusk to be seen. I'd felt terrible we couldn't accommodate everyone and was glad we were running another clinic today. According to Elizabeth, those not waiting to see us had opted for spiritual healing and were in the chapel listening to Dunk deliver his midweek homily. "I've got to leave to interpret for Rev. Dunk. I'll grab someone who knows a little English and have her help you while I'm gone."

She walked back in with a girl who didn't look a day over twelve.

"A child?" I asked.

"Our children speak what English they've learned in my school. Most parents don't, or only speak the very basics. Elena's your best bet. And she's one of the lucky children who wasn't taken by those men."

Most of our patients were men with the aches and pains that accompanied lives of backbreaking labor in the fields. Despite the plentiful local produce, some people were obviously malnourished. They were the ones I assumed were infected with intestinal parasites. With no ability to test, we simply put them on anti-parasitics. The majority of patients, especially children, had skin rashes and superficial infections. Given the hygiene limitations in the village, impetigo—a simple infection of the skin surface—was rampant. Although Engineers International had installed a well a few years earlier, many people still went to nearby creeks to wash their clothes and bathe.

It was almost dark, and we were seeing our final patients. "Got a boil here, Dr. Gil," Sarah said. She was looking at the leg of a man with a distended belly and a large sore on his foot. "I'm gonna soak this thing in water and then see if I can open it."

After putting the man's foot in the water, she moved on to the next patient, a woman with low back pain. All she could offer was a short course of anti-inflammatory medicine. With Elena's help, Sarah told the woman it should relieve her discomfort, at least for a while.

Sarah returned to the man soaking his foot. As she lifted it out of the water, I heard her shriek. "Dr. Gil, I think I'm gonna be sick!"

I rushed over. A roundworm had partially exited the sore. I hadn't prepared Sarah for that possibility. "He probably has intestinal roundworms, which is why his abdomen is distended. The worms migrate to the skin, and females will go to the surface to lay their eggs, especially when the site is submerged."

"I can't do this. Can you take over, please?"

By the time I dried his foot, the worm had retreated back into its subcutaneous safety. I dressed the wound and started him on medication. Fortunately, he was our last patient.

Sarah sat in the corner of the porch, her head nearly at her knees. She gripped both sides of the chair so firmly that her knuckles turned white.

"You okay?"

"I'm lightheaded, but I'll be fine. I don't know—maybe I'm not cut out to see patients on my own, Dr. Gil."

It was my fault for not warning her we might see something unusual and really gross, but the odds of seeing that kind of thing back home would be slim to none. Sure, she would see people with problems that disturbed her, and that's when she'd have to focus on the illness and save her empathy for later. I'd learned if you respond emotionally too often, medicine will consume you, and you'll burn out.

"Listen, I know you're kindhearted, Sarah, but save that for after you've addressed the problem at hand."

"But we've got to be empathetic."

"It's a balancing act. You'll figure it out. And it's not just in medicine, either. Ask Dunk what would happen to him if he took on all the problems of his flock personally."

She looked up and nodded. "Point taken. Thanks."

My sat phone rang. Kevin Morris from INES came on, advising me they were about one hour outside of Campoflores. He said their driver was a local guy named Johnny.

"Johnny seems to know his way around or through every pothole and rut on this road, Gil."

"He was our driver too. Quite a character, right?"

"Copy that. See you soon."

When Sarah and I went back inside the house to share the news about Andrea, there was no sign of Elizabeth or Dunk. I assumed his homily had gone longer than expected—not unusual. *Give that man a pulpit, and he's off to the races.* We walked over to our rooms at the church, cleaned up, and dressed for dinner. It would be our last private time with Elizabeth, and I still had more to learn about Carlos.

When we got back to her house, Elizabeth was working in the kitchen. "Great news, Elizabeth. I got a call as clinic ended. Andrea should be here soon. I'll go outside in a minute to wait for them."

"Marvelous, Dr. Gil. Trust me, you'll hear them when they arrive. Sarah, if you'll please stay here and watch the food on the stove, I'll go get Andrea's parents."

Not long after Elizabeth left, the sound of an approaching vehicle and then Woodstock's unmistakable toot turned our heads to the side window. The van appeared in a flurry of dust. Two men jumped out, and one of them helped a child down from the back seat. She walked slowly, with her chin almost to her chest.

Elizabeth and a couple walked up. The woman yelled. "*Mi Andrea! Estas en casa.*"

Andrea looked up, then rushed into the woman's arms. They both wept, and then the man joined in on the hug.

Yes. Andrea was finally home.

Elizabeth had cooked more than enough food, and she insisted that Andrea, her parents, and Elena stay for dinner. Kevin Morris, his partner Dirk Austin, and Johnny also joined us. It was a joyous reunion celebration.

Before we sat to eat, Elizabeth pointed to Sarah, Dunk, and me, and explained to Andrea's parents that our efforts had led to their daughter's rescue.

They were quiet, but looked at us in a way that made all our efforts worthwhile. Then the father simply said, "*Mucho gracias.*"

Sarah said, "Actually, it was all Dr. Gil. Dunk and I kinda came along for the ride . . . and to keep him safe." She laughed.

Dunk chimed in. "Gil put it in motion, but these two men and their organization did the heavy lifting. God bless them for what they're doing all over the globe to rescue trafficked individuals."

"Cheers to that," Elizabeth said.

When we took our seats, I noticed Dunk was quick to take the one next to Elizabeth. As we ate, I quietly asked Kevin and Dirk about any progress INES had made in finding other girls. Little did I know what they would say and how it would affect all of us.

At the time of their last communication with the rest of the team, before they were out of range, they received word there were leads on several of the girls and some had been found—in Tarapoto, Lima, and all parts in between. Transportation was being arranged to bring them home.

"But how?" Sarah asked. "How on earth do you come into a country you don't know and find victims? Seems to me it'd be like finding a needle in a haystack."

"Good question," Dirk said. "Normally, we don't have this much luck so fast. We caught a major break in this case."

"How so?" Dunk said.

Kevin explained that one of the traffickers had been forced to participate. Seems he was in gambling debt to the crime's mastermind, who threatened to kill this guy's family if he didn't pay. When the boss gave him the option of helping in the kidnapping, he had no choice. Turns out he might have been a gambler, but he had no heart for trafficking. He'd been in charge of noting all transactions between his colleagues and the buyers, but he'd secretly recorded the names of everyone involved in the kidnapping and copied his notes before turning them in to the boss man in Lima. Once he was allowed to go home, and he'd safely gotten his family to an undisclosed location, he turned the information over to the authorities. He'd also recorded tag numbers of the buyers' cars, making it easier for the authorities to track them down. Most of them had been arrested by the time INES had boots on the ground.

Dirk grinned. "They practically tripped over themselves providing very useful intel, trying to beat one another to get the best legal deal. Like they always say, how can you trust your partner when the guy's nothing but a dirty crook?"

Elizabeth took a deep breath and then asked if they had any names of the rescued victims.

Kevin shook his head. "Nothing on our end, at least at the time we lost communication."

"One more thing," Dirk said. One of the men arrested said one buyer was from the States and planned to fly a girl home. Said she was the oldest and most articulate of tHe whole group."

Elizabeth closed her eyes and gasped. Dunk placed his hand on her shoulder.

"Oh, goodness. That's got to be my Luna. Carlos was right after all."

Chapter Fifty-Four

Atlanta

Luna

When my mum and I lived in London, we loved to watch Disney movies. My favorite was *Mary Poppins*, probably because it was set in my home city. I took to calling the stern woman in Beast's house "Ms. Poppins." Maria liked the name, even though she had no idea where it came from.

Several weeks into my captivity, Ms. Poppins informed me we were going shopping. I needed new clothes to look presentable, or so she said. Before we left, she took Maria into the other room. As we walked toward the garage, Beast was sitting at a table eating breakfast. She stopped to tell him she'd done as he asked; Maria was ready for him, and we were leaving. We climbed into the back seat of the big car. Same driver.

A short ride brought us to what appeared to be a shopping mall, identified by a large sign as Lenox. It was like Burlington Square on Piccadilly, only not nearly as stately and ornate. When we climbed out of the car, I noticed the weather had changed—much cooler and less humid—and leaves were falling from the trees dotting the landscape. Like Maria, I'd ignored the time spent at the house, but we'd moved from summer to autumn.

We entered a large clothing store with a children's department. Ms. Poppins handed me several dresses to try on. Most were pink or had pink in them. "His favorite color for his grandchildren," she informed me. She purchased several dresses and a few pairs of shoes.

I thought the outing was over. I was wrong. We stopped at a salon, where I climbed into a chair and a woman cut my hair to shoulder length.

Ms. Poppins looked at my hair from all angles and proclaimed, "Perfect. Much easier to care for and just the way your grandfather likes it."

Before heading back to the house, we had lunch. To the casual observer, we could have easily passed for a mother treating her daughter to a morning out, but they would have missed the pain in my eyes and the absence of joy in my face.

When we returned to the house, Maria was back in our room, in bed and covered with the bedspread. A soft sobbing broke the room's silence. I gently pulled back the covers. She lay with eyes open, staring into what I assumed was a distant and longed-for past. Beast was slowly breaking her down to something less than a human. I had to engage her.

"Maria, talk to me. Did he hurt you?"

More sobbing.

"Okay, try to sleep, and we'll talk later."

Something had to be done. I figured Beast had invested too much in me to hurt or kill me. I was the one who could speak out against his treatment of Maria. I would be David to his Goliath.

I was surprised to find our bedroom door unlocked. I rushed into the main room, past a startled Ms. Poppins, and found him working at a large wooden desk. "You're nothing but a fat, greasy pig. How can you treat a girl that way? Try that with me, and you'll regret it."

Beast looked at Ms. Poppins and tilted his head toward the door. "Take her to the room. Now."

"Come with me, young lady. I warned you not to cause trouble."

I pulled against her grip on my arm. No luck. She was stronger than I'd expected. She pushed me into a windowless room with a single bed with shackles at each corner and ordered me to undress. I complied immediately and pretended to cry, but when she tried to throw me on the bed, I lunged headfirst into her abdomen. She fell to the floor, her mouth wide open and gasping for breath. I grabbed my clothes and ran back to my room.

For three days, we were kept locked in our room. I opened the blinds of the bathroom window and the curtains on the bedroom window, thinking natural light might lift Maria's spirits. A bed of beautifully-colored leaves sat below the nearly bare trees that populated this backyard and the yard behind it. Sunlight streamed in and pooled on the bathroom floor and walls. Ms. Poppins brought food to us, carefully opening the door and peeking in, as though wanting to be sure we were out of striking range. She looked at the bedroom window and told me to close the curtains and leave them closed. I foolishly believed we might be in the clear with Beast.

At night, long after Ms. Poppins made her last room check, I'd open those curtains and look out at the moon. I wondered if my people in the village were also seeing it. If so, it was my connection to home. Thoughts of my mum and the parents of the other girls who'd been taken played through my head, and most nights, I dreamed and prayed of returning home. I had to keep faith that Maria and I would be rescued.

Slowly, Maria began talking again, though in a monotonic voice with no facial expressions. First, she answered questions with only a word or two, but then she spoke of her home in Mexico. Her path to this prison was different from mine, and quicker. Once over the border, she was driven by van across the southeastern states to Atlanta. She never encountered Beast until she met him in the room.

"We must be hopeful, Maria, and have faith that we will be returned to our homes. You must believe your parents are alive and waiting for you." She pressed her lips together, closed her eyes, and nodded rapidly.

She was improving. *God is good.* Yes, He is good, even when we're in the valley of the shadow of death. That's what Father Carlos always told us.

"Maria, do you believe in God?"

"Of course."

"Are you a Christian?"

"I guess so. My family is Catholic, like most in Mexico are, but we don't go to Mass very often. I guess we're not very religious."

"Even though I'm Protestant, we're both Christians. And you don't have to go to Mass to be religious. There weren't even church services in my village until Father Carlos arrived. My mum raised me in the faith. She taught me that Jesus said whenever even a few of His followers are together, He is there too. Do you know what that means?"

"He's here?"

"Yes. We must believe that."

"So if He is here, we're protected by Him?"

I nodded.

She yawned and then climbed into bed. "I'm sleepy."

I turned off the light.

"Luna?"

"Yes?"

"Thank you."

Chapter Fifty-Five

Campoflores

Our departure was difficult. Leaving Elizabeth without her knowing Luna's fate proved emotional. Few words were spoken at breakfast as we thought about our trip back to Lima and as Elizabeth likely considered a future without her daughter. I thought of Alex and how heartbroken she'd be if she lost Chrissy. In a perfect world, parents would never survive their children, but as Dunk often pointed out, life's not fair and there are things we won't understand until we meet our Maker. He frequently quoted 1 Corinthians 13:12 as proof. Honestly, I had to look it up. To put it mildly, my study and knowledge of the Bible had taken a backseat to my medical studies. That needed to change.

Sarah put down her fork and rested her hand on Elizabeth's shoulder. "You've been such a gracious hostess, Elizabeth. Thank you so much. And your story is an inspiration. To give up the life you had and move here, simply out of love for your husband . . . I don't know how many women would do that."

"We felt called to this place, Sarah. Now these people are my people. This is my home and always will be. Regardless of what happens to Lu—"

"I know," Sarah said.

I shook my head. "I think about how much I deliberated over whether or not to make this trip. Now I'm so glad we came and were able to tell you Carlos died a hero, attempting to earn the money he needed to return and search for Luna."

"No, not in Peru . . . he thought she was in the United States."

"What makes you say that, Elizabeth?" Dunk asked.

"When he told me he was going to your state to work, I asked him why he didn't just get a job in Lima. He told me he had a dream in which God

217

told him Luna would eventually be taken to the United States and he was to go and find her. It made sense to Carlos because her lighter skin and ability to speak English would make it easy for someone to transport her without raising suspicion. He wasn't sure where he'd find her, of course, but he knew his carpentry skills would allow him to find work in North Carolina. He never doubted the words he heard God speak, even in dreams, and he felt strongly God would lead him to Luna, so he left just a few days after she was taken."

I leaned in toward Elizabeth. "Wait a minute. You're saying he left everything behind to travel to an unfamiliar country in an attempt to rescue one child? All based on a dream? And that's what you meant when you said he was right after all?"

"Yes. I gave him the photo you found in his pocket. If his hunch was right, he wanted to have a way to show people what she looked like. As I said earlier, they were practically father and daughter."

"No greater love," Dunk said. He leaned into my ear and whispered, "John 15:13."

"Ever since I was with Carlos as he lay dying, I've wondered about him. Can you tell us any more, Elizabeth?"

She stared into space, as though searching for a distant memory. When she looked back at us, she put both hands on the table, seemingly steadying herself. She said Carlos was already living in Campoflores when she and Luna arrived. He was a legend of sorts. Seemed he just walked into the village from the nearby mountain range. Came out of nowhere, like air that rushes into a room when a door opens. "Why he chose Campoflores, they never knew, and he never told them. Of course, I knew it was because of his friendship with Manuel. But people claimed when he started preaching, he changed the village . . . like a light shining brightly on them, lifting their spirits, and giving them a new sense of hope. They grew to depend on him. In fact, the villagers were devastated when he told them he had to leave on a mission to another country. He promised he'd be back but, of course, now I know that isn't to be. He did, however, bring Luna and me to Campoflores, and I do my best to follow in his Christian footsteps and teach the Word."

A knock on the door interrupted the ensuing silence. It was Johnny, smiling as usual.

"*Los sientos.* Almost time we go, Mister Gil. Bags in van. Mister Kevin and Mister Dirk waiting too."

"We'll be right out, Johnny," I said. "Thanks."

I turned to our hostess. "Elizabeth, we can't thank you enough. We'd love to come back and hold another clinic, maybe even get the reverend back in the pulpit." Dunk rolled his eyes.

Sarah hugged Elizabeth. "If there's anything else we can do, please let us know."

Elizabeth looked at each of us briefly, closed her eyes, and sighed. As we walked out, she called my name. I turned and looked back.

"Just find my Luna."

Chapter Fifty-Six

On the road to Moyobamba

Our journey was a rewind of our trip to Campoflores. Kevin and Dirk took the back seat, Sarah and Dunk the middle seat, and I rode shotgun.

"You like Campoflores, Mister Gil?" Johnny asked.

A rut in the road jolted me. "Yes, very much. Hey, Johnny, think you can miss at least some of the ruts on our way back?"

"You funny man." He laughed. "Miss Elizabeth, she very nice woman and, how you say, good Christian?"

Dunk leaned forward. "I agree, Johnny. She's a special lady."

We settled into a rhythm of sways and jostles. Even this early, the stifling humidity pressed down on us. I dozed, occasionally waking to conversation or the screech of a bird hidden in the trees. Suddenly, Woodstock lurched to the side of the road. Johnny grabbed the steering wheel with both hands and pulled hard to the left, trying to avoid hitting a roadside tree.

"Big problem, Mister Gil. Flat tire."

"You got a spare?"

He nodded as he wrestled the van to a stop. We all climbed out, and Johnny lifted the floorboard behind the back seat to retrieve the tire.

"You guys get in the shade and relax," Kevin said. "Dirk, help Johnny with the spare. I'm gonna take a leak." He disappeared into the trees.

As Johnny and Dirk jacked up the van, two men dressed in camo approached in a Jeep. They climbed out, pointed to the flat, and said something to Johnny in Spanish.

"They help us, Mister Gil. We be on road again soon."

Suddenly, the men brandished pistols. One walked over to us, his gun pointed at Dunk and me as he ogled Sarah from head to toe in a way that sickened me. The other held his gun on Dirk while he yelled something to his partner. I didn't understand any of it, but Johnny's eyes grew wide. He stood and put his hands in the air.

"Mister Gil, they take Sarah. Say American woman very valuable."

Sarah began crying and Dunk closed his eyes, silently mouthing what I assumed was a prayer. The man grabbed her by the arm and forced her to the Jeep. I stepped toward him, but he turned and aimed his gun at me. He tied Sarah's hands behind her back and shoved her into the vehicle. As he turned back to us, Kevin lunged from the cover of the trees and bowled over the would-be kidnapper, grabbing his gun as the man fell. When the kidnapper's partner turned toward the commotion, Dirk stood and grabbed a pistol from his waistband and pushed its barrel against the man's neck. It didn't require Spanish for the man to understand he needed to drop his weapon.

As the INES team secured both men with rope they'd grabbed from the back of the van, I ran to Sarah, untied her hands, and embraced her. "Sarah, are you okay?"

She nodded quickly. With her eyes closed and between gasps of air, she said, "Dr. Gil, I was so scared."

"We all were, Sarah." I turned to Kevin and Dirk. "Great work, guys, and thank you so much. What are we going to do with these two?"

"We'll leave them tied up beside the Jeep," Kirk said. Then he grabbed the keys to their vehicle and threw them far into the woods. "When they do finally get loose and find those keys, we'll be long gone."

Johnny resumed his work on the spare tire as though nothing had happened. Once he finished, he said, "Ready to roll."

We all took deep breaths as we pulled away from the scene. I looked back at Kevin and Dirk and thanked them again. Kevin explained they'd been warned by the authorities that marauders traveled this route, preying on anyone they could take advantage of.

"You were lucky you didn't run into any of them on your way *to* Campoflores," Kevin said. Then he added, "Don't want to scare you, Sarah, but had they gotten away with you, you'd likely have never been seen again by anyone you know."

Sarah bit at her lower lip and shuddered. "I don't even want to think about that. Thank you for saving my life."

The men simply nodded, leaned their heads back, and closed their eyes, as though they were going to catch a nap.

Unbelievable. All in a day's work for them, I guess.

Chapter Fifty-Seven

Hillsborough

Alex

Soup surprised me when he called and asked if he could come see us for a quick visit. "Once the Thanksgiving and Christmas seasons roll around, I'll be picking up more shifts to let the family guys off as much as possible. But first, I'd really like to see you and Chrissy and maybe get some shooting in. Of course, if Suzie's free, it would be nice to see her too."

"Perfect timing for us, Soup, but Suzie won't be here. She's in Raleigh for a few days meeting with the newspaper folks."

"Well, I'm coming anyway. Be there tomorrow. Hey, heard anything from Sully?"

"I know he made it to Peru, but he's so deep in the country now, we can't reach each other. I'm probably worrying unnecessarily, but I can't help it . . . and I don't know why."

"I'm just a guy, Alex, so what do I know? But could it be you've never been away from someone you loved so much? Ever consider that?"

———

I reached to the back seat for my Perazzi, and Soup grabbed his Beretta and a gift-wrapped box from the trunk. We were at the range for some target practice the morning after his arrival.

"What's in the package, Soup?"

"You'll see soon enough. Let's go kill some clay pigeons first."

Soup was a marksman. I guess it came with the job. He was shooting pairs of pigeons more successfully than I was hitting singles. But he was patient with me, giving me tips on position, leading the target, and proper breathing—things I'd never thought about when I came out here alone and was happy to hit anything.

"I'm feeling a little self-conscious," I said.

"You shouldn't be. You're doing great. But hey, want to try something different?"

"Sure; why not?"

"Okay, then. Open the present."

"Present?"

"Like I said, I won't be here for Christmas. Consider it an early gift."

Inside the box was a shiny, compact pistol. I'd seen a gun like this at the police station but never held one. "Soup, if I can't hit a pigeon with a shotgun, how on earth am I gonna do it with a handgun?"

"It's not for target practice, Alex. It's for self-defense."

"But I don't—"

"Listen. I know you live in a small town where things are peaceful, but you never know. Bet you never expected to have a bomb go off. Right?"

He had a point. No one's completely safe from crime, even in Little Town, USA. Had he been violent instead of a bag of hot air, even Virgil could have threatened Chrissy and me.

"Soup, I don't know. I don't think I could point a gun at somebody, much less shoot them."

"Most cops never fire their weapons while on duty during their entire career. You only hear about the ones who do. An officer's gun is a deterrent. Most burglars are gutless cowards. When they look down the barrel of a weapon, they melt like hot butter."

"Well, it *is* a nice-looking piece," I said.

"Now you're talking cop talk." He pointed his head toward the door to the facility. "Let's go inside to the target range and try it out."

I had to admit the Glock 19 was comfortable in my hand, and it sure had a lot less recoil than the shotgun. I didn't hit many targets, but at least I got comfortable pointing and shooting.

Soup's visit ended much too quickly. Before he left, he promised he'd squeeze in another visit as soon as possible, especially since he'd missed Suzie this trip. "Might even get down to Charleston sometime to meet her family." When I arched my eyebrows, he said, "Well, Alex, it is Charleston. You know, kind of a destination."

"Yeah, right, Soup. I hear you."

"Now, don't forget," he said. "Practice, practice, practice using that handgun I gave you."

"Copy that, Soup." If you own a gun, you need to talk like you own a gun.

On my way back into the house, my cell rang. Dr. Greer.

"Hi, Alex. Heard from Gil?" he asked.

"Not in three days, but they should be on their way back to Lima now, so I'm sure he'll call or text once he's got cell service."

"Well, just so you know, Miss Wainwright died last night."

"Oh, no. What happened?"

"Don't know yet. Her cleaning lady found her this morning and called Riddick. Later, he told me he went over there immediately and found her lying in her bed, holding a Bible in both hands, and sporting what appeared to be a contented look. My best guess is she had a heart attack. Either that, or her cancer finally got the best of her. You know, Gil's gonna be upset. She wasn't an easy patient, but he'd grown fond of her. I think we should wait and tell him in person."

"Agreed."

———

The pre-holiday seasonal rush hadn't yet started. Between the occasional customers who moseyed in to browse the shelves, I enjoyed the quiet solitude of being immersed in the smell and feel of books. I even found time to reread *Redeeming Love*, my favorite Francine Rivers book. I loved how she used a story from the Bible as a basis for a fiction love tale. My cell rang. Normally, I'd ignore it when I was at work, but no one was in the store, so I checked the ID. It was Bobby.

"Alex, got a minute?"

"I'm at work, Bobby, but it's quiet, so I've got a few minutes. What can I do for you?"

"First, I want to ask you to forgive me for hurting Suzie—"

"Bobby, she has *so* moved on from that catastrophe. In fact, her exact words were 'I avoided a real dumpster fire with that guy.' But she also said she'd forgiven you. If she can, I guess I can too."

"I'm grateful . . . and I'm thankful Gil confronted me. Once I calmed down, I thought hard about my life and my priorities. I messed up, but I wanted to make it right . . . with Jill. I confessed everything to her, and she said she'd give me another chance. Actually, 'one more chance,' is how she put it."

"Good to hear, Bobby, long as you really mean it." The front doorbell jingled, returning my attention to the bookstore. "Listen, I better get back to work."

What could have been a disaster for Suzie and Bobby had somehow worked out. We had Gil to thank for that. It took courage for him to confront one of his best friends.

Courage. That seems to be one of his better traits. I could love a guy for that.

Chapter Fifty-Eight

Atlanta

Luna

I had to find a way for us to escape. *Think, Luna.* I remembered my mum telling us in class to put the brains God gave us to good use. Finally, while I was in the shower, I looked down and something came to me that might actually work.

The day after Maria was taken to the room again and then returned, Ms. Poppins came to the door and summoned me. I meekly walked to the room and got undressed, as she ordered. When she pushed me down on my back and started to lock the shackles, Beast walked in.

"Leave. I want the pleasure of pinning her down."

As he approached, I lunged for his ankles and pulled on them as hard as I could. He lost his balance and fell backward, his head hitting the wooden floor with a loud thud. Ms. Poppins must have heard the racket because she suddenly appeared. As she stooped to check on Beast, I grabbed my clothes and ran out of the room. But not to the bedroom. First, I ran to his study and grabbed a marker I'd noticed on his desk the day I confronted him. When I got to our bedroom, Maria was standing at the door, wide-eyed.

"Quick. Get in. I need to close us in the room." Then, more than ever, I wished we had a lock on the door.

I quickly dressed, then hid the marker in one of the top drawers of the dresser.

Maria shook her head and grinned as I told her about my encounter with Beast. "I could never do that, Luna. You're so brave. I want to be like you."

227

"You are like me, Maria. We're in this together. But we have to fight. We have to resist Beast when we're in that room."

I figured I'd be punished. Other than our freedom and dignity, there wasn't much else they could take from us but food. I warned Maria I'd probably have to go without eating for a few days. Sure enough, that evening, Ms. Poppins came to the door with a single tray that held just enough food for one person.

"This is for you, Maria. Obviously, you can share as you see fit, little girl, but remember, you must eat to keep up your strength and please Grandfather. He wants you to remain strong and healthy." Her eyes narrowed in a way that betrayed pure evil.

Maria nodded. As soon as Ms. Poppins left, we eagerly shared the meager portions. Between bites, I explained my plan. "So listen, if you wake up tonight and hear noise in the bathroom, don't be frightened. It'll be me putting everything into motion."

That night, long after the house quieted and I assumed Beast and Ms. Poppins were asleep, I opened the dresser drawer, grabbed the marker, and went into the bathroom, safe from view should Ms. Poppins decide to come to our room. I grabbed the stiff rubber shower mat from the floor of the tub and, in the biggest letters possible, I wrote HELP US on the bottom side. The sign fit perfectly in the window that looked out on a neighbor's well-manicured backyard. If someone saw it, I prayed they'd heed my plea.

When I turned around, Maria was standing there, grinning. I hugged her and whispered into her ear, "We're going to be free soon, Maria. I just know it."

A glimmer of hope must have stirred in her soul. When we climbed into our beds, Maria began talking more than she'd talked in all the time we'd been together. She told me about her family, the school she attended, her grandparents in Texas, and Socks, the family's cat. "It makes me sad to think about them being so far away."

"When I open the curtains tonight, look up at the moon. Imagine your parents looking into that same night sky and seeing that moon. That's your connection to them."

"But what if the moon's gone?"

"Gone?"

"I mean hidden—by the clouds."

"It's still there, Maria. You just have to look for it."

I watched her smile as she looked out the window. When she finally drifted off, I closed my eyes and fell into a deep and peaceful sleep.

When I walked out of the bathroom the next morning, Maria was gone. I never saw her again.

Chapter Fifty-Nine

On the road to Tarapoto

We stopped in Moyobamba long enough to eat and use the bathroom. Kevin and Dirk were on a tight schedule and needed to rendezvous with their team in Tarapoto at a specified time. Anxious as I was to travel far enough to reach a cell signal, I was sorry we wouldn't have a night to spend in town. We ate quickly at the Peruvian version of a fast-food joint and then hit the road.

About an hour out of Tarapoto, we stopped for a stretch break. One bar appeared. I rang Alex on FaceTime, praying she'd pick up. When her image filled the screen, my heart leaped. "Hey, babe."

"Oh my gosh, Gil. It's so good to see your face. Where are you?"

"Almost back to Tarapoto. Then the short flight to Lima and we'll be headed home. Just wanted to let you know we're okay."

"So no problems? No safety issues?"

"Nope." This was not the time to tell her about our scary road adventure.

As Alex started speaking again, the phone crackled, and our connection was lost. Well, at least we saw each other.

Familiar sights from six days earlier appeared. I knew we were close to Tarapoto. Kevin and Dirk warned us the bad-looking dudes we'd see at the airport were members of their team, not locals seeking to cause us harm.

"Few minutes we be at airport, Mister Gil," Johnny said. "Praise God no more trouble."

A sleek jet sat on the runway, with no sign of the prop plane that carried us to from Lima to Tarapoto. When I told Sarah and Dunk I was going inside to ask about our flight, Kevin stopped me and pointed to the jet.

"That's your ride. You're flying with us."

"But the rescue. Aren't you going to go after more of the kids?" Dunk asked.

"If our private jet's here, it means our work here is done. We're moving on." We must have looked confused because he said, "The team will explain everything on the flight to Lima."

———

I'd never stayed in a hotel as nicely appointed as the interior of that jet. When we boarded, the three of us stopped in our tracks and gawked. It had more leather than a rodeo full of chap-decked cowboys.

"So this is how the other half travel, huh?" Sarah said.

We buckled in, and I looked across the aisle at Dirk. "How in the world did you guys score this beauty?"

He leaned toward me and explained that INES was once called in to find a kidnapped little boy. Turns out he was being held for ransom because his dad, owner of Rent Air leasing service, was extremely wealthy. The INES team located the boy and returned him to his parents, safe and sound. In a show of gratitude, the boy's father donated one of his fleet's jets to the organization.

"The man was filthy rich, including a heart of gold," Kevin added. "We use the jet for international missions because it can handle transatlantic travel. That way, we can touch down on an airport's private landing strip, taxi into a hangar, and leave in big, black SUVs. No one's the wiser and our mission stays under wraps." He turned to the five team members huddled near the back of the plane. "Danny, get up here, please."

Kevin had put Danny Peters in charge of the mission once he and Dirk left with Andrea and headed to Campoflores. According to Kevin, he'd been in Special Ops when he served his country. Once he was honorably discharged, he missed the action so much that he signed on with INES.

Kevin jerked a thumb toward Danny. "Dude's one of the smartest and toughest teammates I've ever served with, and that's saying a lot. Danny, read us in on where things stand."

By the time Danny finished his story, we were circling the Lima airport, waiting for clearance to land. According to Danny, the five team members had continued to get information from the men taken into custody, and that was what had led them to Andrea. All of their devices were confiscated and downloaded. Making all the intel fit into something the men could act on was like putting together a jigsaw puzzle.

"Kevin probably told you these creeps sing like canaries when they're interrogated, just trying to save their sorry hides. They are clever until they're caught. Call themselves the 'Sharks' but they wear hoodies with a dragon logo on the back to confuse people. One of them even ratted on the guy who came to your town to kill the preacher from Peru. Still looking for that dirtbag." He shook his head.

They'd quickly learned one girl had been taken to Lima to be flown out of the country. With Ava and Andrea rescued, that left twelve girls still in Peru who had to be found. Using the information the gang members "volunteered," and the electronic trail the team's tech expert mapped out, they developed a strategy. Each of the five team members partnered with two officers from the Peruvian National Police and pursued their targets.

"Fortunately," Danny said, "the mission was a resounding success. All twelve girls were found and rescued. We found them in some situations that would make you sick to your stomach, but only two were in bad shape physically. All twelve went through medical screening, including rape kits. Two of the girls had to be admitted and treated with IV fluids and antibiotics for dehydration and infection. It's not uncommon for these sex-trafficked girls to get urinary tract and pelvic infections. These two went so long without treatment, the infections spread to their blood. They'll be in the hospital for five to seven days and then taken back home."

"With the other ten girls?" Dunk asked.

"No, the other ten are on their way to board a bus for their trip back to Campoflores."

"A bus?" Sarah said, as she raised her eyebrows.

"Actually, it's a school bus some group in the States donated to a little church in Tarapoto," Danny said.

I thought of Johnny and shook my head.

We landed and taxied into a large hangar housing several small jets. There were two SUVs and one van parked inside the building.

"Guys, we'd fly you back to the States on the jet, but we're headed to another country on a new mission," Kevin said. "The van will shuttle you to the main airport."

Sarah gave Kevin and Dirk a hug. Dunk and I settled on handshakes. "Fellas, we enjoyed meeting you and getting a taste of how you operate," I said. "Don't know how we can thank you."

"We don't need you to thank us. Just seeing the looks on the faces of the people we rescue is all the thanks we need."

As we turned to walk to the van, Kevin grabbed my arm. "Listen, Gil, airport security is running down footage from the time when Luna would have likely arrived at the airport. Takes a while because their systems aren't quite as sophisticated as ours back home, but I'll call you as soon as we get any information we can act on."

"As you guys like to say, 'Roger that.' That'll be a call I'm eagerly waiting for!"

Chapter Sixty

Hillsborough

Alex

As soon as we lost our connection, I ran into Chrissy's room and told her Gil had called and was safe.

"Great, Mom! We've got a buncha stuff to tell him once he gets home. A lot happened in one week: my visit with dad, Soup's visit . . . and, of course, that gun. Yuck."

"I know you don't like that thing, but Soup meant well. Gotta say, I do like shooting it—but never at a person. I'll probably have to dust it off on those rare occasions I practice."

Chrissy went back to Instagram, and I left to do some reading. Dutch strolled behind me, my shadow for the week. I had to admit, though; it was great having him around. As I sat down, my phone rang. Dr. Greer.

"Hey, Alex. Sorry to call you with more bad news, but I thought you should know. We had a scare at the office today right before we closed. Arnie's nurse, Pat, went in to tell him goodbye and found him just sitting at his desk, not moving or speaking, just staring into the distance. I ran in, checked his vitals, and called 911. He was taken to Chapel Hill, where he's being evaluated." There was a catch in his throat. "Alex, I think he had a stroke. Another thing to hit Gil with, but he needs to know as soon as possible. Can you call or text me soon as he's back, please?"

"Of course. I'll contact you as soon as he's home, and I won't say a word before you get here."

Funny how you can go from a high to a low faster than an elevator moves one floor. Gil's FaceTime call had lifted my spirits and sparked a

234

romantic flame in my heart. My obsession with his safety told me God might be trying to make a point I'd been ignoring. But now this. Gil would be devastated. He admired Dr. Schmidt and treasured his counsel. He had to be told as soon as possible, but in person. That, and the news about Miss Wainwright, were likely to unsettle him.

I couldn't read. I put my book down on the end table and gently stroked Dutch's back. Before going to bed, I texted Suzie and Soup to let them know Gil was headed to the airport and would be home the next day.

———

When I was a young girl and needed advice or solace, I always leaned on Tom Waters. This morning was no exception. When I phoned him earlier, he'd graciously agreed to meet me for coffee at the diner. I was talking to Shorty when the clicking of paws on the linoleum told me they'd arrived. I ran over and gave him a quick hug.

As I slipped my arm through his, I said, "Thanks for meeting me on such short notice, Tom."

"Well, Miss Alexis, it's not like my dance card is full, ya know? Besides, Scout would've bitten me if I'd said no." He leaned down and patted the dog's head but kept his eyes in my general direction.

Before we took a seat, Shorty had two steaming cups of coffee on the table. "Morning, Tom. Try the terrific taste of this treasure. But be careful, 'cause it's *caliente*."

"Reckon that means 'hot,' correct?"

"Yes, sir. Just couldn't make 'hot' work."

Tom laughed and turned back to me. "That boy never ceases to amaze me . . . or amuse me, for that matter. Anyway, what's the good word this morning?"

"Gil's on his way home. He should get in later today."

"Wonderful. Now, Alexis, I can't see it, but I can hear the twinkle in your eye through your voice. Guess you've missed him, right?"

"Oh, yes. It's only been a week, but—"

"I understand. It happens when you're away from someone you lo—uh, really like."

"He said everything went great. Absolutely no problems."

"Well, I look forward to hearing about his adventure." Tom leaned in and spoke in a low volume. "You probably haven't heard, but Arnie Schmidt had to go to Chapel Hill yesterday."

"Actually, Dr. Greer called to tell me. But how'd you know?"

"Rich keeps a scanner at the store. Says he likes to keep his finger on the pulse of the town's health, so to speak."

I sighed. Dr. Schmidt's health issue was a great segue to what I really wanted to talk to Tom about. I was worried about Gil—about how he'd handle the double whammy of Dr. Schmidt and Miss Wainwright. After explaining all that, Tom reached over and found my hand.

"Listen, Alexis, Gil's a doctor, and he understands matters of poor health and death. He also understands things happen in this world that only God understands. Things we can question or dislike but have to accept. So, intellectually, he'll handle it perfectly fine. Emotionally, maybe not so much. That's where you come in. Just be there for him. Listen to him. I know you'll do that because you care about him. Like I said, I hear it in your voice."

Another deep breath. Another segue. "You almost said it earlier, Tom, so this might not surprise you, but I am in love with Gil."

He took a sip of coffee and used both hands to put the cup back on the saucer. "No, ma'am, no surprise here. I could tell, even with the limited time I've spent with you two. But Alexis, love's a beautiful thing. It's something that just kinda happens when two people perfect for each other are together for a while. Welcome it. Take it in your arms and relish it. Gotta say, Gil's a lucky young man, but you're a lucky lady too."

"Tom, I feel foolish talking to you about this, but I don't have anyone older and wiser to give me counsel. With no mom or dad around—"

"Dad?" He shook his head and chuckled. "Even if he were sitting right here, you wouldn't want to take his advice on love, would you?"

He had a point. My parents weren't relationship role models, for sure. Probably the best thing would have been to watch what they did inside and outside their marriage then do the opposite. Their failed marriage and mine with Virgil had clouded my view of what a relationship could be. Gil changed all that.

Tom and I finished our coffee, and I gently grabbed his elbow to help him up. "Well, that was a good talk. As always, I appreciate your keen insight." He furrowed his brow, waved me off, and started for the door, Scout at his side.

I really do love that man.

Chapter Sixty-One

Atlanta

O ur flight was uneventful. Despite my excitement about returning home, I slept well. If I snored, Sarah probably didn't hear it. She fell asleep before I did and was still out when I woke up. We had to make a connection in Atlanta, but we planned to use the downtime to freshen up and get something to eat.

As we maneuvered through the airport's busy foot traffic, looking for some place to eat, I glimpsed someone in a hoodie I swear had a dragon on the back. Instantly, my heart pounded and drops of sweat formed on my brow. I pushed through the crowd but couldn't find him.

Sitting over burgers, fries, and Coke Zero, I mentioned it to Dunk and Sarah. "I think they've got at least one person here. Who knows, maybe more? This may be where Luna was brought." I bit at my lower lip. "Possibly other victims too."

"Makes sense," Dunk said. "The Atlanta airport's one of the busiest in the country, with lots of international flights going through this place."

Once we'd eaten, we grabbed three seats at our gate. I watched our carry-ons so Dunk and Sarah could go for coffee. My phone rang. It was INES.

"Gil, Kevin Morris here. Figured you'd be in Atlanta by now. Want you to know we got some intel from the Lima airport's security tapes. Your girl and an older dude were spotted walking to a gate for a flight to Atlanta. We called the airline and confirmed their flight ended there, with no connections."

"So she's here?"

"In all likelihood, yes. It'd be easy to have a girl go unnoticed in such a big city."

"What's the next step, Kevin?"

"We've alerted our team in the States. They'll coordinate the boots-on-the-ground effort to look for her. Also called our teammate in Tennessee. He's already brought your friend up to speed on the intel, so now he's completely read in too."

I thanked Kevin, hung up, and nervously paced between the seats that faced each other in the crowded gate, smiling and shaking my head. People probably thought I was crazy. Dunk and Sarah finally returned. I reached for my coffee, my hand trembling.

"Dr. Gil, is everything okay?"

I filled them in on Kevin's call, trying not to omit any of the details. "I think I'm going to stay here and alert the authorities. We need to get going on this."

Dunk shook his head. "Slow down, chum. What are you going to do alone here in Atlanta? Let's get home so you can map out your role, if any, in all this. You can start by calling Alex's brother to find out where things stand with the INES team. We have to figure this will take some strategic and tactical planning. Be careful not to get over your boots."

Dunk got the expression wrong, but he was right about the need to slow down and plan. Kevin's call had excited me, and I'd failed to think through things logically. It was almost time to board the short flight to Raleigh. We were right on schedule, meaning we'd be home soon. Before boarding, I texted Alex our ETA.

Once we found our seats, Dunk pulled out his Alpha Smart keyboard and began typing notes about our visit. Guess he figured the trip would "preach," as he liked to say.

Before she reclined her seat and listened to her jazz playlist, Sarah said, "It was a great trip, Dr. Gil, but honestly, I'm looking forward to getting back to the office."

"Me too. And I want you to get Miss Wainwright in so we can properly thank her for the trip. Either that or we'll go out to her place one day soon."

"And you're sure she's our benefactor?"

"Yep, heard it straight from the horse's mouth. Dunk told me so when we were in Peru." I leaned back against the headrest and savored a cup of coffee. We descended through blue skies dotted with puffs of clouds, like falling through massive clumps of cotton candy, and landed without even a bump. It was good to be back on Carolina soil.

Alex was as close to our exit as she could get without the risk of some airport security officer escorting her away. Her waving and jumping up and down told me she'd spotted us before we saw her. We embraced. Forcefully. When I tried to release her and back away, she held me even tighter.

"Missed you, sweets," she whispered in my ear, tickling it with a rush of air.

Music to my ears.

As our SUV headed out to pick up Interstate 540, Alex's questions started. She wanted to hear all about our trip, no details spared. Every time I asked her about her week, she shifted in her seat and fired off more questions.

"Alex, you're ignoring my questions," I said.

"No, not at all. It's, you know, Hillsborough. Nothing exciting. I just want to know as much as possible about what you guys experienced."

Her jaw dropped when I told her Carlos was in the States on a divine hunch, and it turned out he was right. "We think Luna's somewhere in the Atlanta area, although she could have been taken almost anywhere. Right now, Atlanta's all we have. Soon as we're home, I'm going to talk to Soup about our next steps."

"Good idea, Gil. Rest your eyes. Your fellow travelers in the back seat have nodded off."

Dunk slept, his head on the top of the headrest and his mouth open. Sarah was leaning against her arm propped on the door. It had been a demanding trip and all three of us were exhausted.

When I next opened my eyes, we were in Hillsborough. We dropped off Sarah and then Dunk. As he unfolded from the back seat and grabbed his bags, he thanked Alex for the ride and told me to keep him posted on Atlanta.

A short drive later, we were in my driveway. "Finally, home sweet home." Movement in the window caught my eye. "Is that Dutch?"

Alex's mouth curled into a big grin. "Yep. Dropped him off before heading to Raleigh. Figured you've missed him more than anyone—except me, of course." She winked, but then her look grew serious.

"Gil, I need to text Jim Greer so he can come over. We've got some news for you."

Chapter Sixty-Two

Atlanta

Luna

Maria was gone. With some combination of anger and fear, I ran out of the bedroom to confront Beast, carrying the stuffed teddy Ms. Poppins had told me to always keep with me. I figured he'd be furious when I ran into the study, but I had little to lose. I stopped outside the study's door. Ms. Poppins and Beast were talking.

"I was duped. She looked so young." He cleared his throat. "She's too, you know, well-developed."

"What should we do with her, Grandfather? Same as the others you tired of?"

"I've posted her information with my sources. As soon as I get a decent offer from someone looking for a more mature girl, she'll be gone."

Absentmindedly, I set my stuffed animal on a side table and rushed into the room. He was at his computer, a cup of steaming coffee and a plate of partially eaten waffles resting on the desk. His smug look failed to unnerve me. Ms. Poppins stood between the two of us, her hands clasped behind her back. She turned to me, her eyebrows lifted.

"Young lady, what are you doing in here?"

Beast stood and glared at me. "How dare you come in here uninvited. Who do you think you are? You're nothing but trash—mere waste, waiting to be deposited on the garbage heap of worthless girls. You can be replaced, and you will be as soon as the next shipment's available."

"I want to know what happened to Maria."

"That's no longer your concern, young lady," Ms. Poppins said as she took a step toward me.

"No. I'll tell her." Beast turned to me. "She disappeared and will never be seen again, all because she was a very bad girl. The same could happen to you."

I forced a laugh. "I'm not afraid of you. The forces of good are stronger than the forces of evil. Even your evil."

"Take her into the room. Now!"

Ms. Poppins grabbed my arm, and I tripped, falling as I tried to break away. Before I could stand, she dragged me to the room. She watched as I undressed, then quickly shackled me to the bed. "Looks like you're ready for him now, slut." She narrowed her eyes and grinned.

Truthfully, I was afraid of Beast, but I couldn't let him see it. He couldn't have that power over me. I said Psalm 23 to myself over and over. He entered, but I wasn't fearful of his evil; I'd found a way to temper it. When he undressed, I mocked him. "You are fat, hairy, and ugly. You can't do what you want with me because you're not a real man—you're a beast."

"Shut up. I'd kill you if you hadn't cost me so much money. But I will break you."

Humiliation must have been a strong force. He was unable to perform as he'd intended. The only satisfaction he got was seeing me naked. He turned away from me, dressed, and left the room.

After Ms. Poppins unlocked the shackles, she grabbed my elbow, forcefully pressed me in the back, and pushed me into my room. I heard her latch the door. *Good.* I wanted to be alone. My fingers trembled as I struggled to button the pink dress. My breathing came in gasps, and I felt my heart beating rapidly.

Did I encourage Maria to push back on Beast? Is that why she's gone? Was it my fault? I dropped to my knees and prayed to God this would all end soon.

They withheld my food for two days. He was trying to break my spirit. Perhaps that would weaken my strength but not my determination to escape . . . or my belief that God would look after me. The sign was still in the bathroom window, undisturbed. All of my fears, hopes, and future were resting on that bathtub mat and that someone out there would take it seriously.

Chapter Sixty-Three

Hillsborough

Dutch planted his paws on my waist as soon as I walked into the house. His tail was wagging and his big tongue lolled around, looking for any spot he could lick. I was dead tired, but Alex's statement startled me into hyperalert. I took my bags into the bedroom. After washing the trip's grime off my face and hands, I returned to the kitchen, where Alex was making coffee.

"Dr. Greer should be here any minute."

"What's going on, and why is Jim coming over?" I asked.

She handed me a cup of coffee and took a seat at the table. "Patience, sweets. I just heard a car door slam."

I greeted Jim at the door. "Come on in, partner, and tell me what's going on."

"Good to see *you* too, Gil."

We shook hands. "Sorry. Left my manners at the airport."

We sat in the living room, where Dutch resumed his usual position at my feet. Alex brought in coffee for Jim and me. He looked at me and then at Alex, who nodded.

"Gil, there've been some, uh, developments that concern the office." He cleared his throat. "I'm not sure how to put—"

"Just say it, Jim."

"Arnie's really sick." As he continued to speak, his words were rendered into an incoherent mumble in the background as my mind went to my senior partner and all he'd done for me. He was my mentor—my guiding light—the one person I went to for advice on medicine and, sometimes, life in general. The father I never had. Now he was gone, at least from the office. Some of the words broke through the fog, however: non-communicative, possible stroke, waiting on test results, guarded prognosis. Tears fell. Alex sat beside me and took my hand in hers.

"This is awful. How's the office staff handling it?"

"We've been busy, of course, with Arnie out and you and Sarah not there, but that's probably been a blessing. Ruth calls me frequently to keep me posted. In fact, earlier today—"

"Ruth. Oh, my goodness. How's she holding up?"

"As well as expected, I guess. Their daughter flew in to be with her. I was gonna say Ruth told me earlier today it wasn't a stroke. His scan showed a large glioblastoma, pretty close to his cerebellum."

"A glio what?" Alex asked.

"Glioblastoma. It's a bad-acting tumor, and this one sounds like it's in a location that won't make surgery possible," Greer said.

I massaged both temples and then stared at Jim. "You said 'developments.' Plural. Is there something else you haven't told me?"

Jim leaned in, his hands on his knees, and quietly said, "Gil, we lost Miss Wainwright."

"What?"

He explained that the autopsy showed she'd had a heart attack. It did help to hear that by all appearances she seemed to have died peacefully.

"I didn't even get a chance to tell her," I said.

Alex moved closer and gently asked, "Tell her what, Gil?"

I explained she was the person who approached Dunk about funding the trip. Not wanting to embarrass her or, selfishly, risk having her withdraw her support if she knew I realized it was her, I never thanked her. "She was such a private person and I figured it'd be best not to make a big fuss about it ahead of time. But Sarah and I were going to talk to her this week and tell her all about the trip and how much good her money did. I was foolish not to thank her when I could have, and now I'll never be able to."

"No way you could have known." Jim shook his head. "Listen, buddy. I know you're tired. I'm gonna head home. I'll see you at the office."

"About that, Jim. We've got a lead on the whereabouts of the missing girl. I need a little more time off so I can go to Atlanta and see this thing through. Is that going to be a problem?"

"Actually, no. The temp we've got working for us right now told me today he could use more work. We can keep him on until you're back."

With that, Jim left. I was lucky to have such a good partner—one who understood what made me tick and why this was so important to me. But I'd sure owe him some favors once I was back at work.

Alex stood and hugged me when I came back from walking Jim out. "Sweets, I'm so sorry all that news got dumped on you, but Dr. Greer and I figured you'd want to know as soon as you got back."

"You figured right, so thanks. I've still got to process everything, but right now, I need some sleep. It's too late to call Soup now. But first thing tomorrow, I'll be on the phone with him to figure out what's going down in Atlanta."

"Now that they've almost found her, Gil, can't you leave the rescue to the authorities?"

"No way. My personal life's been all about unfinished business—no dad and a mom suddenly lost. I've got to finish this, Alex—for Carlos."

Alex surprised me when she smiled. "That's what I thought you'd say, sweets. And I understand. Now, you gonna be all right tonight? I hate to leave you all alone."

"What do you mean, 'All alone?' I've got Dutch." Right on cue, he looked up and licked my outstretched hand.

After Alex left, I wondered why she didn't seem at all surprised or worried about my going to Atlanta. Maybe she understood me better than I'd given her credit for.

Chapter Sixty-Four

Atlanta

Luna

The doorbell rang. It unnerved me, probably because it hadn't chimed since my arrival here. Beast and Ms. Poppins didn't seem like the type to welcome visitors. First, voices. Then, raised voices and what sounded like an argument. The door closed, and the house was silent. Suddenly, Ms. Poppins rushed into my room and went straight to the bathroom. She walked out with my sign, her face red and dotted with sweat beads.

"What were you thinking, young lady? That this would save you? Nobody out there cares about you. No one's coming to help you, either. Put on your nicest dress and comb that tangled mess of hair. We're leaving." She turned to walk out and then looked back. "And be grateful Grandfather sold you. Otherwise, he'd kill you for this stunt."

She slammed the door. I dressed as quickly as I could, but it was difficult with my hands shaking. Beast sold me? I'm being moved to another location? If anyone *is* out there looking for me, this will make it much more difficult. I hated this house, but here I knew Beast wouldn't hurt me, just humiliate me. I closed my eyes and silently repeated the twenty-third Psalm for the umpteenth time.

When Ms. Poppins returned, she grabbed my arm and walked me into the hall. "Go straight to the garage, young lady. No trouble or funny business."

The same big, black car was waiting for me, the driver sitting at the wheel. Ms. Poppins opened the back door, forced me in, and slammed the door closed. Beast sat there. He didn't look happy.

247

"You've been a big disappointment, little girl. Worthless to me, really. Now you've been sold. That's right. You're a commodity—cheap trash that gets dumped on the next person willing to buy you. I'm not even making back what I paid for you." He narrowed his eyes and squeezed my thigh. "I don't want any more trouble out of you. My contacts in Peru know your village. They could go there and take your family or even kill them. Is that what you want? Remember that, and when we get to the airport, maybe you'll behave. You'll walk in with me. If I talk to you, you're to act happy and talk back. We'll be a man and his granddaughter going on a trip. Understood?"

My mum is in danger too? I hadn't thought about that until now. But that was a long way for him to send someone just because he's mad at me. *Maybe he's bluffing.*

I turned my head away, closed my eyes, and nodded rapidly. I was frightened. If I were trash, someone might choose to dispose of me. Then I'd never see my mum and friends again. As much as I hated the thought, I would comply with whatever the next beast asked of me. My fate would be determined by evil men in a spiritual battle with God. I hoped God would win, but my hope was diminishing and my fear increasing.

As we traveled, I recognized some of the landmarks I'd seen on the way to Beast's house, only in reverse order. Much too soon, bright lights filled the sky. It had to be the airport. I was getting closer to whatever my fate would be.

The Lord is my shepherd, I shall . . .

Chapter Sixty-Five

Despite all the things going through my head, I slept well. On this morning, I fueled on coffee and a toasted bagel. After feeding Dutch, I punched Soup's name on my Favorites list. Turns out, he was way ahead of me.

We bypassed the usual small talk, and he cut to the chase. He'd been in contact with his guy at INES. A team was being assembled to head to Atlanta. Soup had already called his buddy on the Atlanta police force, who promised to prepare for the rescue team's arrival. Apparently, this wasn't Atlanta PD's first rodeo with INES. As Dunk and I'd suspected, having one of the busiest airports in the world made Atlanta a frequent crossroads for trafficking victims, if not the actual destination.

"Soup, I know this is out of my lane, but I want to be there if and when the girl's rescued."

"Figured that, Sully. I'm about an hour west of Hillsborough. I'll pick you up, and we'll head for Georgia."

I had an hour to get ready. I called Alex, updated her on my plans, and asked her to keep Dutch again. Of course, she was fine with that. Said she was leaving to stop by the house as soon as we got off the phone. I threw enough clothes and toiletries together to get by for a week. As I grabbed my duffel bag, I heard a car door slam. Alex.

She walked in with her own bag in hand. "Morning, sweets. Up for a little adventure?"

"What are you talking about?"

"I'm going with y'all. You think I'm staying here when I could see Soup and his guys in action? No way! This is like real-life *Law and Order* stuff."

"But what about Chrissy . . . and Dutch?"

"No worries. Suzie said she'd stay with them at my place."

"So this was prearranged?"

"Listen, Gil, before you even told me you were going to Atlanta, I knew there was no chance you'd miss out on the rescue, so I made arrangements with Suzie. Leave your house key under the doormat and she'll swing by to get him later this morning."

I shook my head. "You never cease to amaze me, babe."

Soup arrived a short time later, giving me just enough time to go in and tell Dutch goodbye. Alex ran out to greet Soup. A man I didn't know climbed down from the SUV's passenger seat.

"Alex, Sully, this is my buddy, INES agent Don Calvin. He's the one who got the ball rolling on this rescue mission.

Don was short and stocky, with a square jaw resting on a neck as wide as his head. He sported a crew cut and wore aviator sunglasses. Seemed like a serious dude. You know the type—the only guy in a comedy club not laughing.

"Good to meet you guys. You ready? We need to get on the road," Don said.

While Soup grabbed our bags, I went in to give Dutch a final pat on the head and grab the house key. Apparently, Don saw me slip it under the mat.

"No offense, Gil, but that's not too original . . . or safe."

"We're in Hillsborough, Don. Most houses aren't even locked." I winked at him and climbed into the back seat with Alex.

As we rolled south on Interstate 85, Don turned to Alex and me to bring us up to speed. He planned to rendezvous with two agents already headed to Atlanta. The three of them would meet with local law enforcement and begin scouring police files on traffickers linked to Georgia. They'd focus on any profile that seemed plausible and pursue it for information on current activity. Phone usage, recent travel domestically or abroad, large bank transactions—everything was fair game when it came to finding a missing child, even if the limits of the law had to be pushed. It sounded laborious and a bit far-fetched, but I kept that thought to myself.

Don looked at me. "Tell me what you know about this child."

"Name's Luna. She's sixteen, but her mother, Elizabeth, said she looks young for her age, and short, like her dad. He was Hispanic, but mom's

English, so Luna is fairer than what you'd expect of a Peruvian girl. Here, I've got a picture of her. Will it help?"

He looked at the photo and gave me a thumbs up. "It could help tremendously. If she turns up in a public place like Hartsfield-Jackson International, we can run facial recognition. It's a long shot, but at least it's something."

"Kinda like looking for a needle in a haystack," Soup said. "But hey, if you look long enough, the needle will eventually turn up, right?"

Soon, the monotony of interstate travel lulled me into a fog. I remembered passing the exit to Clemson University, and I heard Don comment about bass fishing on Lake Hartwell, but the sun sparkling on the wind-whipped waters of the lake finally put me under. I guess we'd been on the go so much that I drifted off whenever I could. I woke when the SUV decelerated.

"Where are we?"

"Middle of nowhere in Georgia, Sully," Soup said. "I need a coffee, and we might as well refuel while we're stopped. Let's everybody get out and stretch our legs."

While Soup filled the tank, Don walked over to the edge of the station's parking area and made a call. Alex and I headed into the convenience store to buy four coffees.

"Pretty exciting, huh, sweets?"

"Nerve-racking but exciting—you know, just the thought of possibly finding Luna and getting her home. If you could have seen the desperate look on her mom's face—"

"I get it, Gil. That poor girl's not much older than Chrissy. I'd be destroyed if I were in that mom's shoes. I wanna find Luna, but I hope we find the creep who stole her too. I'll give him a piece of my mind, and I won't be very Christian about it."

"Okay, okay. Calm down. By the way, Soup told me we'd be lucky if they let us tag along on any lead. If they do, we've got to hang back and keep a low profile."

"Fine by me. I'm looking for justice, not heroics."

The three of us piled into the SUV. Don rushed back, a crack in his stoic demeanor. He jumped in and explained the call was from the team in Georgia. "They already have a lead. Someone reported suspicious behavior at a house in the Atlanta suburbs. They're on their way now to investigate. Could be we'll miss all the action, folks," Don said.

Soup looked over at him. "As long as we get the girl, buddy, that's fine by me."

Chapter Sixty-Six

Atlanta

"Heads up, folks," Don said. "We're almost there, but this is where all the traffic from I-85 and I-75 come together, and the interstate does its best impersonation of bumper cars at a state fair."

We crept along until we turned off into downtown Atlanta and made our way to the police station. The building was a blend of glass, concrete, and glistening steel, larger than anything back home. I thought of what Chief Riddick would say if he could see this building, much less work here.

Soup and Don walked in like they owned the place and talked to someone at the front desk. Soon, we were ushered into a conference room by a dowdy, serious-faced female officer whose look seemed to dare anyone to cross her. She told us the team was on the way back to the station—but empty-handed.

"The head's down the hall," she said, pointing. "And coffee's around the corner. We empty, and then we refill." She managed a smirk.

Four men approached us, two in camo and two in police uniforms. The two in camo entered the room first, looking like walking action figures. Seriously.

Don stood and gave them each a hug. "Guys, these are two of my colleagues, Steve Nixon and Trey Wagoner. Two of the best, I might add."

We exchanged greetings and took our seats. Their faces turned all business when they updated us on their mission. Less than an hour earlier, a resident in a high-end neighborhood reported a sign with "Help Me" written on it mounted in an upstairs window of her backyard neighbor's house. She'd gone to the home and was greeted by a stern young woman who didn't act quite right. The woman said just she and her father lived there, and denied that anything nefarious was going on at the house. She had no explanation for the sign, however. But what really worried the neighbor was she spotted a pink stuffed animal sitting on a side table.

"She thought that would be strange in a house with two adults, so she called it in to the station. The department got an emergency search warrant, and we hustled out there," Nixon said. "The woman had no choice other than to let us in, but she was alone. When we went upstairs, there was a bedroom with two single beds and the sign laying on the floor. It was actually written on the back of a bath mat. Down the hall, a door was locked. She refused to open it, so we kicked it in and found a windowless room that contained a single bed with shackles attached to each corner of the frame."

Alex leaned forward. "What are you saying, if I may ask?"

"Something awful has been going on there," Wagoner said. "Maybe your girl or some other victim. We really don't know. We peppered her with questions until she broke down, crying. Turns out, she had been trafficked as a teen but grew fond of her captor, so he groomed her to be his assistant."

"Stockholm syndrome," Soup said. "In a weird way, she's as trapped now as she was when she was taken."

I dropped my head. "So a dead end."

Both agents grinned. "Not exactly. This is where it gets interesting. The house was in a high-dollar neighborhood. You know, the kind of place where security cameras are more numerous than flies on an animal carcass. The system across the street caught what looked like an older man and a child climbing into the backseat of a car. Couldn't make them out because it was too dark in the garage, but as soon as the car backed out, we got the tag number. The footage's time stamp confirms the neighbor's report. Our department's tech folks are tracking down the car and checking for a GPS system. Can't imagine there isn't one, given the late model. Meanwhile, the officers alerted airport security to look for it, just in case they headed to the airport."

"Then let's go," Don said. "If they're bound for Hartfield-Jackson, they're probably about there. We can't take the risk that we miss them and that child's put on an airplane to heaven knows where."

"I agree," Soup said. "We'll follow you there."

Don glanced at Alex and me with what appeared to be a skeptical look. "Listen, Soup, we usually don't allow ordinary citizens on one of our missions. Too dangerous. This operation could go sideways in a heartbeat."

"Understood, Don, but you also don't usually have ordinary citizens who've gone out of the country on their own to help find a missing child. Sully's put his life on hold for this. He deserves to be there. He and Alex will bring up our six from a distance. I promise."

Don looked at us, screwed up his mouth, and shrugged. "Okay. Let's go."

Chapter Sixty-Seven

Atlanta

Luna

I panicked. We were stopped at a traffic light, almost to the airport. I had to either escape or die trying. Even death would be better than being hopelessly lost and enslaved, with no one looking for me. With all my might, I pushed Beast against the car door, jerked on my door's handle, and jumped out of the car. I ran. It was a cloudy day. My eyes were filled with tears, and I didn't see the street curb. I tripped and fell face first. Before I could stand, a hand firmly grabbed my neck. It was the driver.

Beast rushed over and clamped down on my arm, pulling me away from his driver. He looked me over, head to toe. "Lucky for you, little girl, you didn't injure yourself or tear your clothes." He swung hard and hit me in the stomach. I gasped for air as he dragged me back to the car. "Now, behave yourself. I know other ways to hurt you that no one would ever see, and I'll use them if you try something stupid again."

I doubled over in the car, leaning against the door. I was beaten—physically and emotionally. A short drive later put us in one of the departure lanes, passing lines of cars with people hurriedly unloading their luggage. A few police cars marked *APD* sat against the walkway along the airport entrance. No lights, sirens, or officers.

The driver hopped out to get my bag from the trunk. Beast turned to me and said, "Remember, no funny business. I can put you back in this car and make sure you're never seen again."

I nodded.

The airport was a mass of people pushing ahead and cutting through one another with their rolling carts and luggage. It was much louder than I remembered Heathrow ever being, but that was years earlier. Had I yelled, I doubt anyone would have heard. Beast kept his arm resting heavily on my shoulder, his hand squeezing it just enough to remind me of his presence and strength. As we approached the ticket machine, or kiosk, as Beast called it, the crowd thinned and the noise diminished. Not totally, but enough. This was my chance.

As loudly as possible, I screamed, "Someone please help me!"

Chapter Sixty-Eight

Hartsfield-Jackson International, Atlanta

Even though the INES agents were armed, we all passed through security, thanks to two of Atlanta's finest, one male and one female, who met us at the entrance. We probably looked like a strike force walking into the airport, though most people seemed too preoccupied to notice.

"We need to scan all the domestic departures. It's doubtful she'd be taken back out of the country," Don said. "Steve and Trey, each of you peel off with an officer. Soup, you and your friends stay with me." He looked at Alex and me. "Remember, keep a safe distance."

The throng of travelers frustrated us as we tried to hurry. Time was critical. Fortunately, at each gate, people peeled off from the crowd, and it eventually thinned, making it easier to scour the area. Don and Soup walked ahead of us, their heads moving left to right and back again like swivel rockers. Suddenly, Don looked at Soup and pointed. A second later, I heard it.

"Someone please help me!"

Don and Soup rushed toward an older man and tackled him.

Soup pointed to the girl and looked at me. "Is she the one, Gil? Is that Luna?"

"Yes, I think that's her!" I rushed to a young girl who stared at the commotion, her eyes wide and her mouth covered with one hand. I took her other hand in mine, a connection I'd longed for since I'd first learned of Luna's identity. Alex walked up and smiled at Luna.

Then my eyes locked on a creature I determined to be the epitome of evil. Rage rose in my throat and pounded my head. When they got the man to his feet, I rushed up and grabbed Don's pistol from his shoulder holster and pointed it at the man.

"You're an animal and deserve to die!" The gun shook in my hand. Soup lunged and grabbed my arm, wrestling the pistol away. I dropped to my knees and cradled my head in my hands.

Don radioed his agents and gave them our location. Soon, all four of them ran up. One of the officers put the man in cuffs and took him away.

When I stood, Soup was staring at me. "I'm okay, Soup. Not sure what came over me. I'm sorry."

"You're lucky Don's a private agent and not a police officer. Otherwise, you'd be arrested for doing what you just did. What were you think—"

"Can we save it for later, Soup," Alex said. "Come here. I want you to meet Luna."

Luna cut her eyes at Alex. "How do you know my name?"

"Let my friend explain," she said. "Gil, come over here." Her glare told me exactly how she felt about what had just transpired.

I pulled out the photo I'd taken from Carlos's pocket and showed it to her. "My name's Gil. I got this from Carlos and later heard about your village in Peru." Her eyes widened when I told her I'd gone to Campoflores to meet her mom. "You see, Luna, Carlos left Peru to look for you, and we just picked up where he left off. Someone's been looking for you ever since you disappeared."

Tears leaked from her eyes. "What about the other girls? Is someone looking for them too?"

"They're all safe and back home, or on their way," Alex said. "You're safe now, too, and you'll be on your way home soon. First, some very nice people need to check you to make sure you're okay, but I'll stay with you the whole time."

Alex took Luna by the hand and followed the female officer toward the airport's exit.

———

Don explained to the officers our personal involvement in the search for Luna. They allowed Alex to ride with them on the drive to the nearest hospital. Soup and I followed. Later, Alex told me the female officer took Luna's entire statement regarding her abduction and imprisonment. As she recalled what must have been the worst of her experiences, especially how she'd stood up to the man she called Beast, she teared up and Alex said she felt the girl's hand trembling in hers.

Alex and the female officer stayed with Luna in the hospital's emergency room while Soup and I sat in the waiting area.

Soup leaned into me, his voice low and serious. "Sully, what in the world got—"

"I know, Soup. I was reckless . . . and I'm sorry. Honestly, I barely know where the trigger is on a gun, much less how to fire one."

He shook his head.

Finally, Alex came out to update us. "The doctor just examined Luna and got some samples for body fluid testing. Good news: she told the police officer she saw no evidence of physical trauma, but that test results would be sent to the station once available." She then grabbed my arm and said, "Sullivan, can I see you for a second?"

We walked over to a quiet corner, and Alex glared at me. "Gil, for Pete's sake, what did you almost do in there, and why?"

"As I told Soup, I'm sorry. But when I saw that man, every pent-up feeling I had about my father, my childhood, and what happened to my mother erupted, and I lost it."

Her grip on my arm softened. "Know what, Gil? I get it. Who knows, but maybe I'd done that if you hadn't beaten me to it—even after I'd promised Chrissy I'd never point my gun at another human being."

"*Your* gun?"

"Long story for a better time. Let's focus on Luna now."

The officer and a nurse walked Luna out to us. "Medically, there's no reason for this young lady to stay overnight. The doctor's releasing her," the nurse said.

"Luna, is there anything, and I mean anything, you want right now?" I asked.

"I really want to go home, but right now, I'm hungry. They didn't give me much to eat at that house."

Soup and I followed the officer, Luna, and Alex out of the ER. Alex kept her hand on Luna's shoulder as we walked. The officer's cell rang. She said little but nodded as she listened. She looked at me and grinned after she secured her phone.

"Apparently, sir, our little rescue operation's already made the news . . . and not only locally. Seems a Congressman Culpeper has already called the State Department's Office of Children's Issues. You've been made temporary guardian of Luna."

"Meaning?"

"It means she'll stay in your care, Gil, until you get her back to Peru," Alex said.

"I hadn't even gotten that far in my hopes of finding Luna and getting her home. But I'll scramble to get a couple of hotel rooms and, hopefully, tickets to Lima for tomorrow."

The officer shook her head. "No need, sir. Your congressman has booked two rooms at the Marriott, and there are three first-class tickets on a flight out of Atlanta to Lima, first thing tomorrow morning. You two must be good friends."

"It's a long story," I said.

Soup shook his head slowly. "Unbelievable. Everything's falling into place as though it was ordained."

"Maybe it was. I texted Bobby before we left to come down here, updating him on our progress. I guess he contacted his dad, who put everything into motion. This really *is* unbelievable!"

As we went through the cafeteria line, I held Alex back and let the police officer stay with Luna. "Listen, I know you've got Chrissy at home, so you can head back with Soup in the morning if that's what you'd like, but I'd love to have you—"

"Go with you to Peru? Heck yeah, sweets. Wild horses couldn't keep me from making that trip."

"I don't think that's the actual expression, babe."

"Whatever."

By the time we finished eating, it was late. When her replacement arrived, we thanked the officer, who'd stayed long past her duty shift to make sure we got squared away. Alex and Luna climbed into the patrol car, and Soup and I followed them to the Atlanta Marriott Marquis, where I hoped we'd all get some much-needed rest.

Chapter Sixty-Nine

Soup and I dropped our bags on the floor and sat on the queen beds.

"Well, Sully, how'd you like our little adventure?"

"Not the way I'd want to make my living, for sure. I'm more of a work from office, Rotary Club member, church-on-Sunday kind of guy."

"Different strokes for different folks, right?" He shrugged.

"Yeah. By the way, Alex mentioned something to me about her gun. You know anything about that?"

"When I visited her recently, I gave her a Glock as a present."

"You can't be serious, Soup."

"It was just for target practice. Well, maybe for home security too. But she said she could never point a gun at another human being."

I shook my head. "I'd have said that about me too . . . until now."

———

The next morning, after telling the officer goodbye and leaving the hotel, we crawled along in sluggish traffic, making our way to the airport. As we drove up, Luna closed her eyes and rapidly tapped her hand on her thigh. Alex must have noticed too.

"Luna, it's okay," she said. "You're completely safe with us. We're going to have very nice seats on the airplane, with good food, room to stretch out and nap, or even watch a movie. Would you like that?"

Her hand quieted, and she opened her eyes. She nodded as her mouth curved upward.

Once we arrived, Soup unloaded our bags and told us goodbye.

Alex grabbed his arm. "Come here and give me a hug, big guy."

"Soup, I don't know how to thank you," I said.

"Wouldn't have missed it, Sully. Hey, y'all call me when you get back home, okay?"

When we boarded the plane, a flight attendant ushered Luna to her seat and handed her a blanket and pillow. There was a cup of steaming hot chocolate topped with marshmallows waiting for her.

I looked at the attendant, my eyes narrowed and brow wrinkled.

"We were told we'd have a very special passenger on board today, and we want her to feel right at home."

I was exhausted but couldn't fall asleep. Luna was engrossed in a movie that seemed to be providing her some much-deserved entertainment. That brave girl had been through more terror in three months than some of us experience in a lifetime.

Before I knew it, we were dropping altitude as we approached Lima. After landing, we grabbed our bags from the overhead compartments and deplaned, ready to search for a flight to Tarapoto. I figured if we could get there, we could find Johnny, and he could get us to Campoflores.

Two airport security officers approached as we entered the gate. Luna flinched when she saw them, but Alex reassured her everything was okay.

"Is there a problem, officers?" I asked.

"Not at all, Dr. Sullivan. We're here to take you to your next flight."

"How do you even know who I am and where we're—"

"There's a private plane reserved for you in one of the nearby hangars. It was arranged by some outfit called INES, and it's fueled and waiting to take you to Tarapoto. We've got a shuttle van that'll take you over there. Ready to go?"

I looked at Alex with my arms extended, palms up, and shrugged. "Unbelievable."

On the short flight to Tarapoto, Alex sat with Luna on one side of the aisle, and I took the one-seater on the other side. Alex leaned over and brought me up to speed on things back home, including her call from Bobby.

"Alex, we both know he sometimes says the most expedient thing that comes to mind, but I hope now you believe him."

"Listen, sweets, since my disastrous marriage to Virgil, I've learned to read guys like a book and, yes, I believe he's totally sincere."

"What about me? Have you read me yet?"

"Oh, yeah."

"And?"

"I'm waiting on the sequel." She winked and reached for my hand.

———

As the landing strip at the Tarapoto airport came into view, I did a double-take. We were still a few thousand feet in the air, but I was certain Woodstock was parked outside the building, with a yellow school bus sitting behind it. *Good. Johnny must be here.*

I nudged Alex. "I think you're in for an entertaining ride to Luna's village. Lean over her and look out the window. That's the van we nicknamed Woodstock—our ride to Campoflores."

The plane landed and taxied as close to the little airport as the pilot was willing to get. We grabbed our bags and walked toward the building. Suddenly, Luna froze and then covered her mouth with both hands. Elizabeth was walking toward us, then running. Luna ran to her and melted in her arms, the two of them becoming one embrace of pure love. We heard sobbing but no words because . . . well, because words weren't needed. Elizabeth looked at me through her tears and mouthed, "Thank you."

After I introduced Alex to Elizabeth, we followed her and Luna into the building. We were surprised by a mass of kids and adults clapping, crying, and cheering. I spotted Johnny. He ran over and hugged me.

"Mister Gil. Good to see you, *amigo.*"

"You too, Johnny, but who are these people?"

"Twelve of the girls and their parents, Mister Gil. They not able to wait longer to see Luna, so we bring them here for, how do you say . . . big party!"

"Wonderful. Oh, this is my special friend Alex. Alex, meet Johnny."

"Nice to meet you, Miss Alex." Johnny whispered in my ear, "She very pretty."

In all my life I'd never seen such a happy group of people rejoicing over one lost child. There was music, singing, and dancing, and tables overflowing with food and pitchers of juice. I later learned INES had arranged everything. I regretted Don wasn't there to see the look on everyone's faces, but I suspected he knew what we were witnessing.

Luna and Elizabeth broke away from their friends and walked hand-in-hand over to Alex and me. Elizabeth started to speak, but she was crying so hard she had to pause. Finally, "Gil, thank you seems so inadequate. God bless you." We embraced.

Luna wrapped her arms around Alex. "Thank you for being my new friend and staying with me, Miss Alex. Please come visit me in my village."

Through tears, Alex said, "Luna, I'd be honored. I just might do that."

Luna looked over at me and then back at Alex. "You can bring Dr. Gil too." Then she looked back and winked . . . and that's when I knew she'd be okay.

I took Alex by the hand and said, "Let's go outside. This is their moment." We sat on a bench bordering the tarmac and stared at the forested mountains in the distance.

"I've never seen anything like that," Alex said, shaking her head.

"It's unmitigated joy, isn't it? The kind of thing you see in movies with happy endings."

"Happens in real life, too, sweets." She moved closer to me, a whisper away. "I've longed for that joy in my life, and it was right here, waiting on me."

I looked at Luna and the others inside the building. "You mean their joy? Well, then, I'm glad I brought you along, Alex."

She rested her head on my shoulder. "No, silly. You. You're the joy in my life." She took a deep breath. "I love you, Gil Sullivan."

I opened my mouth, but no words came out. Thank goodness, the pilot walked up and spared me the effort.

He nodded once. "Sorry to interrupt, but we need to leave if you two are going to catch your flight back to the States."

I looked at Alex and took her by the hand. "Let's go home, babe."

Epilogue

Back home

We landed in Raleigh-Durham, but I don't think my feet touched down for a couple of weeks. Although the trip was exhilarating, it was good to be home. Even though I loved my time in Peru, this was where I belonged, with the friends, co-workers, and patients I treasured. I recounted our adventures in Peru and Atlanta to anyone who would listen. Honestly, with each telling, I made it sound more dangerous and adventuresome—like the fish that got away getting larger each time a fisherman tells his tale. I guess I couldn't help myself. But what really mattered was the satisfaction of knowing I'd completed Carlos's mission. I'd finished the race and kept his faith in me, to borrow from Apostle Paul. Even more important was the joy of knowing Luna was back where she belonged, with a mother who'd longed for her return.

I settled back into my routine—working full-time, Monday through Friday and some weekends, and then church on Sunday. On this day, Alex and I sat in the sanctuary, listening to Dunk's sermon. He'd chosen as his Scripture passage Luke 15, the Parable of the Lost Sheep. Coincidence? I wasn't sure, but I planned to ask him. It reminded me of Carlos. He'd left the comfort and security of his home and set out to find Luna, that one lost child. In doing so, he lost his life, but she was ultimately saved from an existence I didn't want to even imagine. On our way out, Dunk stopped me.

"I got your prayer request for Dr. Schmidt, Gil. Glad to hear he's responding to radiation. We'll keep his name on the prayer list. Have you got a few minutes to chat in my office?"

I looked over at Alex, who nodded and said she'd run Chrissy home and then come back to the church for me.

"Sure, Dunk. I'll meet you there."

After he finished greeting parishioners, Dunk walked over and joined me in his office. He waved me to a seat beside him in the mahogany chairs that sat facing his desk.

"Gotta ask, Dunk. Was that sermon for me?"

"Actually, yes. I know you've been through a lot, what with honoring Carlos's wish and finding Luna, and I admire you for seeing it through. We'll never know, but I suspect Carlos had in mind the lost sheep parable when he dropped everything and pursued those kids."

"Yeah, I thought about that too . . . not that I wasn't listening to your sermon, of course."

"Oh, of course! Anyway, I want you to know how proud I am of you and what you accomplished through sheer determination."

"Thanks, Dunk. That means a lot."

Alex and I drove straight from church to the Dome in Chapel Hill, where we met Bobby and Jill Culpeper for an upscale lunch. It was still Bobby's go-to restaurant—but now in a good way and with the right person. While we were eating, he put his fork down and rested both palms on the table.

"Big announcement, ladies and gent." He looked at me. "Gonna be kind of a part-time resident in your fair town, my man."

I raised my eyebrows. "What are you talking about, Bobby?"

"I'm keeping my practice in Chapel Hill but only doing patent law three days a week. I've rented an office in Hillsborough, where I'll work one day a week."

"Doing what?"

"General practice and pro bono work. I figure with Alex going to work for the Department of Social Services, she'll be able to drum up some business for me. The way I see it, I've been given more in life than I deserve, and it's time I give back a little."

Alex placed her hands on top of Bobby's. "I love hearing this, and I'll definitely send you some business."

Bobby looked at Jill and then me. "Also, by cutting back, I can spend more time at home, focused on what's really important."

Gee, the miracles just keep on coming.

———

One of Bobby's first clients in Hillsborough was Miss Wainwright's estate. He summoned Jim Greer and me to his office for the reading of her will. We weren't quite sure why we were there, so we were shocked to learn she'd left almost everything to our practice, with specific instructions to build a new and larger clinic. Jim and I looked at each other, speechless.

As we prepared to leave, Bobby handed me a sealed envelope. "She also mentioned a charity in her will."

Once back at the clinic, in the solitude of my office, I opened it and found a letter, penned in what I recognized as her shaky handwriting.

My dear young man,
When you read this, I'll no longer be around to burden you. I know I was difficult, but I was lonely and angry. No one cared for me except you and your clinic. You used to listen to my heart, but in the end, you also changed it. All of your talking finally penetrated my soul. For that, I am grateful.

I know your trip will be a success. That little girl is lucky to have you looking for her. I plan to watch it from above, in the company of angels, as Reverend McElroy always put it.

You are a wonderful physician, and you need to take care of yourself so you'll be around for a long time to care for others. A bigger clinic will allow you to hire more doctors. Maybe you can lighten your load and look after yourself for a change.

One more thing, young man. Just so you'll know I really was paying attention, I've left a nice little sum for the women and children's shelter you used to talk about. They'll no longer have any problems with funding.

Eleanor Wainwright

I finished the letter through a puddle of tears . . . and gratitude. Most ministry is one-on-one. Not many of us choose to be preachers, but all of us can be evangelists. After all, we were called to spread the Word, as Dunk liked to say. Somehow, I'd reached Miss Wainwright without even knowing it. I was grateful to learn she knew where she was going and she died at peace.

———

The next day, I had a typically busy January schedule at the office. Flu season. With a full slate of patients, we'd likely work through lunch. Mid-morning, Sarah gently grabbed my elbow and pulled me into the dictation cubby.

"Just a heads up, Dr. Gil. George Owens is on your schedule this afternoon. It's a follow-up visit for the sinusitis he came in for when you were in Atlanta."

"I don't typically recheck patients with sinusitis."

"I know, but Dr. Greer thought he'd benefit from another look, and so did I. You know, to sorta keep an eye on him. Granted, he was sick that day, but he looked terrible—haggard and unshaven, almost a walking skeleton."

I frowned and went back to work.

We were so busy that the afternoon flew by. George was a no-show. Before she left for the day, Sarah called the Owens residence to check on him. The call went to voicemail, but the box was full. I was worried.

Driving home that evening, I replayed Luna's rescue. A missing person or a lost soul are worth dropping everything to search for. Luna was that "one" for Carlos. Circumstances led to him handing off the baton to me, and finding her had been well worth our effort.

Although my medical practice was my passion, I'd inadvertently stumbled upon an experience that satisfied a deeper need within me . . . and helped someone else as well. Perhaps God gnaws at our hearts with new passions, sometimes when we least expect it. I needed Dunk's advice.

———

We were at Shorty's for lunch the next day. I rested my coffee cup on the saucer and leaned in toward Dunk. "I love medicine, but now I've got this itch to do something more. Yet, I can't go all over the world searching for adventures like we had in Peru."

He reached across the table and gently placed his hand on my forearm. "Here's the thing, Gil. All of us have an opportunity to follow Jesus's example of the shepherd. And you might only need to go across the street, not to another continent. Think of some of the challenges you've faced with a few of your patients. You see, some people think they've reached the final page of their life's book and don't realize there are still chapters to be written. We just have to encourage them to keep writing. Think about that."

I thought of George Owens, and a lump grew in my throat. Finally, I said, "Great advice, Dunk. I'm grateful you're my pastor . . . and my good friend."

Maybe, just maybe, George was destined to be my "one." Maybe it would be someone else. Only time would tell.

I guess I still had more chapters to write in my own book.

Acknowledgments

While the writing of a novel's manuscript is quite the solitary process, paradoxically it requires a team of folks to take the document from a laptop and shepherd it through what's required for it to become a book. I have many people to thank.

Terry Whalin, my acquisitions editor at Morgan James Publishing, once again advocated for me at the publishing board. Naomi Chellis, Emily Madison, Jim Howard, David Hancock, and many others who work behind the scenes at Morgan James have my utmost respect and gratitude. You are a great team.

I can't say enough about my editor, Cortney Donelson, whose work far exceeded my expectations and whose expertise made the final product much better. Thank you so much, Cortney. You're the best.

A big shoutout goes to my beta readers: Debbie Ankeney, Joy Ankeney, Joy Ball, Tom Bridges, Laurie Herlich, Donna Thomas, and Stephanie Vanderford. Thank you for plowing through a longer and rougher first draft and giving me helpful feedback. I hope you enjoy the final iteration!

My thanks also go to my two expert advisors. Award-winning marksman Tom Cutler instructed me on all things "guns" and competitive shooting. I was clueless, but Tom was patient. Joy Ankeney offered professional advice on social work issues pertinent to the story and corrected my inaccuracies.

I'm grateful for my pastor, the Rev. Peter McKechnie. Peter, something you said in one of your sermons gave me what I think is the most poignant line in the entire book. I treasure your friendship and spiritual guidance.

Of course, a special mention goes to my daughter, Dr. Stephanie Vanderford, who patiently served once again as my unpaid technical advisor, and to my wife, Carolyn, who never complained when I went off to my study, laptop in hand, to "do work." You two ladies rock my world and make life worth living.

Finally, my utmost and highest gratitude goes to Jesus Christ, my Lord and Savior. How thankful I am that He treats each of us as "the one" for whom He goes searching. I pray He will find each and every one of you.

About the Author

Tim Eichenbrenner is a native of southeastern Virginia. He now lives with his wife, Carolyn, in Charlotte, North Carolina, in a home ruled by their cocker spaniel, Gracie. Tim practiced general pediatrics for thirty-eight years before retiring and starting his writing career. The foundation of his writing is his Christian faith, influenced by his work experiences and emboldened by his personal faith journey. *In Search of the Hidden Moon* is his second novel.

You can find Tim on Facebook, Instagram, LinkedIn, and his website, timeichenbrenner.com, where his blog, "Tuesday Thoughts," posts every other Tuesday.

A free ebook edition is available with the purchase of this book.

To claim your free ebook edition:

1. Visit MorganJamesBOGO.com
2. Sign your name CLEARLY in the space
3. Complete the form and submit a photo of the entire copyright page
4. You or your friend can download the ebook to your preferred device

Morgan James BOGO™

A **FREE** ebook edition is available for you or a friend with the purchase of this print book.

CLEARLY SIGN YOUR NAME ABOVE

Instructions to claim your free ebook edition:
1. Visit MorganJamesBOGO.com
2. Sign your name CLEARLY in the space above
3. Complete the form and submit a photo of this entire page
4. You or your friend can download the ebook to your preferred device

Print & Digital Together Forever.

Snap a photo

Free ebook

Read anywhere